FIRE STAR

CHRIS D'LACEY

SCHOLASTIC INC.
NEW YORK TORONTO LONDON AUCKLAND
SYDNEY MEXICO CITY NEW DELHI HONG KONG

This book was published in hardcover in the United States by Orchard Books in 2007 and in Great Britain by Hachette Publishing Group, Ltd., in 2005.

ISBN 978-0-439-90185-7

25 24 23 22 21 20 14 15 16/0

Printed in the U.S.A. 40

This edition first printing, January 2008

The text type was set in Sabon.

Book design by Alison Klapthor.

For Jay

Shall we commingle?

Thank you to everyone who has helped to produce and support this book: Team Orchard (thank you, Penny, for stepping in so late), Kathy Hector, Derek & Susan, LWC, Sandy and her staff at Browsers Bookshop, Shelley at Harborough, Merel Reinink, and Marshall — they still love the Web site, mate.

Also by the author:

The Fire Within

Icefire

The lights that shine so softly through our firmament are the patterns involved in unfolding. Pick out a pattern and you have the key to meaning, the means for healing and all the help you need to find the way . . .

Gifts of Unknown Things by Lyall Watson
(Hodder & Stoughton Ltd, 1976)

There is a sign in the heavens
Another light in the darkness
A better time is beginning
There is a fire star coming

I see the mark of the ice bear
In the tears of the dragon
And you'd better start wishing
There is a fire star coming

Stay with me,
my love . . .

Part One

The Shooting

Boom. Boom. Boom. Ingavar's paws thumped loud against the ice as he fled from the drone of engines high above. His chest was on fire. His stout legs ached. He'd been running for almost as long as any bear could manage.

Open water. He must find open water. The threat from the sky was drawing close. Men. Men wanted his pelt, he knew. There was only one possible route to safety: If he reached a lead of water, they might leave him be. If their bullets lodged deep in his back as he swam, the ocean would take him and they had lost; if they shot him down on solid ice, his pelt was theirs.

Pweoww. The first shot landed a body length ahead, blowing up a wide corona of ice. Ingavar's momentum took him straight through it. The shattering halo of bitter-sharp crystals cut into his shadowed, battle-scarred snout, stinging his eyes and ripping at his gums. He snorted and veered away. But that was exactly what the men had intended, he knew it when he saw the ridges up ahead. They were turning him toward uneven ground, where his cover was better but his run would falter.

Water. He *must* find open water.

The second shot grazed his ear. He veered again, this time into the pain and away from the snare of the glistening ridges. The scent of the ocean was strong in his nostrils. The ice beneath his paws was thinning, he could tell. There were noticeable shudders and his footfall was ringing. Any bear worth his weight in seal knew how to judge the thickness of the surface. A few more strides and he could rear and break through it, swim below the crust if he needed to.

The third shot thudded into his shoulder. The force of the impact slammed him to his knees. His front legs buckled underneath his belly and he skidded forward with his chin against the ice, until his balance gave out and he fell, panting, onto his flank. There he lay, heat rising from his scissored jaws, claws extended and scrabbling for a foothold as if they had not yet given up hope. But it was over. Ingavar knew it. His senses were swimming. His leg was gone. Deep at the root of the angry red channel which the bullet had hacked through fur and muscle, the poison was spreading inside his lung.

His eyes closed.

In the air, he could still hear the buzz of the plane. It seemed quiet compared to the beat of his heart. His chest throbbed against the creaking ice. Blood pooled in the side of his mouth. Sickness claimed his seal-starved belly. The plane circled like an irritated skua. Why? What were they waiting for? Why didn't they close and shoot again?

He opened his eyes. A wisp of fog streamed across his gaze. A mist was gathering. A mist. How, when the morning sun was bright overhead and there was no wind rippling through his fur? Dizzily, he rolled his head and scented. The air was moving in a quick white spiral. Snowflakes danced and kissed his shoulder. The blue sky turned by pieces to white. A blizzard had come from nowhere to cover him. He snorted with disbelief and his claws pierced deep into the yielding ice, to mirror the distress gouging through his heart.

A blizzard. Too late. *Just too late.*

He closed his eyes for a long time then.

He woke to the sound of his labored breathing and the creaks and groans of the grating pack. The air was brittle with a hazy cold. Moonlight stroked the shifting ice. The burning pain had receded in his shoulder, but so too had all sensation of movement. He rolled over and tried to stand. But his ruined body was far from ready and he crashed before he was halfway righted.

"Why do you hasten your death, fool?"

The voice sent a wave of fear through his head. Instinctively, he growled, raising a bolt of agony in his chest. He lay back his head and quietly whined.

"Be silent," said the voice. There was a harshness in it that bordered on cruel.

Ingavar widened his arc of vision. Just ahead, along the axis of the lie of his snout, was another bear. It was sitting paws together as bears often did, tilting its head down, staring at him. It looked like a dumpy, elderly female — and yet its scent was completely wrong. There was not a trace of the ocean about it, no sweat of motherhood in its fur, no rotting seal meat on its breath. And though it spoke in the everyday language of the Nanuk, the words did not have the guttural rasp that would single out its territories or its origins.

"What are you?" Ingavar said.

The bear changed into an arctic fox.

This caused Ingavar to jerk again. A column of pain reared in his lung, forcing a splutter of blood from his mouth. He shuttered his claws and slowed his breathing. The fox, meanwhile, had circled to his side, where it stopped and lifted a nonchalant paw, flexing it as though to test the range of movement. It flagged its gray-white tail and sat.

"I know you," it said, in Nanuk again.

Ingavar ground his teeth. Was this death? Was this the far side of the ice? He blinked and tried to concentrate. Through tight slit vision he saw the fox yawn.

"You were born into the line of Ragnar," it said. "One of the nine which ruled this . . . waste."

Despite the suffering, Ingavar growled. How could this non-thing know about that?

"Ah, that offends you, doesn't it, bear? Your ancestor was a fighting legend who took the lives of endless men. And here you lie, dying at their hand. How does it feel to be so *useless*?"

Hearing this, the bear let out a terrible roar and pawed the ice in an effort to stand. But the noose of pain about his stricken shoulder tightened once more and he fell back howling.

The fox was quickly behind him then, leaning over, speaking into his ear. "I can save you," it said, seducing him with whispers. "Remember the blizzard that shielded you?"

Eyes closed, Ingavar curled his lip.

"That was my doing. One sweep of my . . ." Here it paused and tested its joints again. ". . . paw. I can heal you, take away the misery. Send you back to gain your revenge."

"What are you?" the son of Ragnar repeated.

With a laughing snort, the fox turned into a black-eyed raven. It leaped aboard his shoulder and clinched its talons. "Move and I'll take your eye out," it said.

Ingavar looked ahead. The wind was still circling, constantly shuffling the surface of the ice. This beast, this demon, whatever it was, had invaded a world he recognized as real. He had no choice but to trust that it could carry out its threat with ease.

"Help me, bear, and I will spare your life."

Ingavar gave the slightest of nods.

"You know of a place that men call Chamberlain?"

The ice bear twitched his snout. What did the places of men mean to him?

The bird responded with an angry squawk and

poked his skull just above the eye. "On the north migratory route. I've seen your kind there, beggaring for food from the trash dumps and tips."

Ingavar grunted. Now, he knew. As a yearling, his mother had taken him there.

"Good," said the raven, dribbling spittle. "There is a man there, nothing more than a boy. He has something I need. Something precious. He wears it like a charm around his neck. It is a tooth, bear. Do you understand?"

Ingavar's eye rolled slowly in its socket.

"A bear's tooth," the bird said impatiently.

The shape of the eye grew long and narrow. The only fabled tooth that Ingavar knew of was that which had fallen from his ancestor's mouth in the ancient times of wars against men. But that was sacred. And surely lost. All the same, he queried it. "Ragnar tooth?"

"Yes, you hopeless bucket of blubber. Deliver it to me and you will walk again."

Ingavar took a moment to think. What did this trickster want with a tooth that was a symbol of everything bears revered? And even were he able to reach the dump town, how would he know or draw close to the boy — or steal the tooth — when hunters were everywhere?

The raven read these doubts in his face. "In Chamberlain, bears are protected," it said, and yet there was such resentment in these words that Ingavar knew this raven could never be trusted. But his curiosity was as strong as his instinct to survive. If he was going to walk again, he must, for now, heed the bird's will. He grunted to show he understood.

Again the bird spoke. "There is a girl in Chamberlain who travels with the boy. You will take her a sign from me. One touch of your paw will be enough. She will steal the tooth and hand it to you. You will hide it under your disgusting tongue, then find a way back to the open ice, where I will be waiting. Is that clear?"

Ingavar shook his head.

"You refuse?" The pointed feathers on the raven's neck rose as it closed its talons in anger.

Ingavar winced and juddered a leg. "Nurr. Girl? Ingavar, how know?"

"Ah," said the raven. And it hopped off his side and onto the ice, where it changed into the shape of a human woman. She was as old as the sky and nearly toothless, dressed in the furs of the Inuit natives. In one hand she held a broken bone. Before Ingavar could even narrow his gaze, she had brought the jagged end crashing down upon his head, blooding his fur with three short scars. Ingavar roared and lashed out wildly, but caught nothing but air between his claws. The woman stepped back and called him a fool. Then she ordered him to stand.

And Ingavar found he could.

The blow, though savage, had drawn the fire from his injured limb and allowed a limping strength to return.

The woman pointed the bone at the ice. A small segment melted and water bubbled up out of the hole. "Look down," she said.

Ingavar bent, then recoiled instantly from his reflection. No! What had she done to him?

"The scars will fade by morning," said the woman.

"But she alone, the girl, will sense them and be drawn to you. She carries the mark of Oomara on her arm. Touch her, once, that is all you have to do. With it, your strength will return in full."

Ingavar backed away, shaking his head. "Boy?" he queried. "What of boy?"

"The boy?" the woman said, and at first she just sneered. Then her raven black eyes descended into evil. "The boy is nothing. Kill him," she said.

A Letter Home

When the mailbox rattled at number 42 Wayward Crescent, one of two things tended to happen. Either Lucy Pennykettle would come rushing downstairs crying, "It's OK! I'm here! I'll get it!" or a small green puffler dragon called Gwillan would zip down the hall, pick up the mail, and fly it quickly into the kitchen.

That morning, it was Bonnington's turn. The Pennykettles' large brown tabby cat was stalking a spider that had scuttled behind the Swiss cheese plant in the corner of the hall when the letter from Manitoba, Canada, dropped through the box and landed neatly between his ears. Gwillan was down the hall in a flash, only to discover that Bonnington had pounced and pinned the letter hard to the carpet as though he had caught a falling leaf.

Hrrr, went Gwillan from the lip of the plant pot, anxious to do his duty and transport the letter to the Dragon's Den where his mistress, Liz, was working that day.

This did not impress Bonnington much. He had never got to grips with dragontongue. He merely twitched his whiskers and sat on the letter. It seemed the obvious thing to do.

That was how Lucy found him two minutes later. By then, Gwillan had reported to the listening dragon on top of the fridge. It in turn had sent a message to the guard dragon, Gruffen — head of household security — and he had hurred in Lucy's ear. Down the stairs she had come.

"Up," she said, scooping Bonnington into her arms.

Gwillan zipped to the carpet and grabbed the letter between his jaws.

"Show me," said Lucy.

The dragon hovered mid-flight so she could read the postmark.

And, of course, once she saw the Canadian postmark, great excitement followed. "Mom!" she screeched. "We've got a letter from David!"

All around the house, dozens of dragon scales clattered and clacked as heads were turned and eye ridges were raised and tails were flicked in expectation. David Rain, the Pennykettles' absent tenant, had sent a message home — from the land of snow and ice, from the Arctic.

Bonnington, whose fragile half-bitten ear did not take well to the squeals of the average eleven-year-old, hissed in protest and scrambled away.

Lucy pounded up the stairs, Gwillan flying at her shoulder. Breathlessly, she burst into the Dragon's Den, where Liz was wiping clean a paintbrush.

"Mom, please can I read it? Please?"

"No," Liz said, whipping the note from Gwillan's jaws. "David gave me alone the right to read his mail." And she took a silver dagger off her workbench and carefully sliced the envelope apart.

Lucy plonked herself onto a stool. "It's got a picture of a big fat pigeon on the stamp."

"I think that's a ptarmigan," Liz said, knowledgeably, withdrawing two sheets of thin, folded paper. "Shouldn't you be calling G'reth and Gadzooks?"

"Oh, yes!" Lucy sat bolt upright and hurred at Gwillan, who set off straightaway for David's room. G'reth, the large-pawed wishing dragon, passed him on the stairs. He found Gadzooks, David's inspirational writing dragon, in his usual place on the windowsill in the tenant's room.

Hrrr, went Gwillan, as politely as he could, for the writing dragon seemed deep in thought and might not take kindly to any interruption from a lowly puffler.

Gadzooks nodded to show he understood. He was busy using the tip of a claw to make a pattern of dots on the misty glass. Turning a page of his writing pad, he copied down the arrangement of the dots. A lower page of the pad fell open. It, too, was speckled with a similar pattern. It was none of Gwillan's business, of course, to ask what the fabled dragon was doing, but it worried him to see a fellow being frowning the way Gadzooks was now. So he bothered to ask, was everything all right? Gadzooks tucked his pencil behind his ear and said he was puzzled by the movements of the stars. Gwillan returned him a look of great awe. He could see no stars in the morning sky, but who was he to doubt Gadzooks? He blew a smoke ring and led the way upstairs.

"About time," Lucy chided as Gwillan settled neatly on her shoulder.

Gadzooks landed by the potter's wheel. He glimpsed along the shelves of waiting dragons and settled his gaze on one in particular. Gretel, the headstrong potions dragon, had come to the front of the small wooden cage in which she'd been imprisoned for the past two weeks. He looked at her anxiously, noting the bitterness clouding her eyes. It pained him to see her caged like this. Surely it was dangerous to breed resentment in a clever and powerful potions dragon, even if her quiver of flowers had been removed? He glanced to the near side of the bench. In a basket filled with tissues and straw lay the stationary figure of the stone dragon, Grockle, the cause of Gretel's detention. Why was it wrong, Gadzooks had often wondered, to take pity on a creature born without fire? Why should this dragon not be revived, as Gretel had only been trying to do? If his master, the David, was here today, would he approve of Gretel's punishment? And worse, if Zanna, the mistress of Gretel, herself away in the Arctic lands, could see her dragon clutching at bars, what terrible outcomes might result?

"Pay attention, everyone, here we go." Liz flicked the first page and started to read. *"Dear Liz, Lucy, Bonnington, and dragons. How are you? How's the weather in Scrubbley? We're frying eggs on the sidewalk up here."*

"How?" Lucy queried, turning up her nose. "I thought it was really cold in the Arctic?"

"He's teasing," said Liz. "Listen, he says so: *I'm teasing, of course . . . there are no sidewalks in the Arctic!* OK, *here's the truth: It's cold enough to freeze the feathers off a penguin, not that you'd see any penguins here, but you get my gist. I have to sleep in socks and a woolly hat if I don't want frostbite on my extremities —*"

"What does that mean?" asked Lucy.

"His toes and ears," said Liz. She gave a quick cough and continued: *"Zanna was moaning the other day because it was so cold her best black nail polish cracked. Oops, she's just read that over my shoulder. Now she's giving me one of her Gothic looks. I'll change the subject.*

"We are having a fantastic time. The polar research station is a bit basic, but we get by. The food is good. We eat WARM, thick oatmeal for breakfast every morning and have steaks the size of Lucy's flip-flops for dinner."

"Yuck," went Lucy.

Her mother read on: *"The base is a sprawling single story building, right on the edge of Hudson Bay. It's about ten miles south of the town of Chamberlain, a place we are dying to visit. Polar bears come to Chamberlain sometimes! They congregate out on the scraggy tundra and raid the trash dumps. Imagine that? A squirrel in your garden is one thing, but a real live polar bear? Wow! Dr. Bergstrom, our instructor, says we will fly out and see them soon, before the sea in the bay completely freezes over and the bears head north to hunt for seals. We would have done it a week ago but he was called away to some important meeting, so we are stuck for the moment working in the lab.*

"We spend our days analyzing ice samples. Some of them date back hundreds of years. Zanna is checking for increases in toxic chemicals called PCBs, which can poison bears and other forms of wildlife, and I am melting ice cores down and making the tea — I mean, making interesting graphs to monitor the levels of something called beryllium 10. This is to do with global warming. Dr. Bergstrom thinks that changes in the levels of beryllium 10 coincide with an increase in sunspots or flares, which might be warming the Earth and making the polar ice cap melt. That's scary, especially for bears. Every year, the ice in Hudson Bay melts earlier but takes a little longer to refreeze. This means that bears are fasting more and more and will reach a point, maybe in the next fifty years, when they will not be able to survive their time ashore and will die of starvation out on the tundra. It's hard to believe that the natural

world we take so much for granted is constantly under threat from climatic change and that creatures like polar bears could so easily become extinct. No one here wants to see that happen. So we are busy searching for long-term answers, feeding the data into our computers to try to predict how long the polar ice will last. The weird thing is, the best model we've created, based on the sampled information we have, indicates that the Earth is about to enter a meteorological phase that mimics a period four and a half BILLION years ago when the planet was first created. . . ."

There was a clink.

Liz stopped reading. "What was that?"

"Gadzooks has dropped his pencil," said Lucy.

Gwillan flew to the floor and retrieved it for him.

The writing dragon hurred in embarrassment and made gestures to Liz to carry on reading. He glanced lightly at Gretel, who tilted her head to look at his pad. Gadzooks gathered it under his arm, keeping his star patterns carefully hidden. Gretel shuffled her scales, but didn't make a sound. She had not spoken now for several days.

Liz read on: *"If I'm honest, the work is slightly boring, but we all feel proud to be doing something positive for the northern 'biome' as people tend to call it — or Gaia, the Earth goddess, as Zanna tells everyone, including our Inuit colleague, Tootega. He's a strange character. His face is as wrinkled as an old leather boot and he smells of fish, and seal, and worse! He works, among other things, as a guide for Dr. Bergstrom and says he will take me out on a sled and let me drive his dog team one day."*

"Wow," went Lucy, very bright-eyed.

"Zanna is totally miffed about this because he hasn't said he'll take her as well. Tootega and Zanna don't get along. He seems to be a bit wary of her, probably because she never stops pestering him about Inuit mythology. She mentioned dragons the other day and he gabbled some words in his native tongue, made a strange sign, and walked away."

"That's not very nice," said Lucy.

"No," Liz muttered. "Nor is this: *Oh, by the way, if you're wondering what this red spot is I've arrowed, it's a drop of Zanna's blood —"*

Lucy and a host of dragons leaned forward. Gretel raised her scales and sniffed.

"The scratch on her arm hasn't healed," said Liz, reading a few lines ahead.

Lucy sat back looking concerned. "The scratch that Gwilanna made? The one that looked like the dribbles of ink on David's book contract?"

"Yes," said Liz. She interchanged the pages, deep in thought.

Gretel ran her claws down the bars of her cage.

G'reth, on the windowsill, shuddered uncomfortably.

"He goes on to say that the other students in their party are all doing fine and that Zanna and one of the other girls are making eyes at a handsome helicopter pilot named Russ —"

"She's David's girlfriend, she can't do that."

"I'm not worried, he writes, *'cause she tells me she loves me about ten times a day, in front of anyone*

who'll listen; she hasn't changed much. She says hi to you all and please will someone give Gretel a hug because she misses her and wonders if she's feeling OK. Zanna's been having trouble sleeping. When she wakes, Gretel is always on her mind."

"Oh," said Lucy, glancing at the cage. "Do you think she knows?" Her face began to redden.

"I doubt it," said Liz. "She's not attuned enough yet. But Gretel's giving out a powerful auma. It would be strange if Zanna wasn't picking up something."

Lucy bit her lip. "What are we going to do when she comes home, Mom?"

"Tell her the truth, that Grockle will suffer if he's brought into this world, and therefore Gretel had to be restrained. She understands that, don't you, Gretel?"

Gretel pulled back into the shadows so that no one could see her violet eyes blazing.

"Last paragraph," said Liz. *"Please give Gadzooks a tickle as well. I haven't heard from him in ages; I hope his pencil hasn't gone blunt. I've been writing a bit of my Arctic saga, but it's not coming out quite the way I predicted. I suppose I shouldn't expect too much when my inspirational dragon is thousands of miles away. Oh well, another three weeks and I'll be there to wipe the mist off the windowpane for him. OK, we're going outside to watch the sunset now. This is one of the highlights of our day. It's beautiful to see the inlets and waterways turning a deep dark orange and to listen to the geese as they flap across the bay. If my camera batteries last (they turn gooey in the cold) I'll be bringing you lots of pictures. The other night, Zanna and I took a walk around the base in our thermal clothing, watching the northern stars coming out. You wouldn't believe how clear they are up here. They look like sparkling Christmas ornaments. You want to reach out and pluck them and put them in your pocket. That's how close they seem. There's one that's low and beautifully yellow. I don't know what it's called — I'll ask Dr. Bergstrom when he comes back, but every time I look at it I feel as though it's lighting up a candle in my heart. I love this place. I could stay here forever, but I'd miss you all too much and that would never do. Oops, I've gone all sentimental. On that note,*

I'll go! Love to everyone. See you soon, David xxx. P.S. Hrrr! P.P.S. If my money has arrived from Apple Tree, please will you deposit the check for me?"

Liz folded the letter and put it back into the envelope. "Well, he seems happy enough."

"I'm going to write back now," Lucy chirped.

"Good idea. I'm sure he'd love to hear from you."

"I won't say about Gretel."

"No, I wouldn't."

"What should I say about his money for *Snigger?*"

Oddly, Liz seemed flustered by this. She pushed her red hair behind one ear and put the letter from David away in a drawer. "Well, nothing. It hasn't come yet."

"OK," said Lucy, with a breezy shrug. "I'll say it might arrive by the time he reads my letter."

"All right," Liz agreed. But in her heart she knew that the money would not come. How could it, when the publishing contract David had signed and she had promised to mail on his behalf was hidden in her drawer, along with the letter he had just sent home, and the one from his editor, Dilys Whutton?

A Strange Companion

He had been walking alone for six whole days when the old bear came to join him. Ingavar had paused to slake his thirst when the air behind him rippled with the clammy scents of another male. Lazily, he turned his head. There was rarely any sense of impending threat to an adult bear of his size and age, and though his foreleg was wounded, his nose was still sharp; the scent would be coming from many paces back.

Or so he thought.

As he turned, he immediately saw that the animal was half as close as he'd expected, almost as if it had landed from the sky. He swung around to face it, taking care not to show any hint of pain or impaired movement. But the old bear displayed no signs of aggression, and continued to pad belatedly forward, following Ingavar's tracks in the snow.

To the younger bear's amazement, it stopped within easy reach of a charge. Then it, too, bent down and slaked its thirst. "You have walked a long way," it said, snow falling out of the side of its mouth.

Ingavar squinted darkly at the bear and raised his head in a threatening stance. After what he had seen six days before, he was not prepared to take risks with strangers. "Move on," he growled, and flicked his snout in a bearing south of his chosen tracks.

The old bear dipped its head to acknowledge Ingavar's physical dominance. Then it grunted and ate more snow. "Why would I want to walk that way when it would bring me into the clutches of men?"

This, of course, made Ingavar twitch. It was many years since he had visited the dump town and his pathway there was admittedly unclear. And now here was this potbellied, straggle-haired lump giving him rough directions to it. He stood, paralyzed by indecision. If this bear was right, how could he think of changing course without invoking meddlesome questions?

The old bear settled down, tucking its hind paws under its belly. It yawned and turned a paw, raking its tongue between the outstretched claws. "You seem confused, Nanuk."

Ingavar ground his teeth. This visitor was bold, he had to give it that. He had not been spoken to as "Nanuk" in years. Although it was a word which described all bears, it was only ever used when an adult spoke down to a younger one, usually in a scornful manner. This bear had used it in a friendlier sense, and that made Ingavar strangely unsettled. "Why were you following me?" he asked, letting the words rumble out of his throat.

"I was curious," the old one said. "The pattern of your tracks suggested you were limping. Now I see your wounds and I understand why. What I don't understand, when the sea ice is freezing and the seal grounds will soon be full, is why a bear so strong in tooth and claw is heading toward land when every other bear will be eager to leave it."

"Who are you?" said Ingavar, swiping the ice, his ego now as ruffled as the fur on his back.

The old bear continued to groom in peace. "My name is Thoran," he said.

Ingavar turned his snout away and gave a swift, derisive snort. He might have guessed this bear would carry the name of the first white bear to walk the ice. Some mothers would never understand the ridicule they put their offspring through. He swung his head again, north this time. "Move on, old bear. Go to the seal grounds, while you still have the strength to catch one."

Thoran shook his head and yawned. "I am tired. We should rest awhile."

"We?" Ingavar barreled his chest.

"There is a blizzard approaching. What point would there be in battling the wind on three good legs and a scratching limp? If you have sense as well as strength, you will lay your injured shoulder against me and let me protect you from the cold."

Blizzard? Ingavar pricked his ears. From the north came the faint but definite whistle of an angry wind. Not only that, a few loose crystals were racing across the surface of the ice. The visitor was right, a blizzard *was* coming. Ingavar blew a throaty sigh and forced his canines into his lip. Once again, this heap of old fur had surprised him. "Why?" he said to Thoran. "Why would you protect me?"

Thoran laid his head down flat. "In Ragnar's time, bears thought nothing of sleeping in packs. You are a son of Ragnar, are you not?"

Ingavar narrowed his gaze.

"Lie down, Nanuk. You need to rest."

The wind moaned and clipped the tips of Ingavar's ears. What could he do but give in and accept the older bear's wisdom? Blowing the pride from his overworked lungs, he buckled his knees and let himself flop, pressing his injured, aching shoulder into Thoran's warm, dry flank. And as the grazing edge of the blizzard came upon them and the snowflakes began to number and stick, he drew himself up in a bulging heap and pushed his long snout deep into the pit between Thoran's open foreleg and belly. He was exhausted and had no wish to speak, but as his eyes grew heavy with the prospect of sleep, he used his throat to rasp four words. "My name is Ingavar," he said.

And then he slept.

LUCY WRITES BACK

True to her word, on the same day that David's letter arrived, Lucy sat down at the kitchen table and spent the next few hours penning a reply. There was much sighing and clucking and frantic crossings out, coupled with balls of crumpled paper flying hither and thither around the room. Bonnington had to paw one out of his dinner bowl, Liz closed the washing machine door on another (Lucy's white school ankle socks came out a shade of gray as a result), and the listening dragon on top of the fridge narrowly escaped being clouted by a bundle that also contained a lot of pencil shavings (Lucy liked to write her letters out in pencil first).

But eventually she settled with a bright blue pen and a notepad with a picture of two red squirrels. In her neatest, most confident handwriting she put: *This is Hermione. Her friend's name is Crispin. They are the king and queen of the pine forest. They used to be gray and nobody liked them until a magic owl turned them red. I think you could do a good story about them.* Then she got on with the proper business of reporting all the news from Wayward Crescent.

She mentioned first how *quiet* things were, mainly due to the fact that their annoying neighbor, Mr. Bacon, had decided to go on a three-week cruise to somewhere called the Gulf of Mexico. *He says he will bring me some jumping beans,* she wrote, *but I would rather have a stick of rock from you. I told Mom you promised to bring home some rock with ARCTIC written all the way through it. Do not let me down!*

And so it went on. By midafternoon she was starting the fourth and last quarter of the notepad when Liz announced she was going shopping and did Lucy want to come? Lucy was deeply engrossed in telling David about the colors of the trees in the library gardens, and how she had gathered a variety of leaves and pressed them in her copy of *Snigger and the Nutbeast,* and here was a small horse chestnut leaf she had found right over Conker's grave, which she was sending to him to remind him of Scrubbley. No, she didn't want to go shopping, thank you, but was it OK if she ran to the post office just up the road and delivered her letter before they closed?

Liz said she could, as long as she was careful and came straight back. Oh, and would she mail the letters on the bench in the den?

Lucy finished off by writing, *Gadzooks is missing you lots, but not enough to shed his fire tear, don't worry!! He's making drawings of stars, Gwillan says. Isn't that funny, you talking about stars and him drawing them? I will go and have a look at his pad when I have done this. I will tickle his scales until he goes tee hee hee like you do when you laugh. Have you told Zanna you do that? He does, Zanna, honest! It's very embarrassing. He snores, too. I have to run now or I will miss the mail. Oh, I nearly forgot. Your money hasn't come, and Mom says Gretel is . . .* She paused to chew her pen and think. What could she say, truthfully, about Gretel? Bending her head again, she wrote . . . *pining for Zanna, but we are keeping an eye on her. I think it will be good when you both come home. Please send another letter if you have time. Lots of love from Lucy xxx*

"Now, I need his address," she said to Gwillan. "Fly upstairs and get the letter, will you?"

Hrrr, went Gwillan, shaking his head. The letter, he reminded her, was put into a drawer. G'reth or Gruffen might be able to open it, but not a little puffler dragon like him.

Lucy tapped his snout. "OK, I'll go."

In the Dragon's Den, she picked up two letters her mother had left by the pottery turntable, then opened the workbench drawer. At first she didn't notice the large brown envelope underneath the white one, franked with a picture of Apple Tree's famous award-winning character *Kevin the Karaoke Kangaroo.* But as she grabbed David's letter and went to close the drawer, a dragon's voice rumbled and she hesitated and turned.

It was Gretel, holding tight to the bars of her cage.

Lucy went over and crouched beside it. "You know I can't let you out."

Gretel shook her head. *Hrrr,* she said.

Lucy frowned. "What do you mean, you know why Gadzooks is unhappy?"

Gretel rolled her eyes toward the drawer.

The guard dragon, Gruffen, fluttered back there to investigate. Scotch tape, scissors, and some envelopes, he hurred.

"I know, I've just seen them," Lucy said.

Hrrr, said Gretel, meaning she hadn't seen *everything.*

So Lucy went back and had a proper look. And that was how she discovered the stamped and sealed envelope addressed to Dilys Whutton, Apple Tree Publishing. "That's David's contract," she muttered. "Mom's forgotten to mail it. That's why he hasn't got his money yet."

Hrr-rrr, Gretel said, crossing her paws behind her back as if she had done the house a great service.

Lucy said, "Does Zookie know?"

Gretel raised her shoulders.

Lucy hummed and dented her chin with a finger. "Perhaps he sensed it and that's why he can't properly write things for David?"

Gretel gave her a wide-eyed look.

"I still can't let you out," said Lucy, feeling an awful pang of guilt as Gretel dropped her wings and shuffled out of sight.

"I've got to hurry," Lucy told herself, glancing at the clock. And without ever thinking that her mother might have had a very good reason for keeping the contract hidden from the world, she put on her hat and coat and gloves, and hurried to the post office to have her letter weighed. Then she put all the letters in the mailbox.

And that was when the trouble began.

A Sign in the Sky

When Ingavar woke, the moon was out and he was coated with a shallow crust of ice. Thoran had already risen and was sitting not far away, staring fast into the dome of the night.

"It is time," he said, without turning his head.

"For what?" said Ingavar. He raised himself clumsily and shook away the snow.

Thoran began to walk.

"Hey, hey, where are you going? Come back." Ingavar's voice was suddenly taut with a mixture of anxiety and irritation. Thoran had moved off along the route he claimed would lead to Chamberlain, the dump town.

"Ragnar was never one for stars," he said. "He was guided by impulse, and that was his downfall. I pray that you and I will be more fortunate."

Ingavar ran on ahead and turned. He walloped the ice, forcing the old bear to stop and sit. "Go back, Thoran. We are not together."

Thoran looked deep into the younger bear's eyes. "I am following a sign," he said. "It seems it may take me into those territories overrun with men. If that is your intention, too, son of Ragnar, you may do well to keep me at your side. Men fear bears. That you know. And what they fear, they sometimes kill. In the dump town, they will be tolerant of us. I am old and easily pitied. But any men with knowledge of the ancient legends might not be so generous to a bear with the mark of Oomara in his head."

At this, Ingavar started wildly. He swept away, looking for a mirror, for water. The lying, sniveling, cheating raven had said that none but the girl would see the mark!

Thoran continued on his way. "Do not vex yourself," he called. "The scars are only clear to those, like me, who can read them in your auma."

Auma? Ingavar had heard this word, but knew nothing whatsoever of its meaning. Once again he loped on ahead, shuffling backward to make sure Thoran had to face him. "You talk in many riddles, old bear."

"The path to wisdom is not always straight," said Thoran.

Ingavar blew a cloud of vapor. "What is auma?"

"Your spirit; the fire inside you."

Ingavar narrowed his eyes in confusion. He had never been one for talk of spirits. What he couldn't hit, he was wary of. "You said you were following a sign. What did you mean by that?"

Without breaking the rhythm of his stride Thoran said, "Look up, Nanuk, what do you see?"

Ingavar glanced at the widely spaced dots. "Stars," he grunted.

"Can you read them? Do you use them to find your way?"

Ingavar snorted low between his paws.

"No. A true son of Ragnar, then?"

"And what are you? A Teller's cub? A dainty son of Lorel?"

Thoran, if he was angered by this, did not growl or stoop to show it. Instead he said chillingly, "One day, Ingavar, you will know. Look between the three stars that point down like a snout and the cluster just to the right of them. What do you see?"

Frustrated, Ingavar turned and squinted. Had no one ever told this waddling fool that bears used their noses, not their eyes, for distance? Nonetheless, he singled out a pulsing, yellow star.

"Good," said Thoran. "That is the sign. Watch it carefully. Let its auma join with yours."

"It has fire?" asked Ingavar, who had never thought that stars were anything more than the eyes of his ancestors watching over him.

"It *is* fire," Thoran replied. "All of them are. But the one that I am following is special. It has not appeared for many, many turns of the ice."

Curious now, Ingavar walked a few paces ahead as if he would like to put out his tongue and swallow the star up whole, like a snowflake. "How do you know this? *Are* you a Teller?"

"Of a kind," said Thoran.

More riddles. Ingavar shook his fur. "Then what does this *fire star* mean for us?"

Thoran slowed down and padded to a halt, raising his gaze in reverence to the sky. "You and I and all that we are, came from the center of these lights, Nanuk." And while Ingavar continued to stare and wonder, Thoran let his auma join with the fire star. His claws reached deep into the pure white ice as if he was searching for a long-forgotten memory. Into his mind came thoughts of an island. An island far away where a giant creature lay sleeping in stone. "Gawain," he whispered alone to the sky. And it may have been a trick of the changing moonlight, but his forehead was suddenly ablaze with fire, and three deep scars that men and bears called the mark of Oomara were alive, then gone, in the blink of the night.

Joining Dots

"You did what?" Liz lowered her shopping bags and threw her daughter such a look of deep shock that Lucy felt compelled to pull a tissue from her sleeve and blow her nose to avoid eye contact.

"It was in your drawer — with a stamp on and everything."

"Yes, and that's where it should have stayed."

"But you *promised* you would mail it and I thought you had. Instead, you hid it and you didn't even *tell* me. That's sneaky, Mom. David will go mad."

Liz sank into a kitchen chair, rubbing her brow. "Something wasn't right about that contract, Lucy. It was tainted with Gwilanna's magics, I'm sure of it."

Lucy settled nervously against the workbench. She

thought back to the day that David had signed the agreement with his publisher, then left to go to the Arctic. The ink in his signature had run down the page, which was odd because the pen he'd used had not been "globby." The ink had run to form a strange kind of sign. This was what Lucy queried now: "Just because of that dribbly pen mark?"

Bonnington leaped onto Liz's lap. She stroked him idly and quietly said, "Yes."

On the fridge top, the listening dragon stirred. Within seconds, it had transmitted the information around the house. Dragon scales everywhere nervously rattled.

"I did intend to mail it, but I changed my mind. I was planning to talk it through with David when he came home. It would have been easy for his publishers to draw up a copy contract. Now, I don't know what's going to happen."

"It's just a piece of paper," Lucy protested.

Liz set her gaze into the middle distance and shook

her head slowly, deep in thought. "No, I think that mark's significant. Gwilanna's using it to set something evil in motion, something to do with David's writing, perhaps. Mailing the contract probably represented the final commitment she needed for her spell."

"But . . . ?"

"Shush, it's all right." Liz clutched her hand. "Whatever it is, we'll deal with it. But we should be on our guard. And David needs to be alerted now."

Lucy pushed the cordless phone across the table.

"Not just yet. Go and call Gadzooks. I want to talk to him. He seemed ruffled this morning. I want to know why."

Lucy turned on her heels, then back again. "What about Zanna? She's got that mark. Is she going to turn into an evil sibyl?"

"I don't know," said Liz, hugging Bonnington to her. "Go and bring Gadzooks — and tell Gruffen to keep a close eye on Gretel."

* * *

Meanwhile, on the windowsill in David's room, G'reth and Gadzooks were engaged in another important conversation — about the origins of the universe. G'reth, by virtue of his gift of granting wishes, had vast experience in the workings of the universe — but as to its origins, there he was stumped. He felt sure that the universe had not always been in being and therefore something had created it. But what?

Gadzooks tapped his pencil against his pad. In his opinion, he said, the answer to the mystery was in the stars.

G'reth raised an eye ridge and glanced into the garden. The sky was barely gray. No stars were visible yet. Why did Gadzooks want to know this, he queried?

The writing dragon chewed on his pencil, making another score in its end. The David was thinking about it, he said.

At that moment, Lucy walked in and asked Gadzooks to come to the kitchen.

Seeming grateful for the chance to cease his pondering,

Gadzooks laid his pad and pencil on the sill and flew straightaway to Lucy's shoulder.

G'reth blew a smoke ring and rattled his scales. He'd been hoping to assess his brother dragon's thoughts on this worrying business concerning Gwilanna, but for now the moment was gone. He drummed his claws and looked along the sill. His gaze alighted on the pencil and pad. He had always been entranced by this simple device of writing things down and having them happen. Curious to know just how it worked, he pottered over and peered at the pad. He picked it up and let it fall open. The pages fluttered and came to rest at a relatively simple pattern of stars. G'reth couldn't help it; he picked up the pencil. He turned the pad left. He turned it right. He looked at its reflection in the windowpane. Then he did something rather odd. He put the pencil onto the pad and began to join the dots in their mirror image. And who knows what force was guiding his paw, but as a shape began to emerge, so G'reth came to have the sudden understanding that the universe was born from the very same place that Gadzooks received his inspiration. In other words, the force which created words and matter was one and the same.

What's more, as he continued to draw, he realized with some degree of surprise that his work was not done. Before the David had traveled north, he, G'reth, had granted a wish that his master should learn the secret of the fire tear of Gawain, the last true dragon to inhabit the Earth. David had made a great discovery — about the relationship of ice to fire. But it was not the *whole* story, just a fragment of it. G'reth could see that now. For the David to understand the secret in full, he needed to step back further in time and learn where the dragon's fire had come from. In essence, that was simply answered: Gawain's fire had originated at the center of the Earth. But where had the Earth itself come from? And how had the fire been born at its center? That was the real mystery.

Snap! G'reth gave a startled *hurr* and looked down anxiously at the pad. His concentration had been so deep that the pencil tip had broken beneath the weight of the pressure he'd applied to it. Yet to his surprise, the joined up star dots had formed a message. Not much of a message, it had to be said. But an interesting one. Just a single letter:

G

At the Water's Edge

Lights. Not high in the sky, but lower down, twinkling on the far horizon. Thoran slowed to a halt and tipped his glistening nose toward them. "That is the dump town, the place that men call Chamberlain," he said.

Ingavar drew up close alongside, testing the strength of the ice underfoot. Since dawn, their pursuit of the pulsing yellow star — which Thoran claimed he could sense in daylight — had been hampered by stretches of open water, steadily increasing in number and size. Several times they had had to change course, so that Ingavar would not need to swim between floes. Now, even that was not an option. The ice was fragile here. With one stout lunge this loose foundation would splinter and crack and they would sink to their necks in ice-cold water. Ingavar's shoulder could not take that.

"What do we do?" he asked, his voice tarred deep with pain and frustration.

"We wait for the sea to sleep," said Thoran.

Ingavar pushed his face into the wind. It was bitterly cold, so cold that his snorts of vaporizing breath were turning to frost as they blew back against his thinning snout. The description of the forthcoming freeze amused him, but the sight of so much water did not. All he could see between himself and the lights that marked the edge of the land were several miles of undulating peaks, dotted with chunks of unfused ice. "It might be days," he said, thumping the surface again to be sure.

"Then why waste your energy pushing and prodding like an ignorant cub? Everything has its time, Nanuk. The stars travel slowly. So will we."

Stars. To the amber eye of the ordinary bear they were hidden in the reddening dusk of nightfall and the knotted clouds lying dormant overhead. Almost a day had passed since Thoran had spoken of following a "sign." Ingavar had spent a large portion of that time walking alone and pondering this. Was it simply coincidence that he should be seeking out the tooth of Ragnar when there was a new star above the dump town? No, not a new star, a *returning star,* if the old Teller was to be believed. Ingavar growled and blew away a sigh. He scraped the ice into a ridge below his paw, feeling its wet bite soak around his claws. His mind had been dizzy with fragments of myth and legend all day. The ice, its texture, its coldness, its ubiquity was all that was keeping his sanity intact. The same could not be said of his patience. He trod the mound flat and swung his body sideways, limping back and forth along the jagged waterline, never taking his gaze off the lights.

Thoran, watching him, stretched out his paws and allowed his body to sink to the ice. "Your injury is growing worse," he said. "And still you are anxious to walk, not rest." He yawned and looked across the water at Chamberlain. "For every light you see, there are at least four men. It must take a quest of great importance to risk surrounding yourself with them."

Ingavar breathed in, tightening his jaw. Thus far on their journey, Thoran had not pressed him for information regarding his purpose in Chamberlain. To hear it voiced now, when they might be stranded for a number of days with only words and the wind for company, made Ingavar very uneasy. The old bear had cleverness wrapped around his tongue. No doubt he would have some reproving words to say about a settlement made with a changeling raven. But that trade was hidden in Ingavar's heart, as sealed as a mother bear in her den. He dared not let it out, nor, despite Thoran's kindness through the blizzard, drag him into potential danger. So, with a false air of severity, he said, "When we reach the town, we go our own ways."

Thoran responded with a courteous nod. "Do you know what they will do to you, when they catch you?"

The young bear stared ahead in silence.

"They will shoot you down again, Nanuk. This time

with a potion to make you sleep. Then they will cage you and ridicule you. If fortune is with you, they will use their machines to fly you back to beyond where we met. Or they may cage you for the rest of your days. Tell me, son of Ragnar, where would be the honor in that?"

The wind coursed through Ingavar's fur. He flexed his shoulder so the cream hairs rippled. "I will be stronger in the town," he said.

"You speak like a bear with vengeance in his heart."

"All bears have a score to settle with men."

"So you know the legend of Oomara?" said Thoran.

But Ingavar fell into a brooding silence and Thoran decided he would press him no further. "Rest," he said. "Before morning, the fire star will guide us across the water."

"How?" Ingavar demanded grumpily.

But by then, Thoran was asleep once more.

A Special Treat

"Wow," said a voice. "So that's what you get up to when you sneak in here . . ."

"Thank *you,*" said David, clicking his mouse. The story of Thoran, Ingavar, and Chamberlain vanished to a box on the toolbar at the bottom of the computer screen.

"It's good," said Zanna, looking over his shoulder. "Put it back up. Let me read some more. How much have you done?"

"Four chapters — nearly enough, if I hadn't been interrupted." He closed the laptop shut. "I think my ice samples call."

"No, they don't," she said, and plopped herself in his lap.

"Zanna, cut it out. This is Bergstrom's office!"

"Oh, getting picky now, are we?" She tossed her long black hair aside. "You didn't complain when I came to keep you warm last night, author boy."

"That was different. *That* was private. Come on, Tootega might be in the lab."

Pouting, she reached out and pushed the door shut. It settled in the frame, displaying a poster of an Arctic landscape bathed in a dusky, purple light. "*Blurghh* to Mr. Inuit grumpy guts," she said, sticking out her tongue and waggling it. "Have you seen that necklace he's wearing today? It's a shaman's charm, full of bones and pouches and hanks of fur."

"I hear they're all the rage up here."

"You can joke," she said, "but it's not funny for me. He thinks I'm an evil spirit."

"Don't be dumb."

"I'm not joking. You've seen how he avoids me. He clocked this yesterday and flipped."

She pushed back the sleeve of her chunky knit sweater. On her arm was the legacy of her fight with

Gwilanna. Three sticklike lines, climbing in a curving ragged stroke from just behind the elbow to halfway down the forearm.

"That's a mess," said David, screwing up his nose.

"Thanks. You look great in the mornings, too." She pulled her sleeve back down to her wrist. "I saw Manorski, the medic, yesterday, to try to find out why it won't heal over. He thinks the lacerations are infected, that's all. He's given me some antibiotic cream. I have to rub it in three times a day until the sibyl Gwilanna goes up in smoke."

"Good," said David, hoping the metaphor would prove correct. Zanna had always refused to accept that the marks were anything more than deep-lying scratches. So why, David wondered, was Tootega so very jumpy around her? And why had he himself been so unnerved when he'd seen that near-identical arrangement appear in the head of a bear on a poster in Henry Bacon's study? He glanced at the laptop. The sign had driven his urge to write, about Ingavar and Thoran and the history of the Arctic. But that was just a story, a saga in his head. Imagination coinciding handily with reality. A spooky synchronicity, nothing more.

Wasn't it?

Zanna caught his eye and looked back at the machine. "What?" she queried.

And that was one good reason she should not go reading his story yet: If she knew he'd based his "mark of Oomara" on her injury she'd go totally ape. "Nothing," he said, tugging her around with a fistful of her sweater. "You look good like this, all kind of . . . homely."

"David, I look like a seal," she said. "Arctic clothing is not very flattering."

He had to smile at that. Back home, she would have been midriff bare, bangle heavy, head to toe in purple and black. What a change a climate made.

"Story," she said. "Tell me something about it. On the flight over you said it began with a mother bear and cub sitting on the pack ice near the Tooth of Ragnar, talking about their ancestry and stuff."

"It did," said David, "but since we've been up here

I've had some new ideas. Everything I've written has been about these two male bears — one old and wise, the other young and aggressive — crossing the pack ice."

"Migrating north?"

"No, that's the twist. They're coming in to town, not away from it. They're following a star. Well, the old one is."

"Whoa, the baby Jesus lives in Chamberlain?"

"In an igloo next to the inn. Try again."

"Um, the star's a comet on a collision course with Canada? It's going to wipe out all the bears unless someone stops it?"

"Surprisingly, no. And that wouldn't be too kind to our hosts now, would it?"

"Sorry, Canada," she said, saluting the flag on Bergstrom's desk.

"That's the flag of Norway," David groaned. "The clue's in the missing maple leaf."

"Never in the Girl Scout guides. Flags are not my strong point. OK, why's the other one coming?"

"Other what?"

"Bear, knucklehead. If one is a wise pack leader from the East, what's the other guy's agenda?"

"Oh, Ingavar. He's been shot in the shoulder. He's coming because . . . he wants to be healed."

"By the good kind fair-haired Dr. Bergstrom?"

"Something like that."

"Really? Is Bergstrom in it?"

David glanced at the laptop again. "There might be a character based on him."

"Don't be cagey. Zannas like truth." She tugged a finger at the neck of his sweater.

He told her a partial truth: "I'm waiting for Gadzooks to decide."

"Cool. You've pictured him?"

"Hmm. Kind of. He sent me a cryptic letter this morning."

Zanna shook with surprise. "That's some smart dragon. How much writing can he get on that pad?"

"Not *Dear David, how's it going?*, you doofus. A letter from the alphabet."

"Was it *Z?*" she asked brightly, showing her perfect, dentist-daddy teeth.

"No. It was *G.* No words or phrases. Just a capital letter *G.* I'm still trying to work out what it means."

"Dragon name. They all begin with a *G.*"

"Great, that narrows things down a bit."

She slapped his shoulder. "Don't get smart. Maybe he's trying to tell you something. About Grockle, say — or Gretel?"

"Stop fishing," said David, shaking his head. "I didn't get any bad vibes from him and it didn't feel specific to any one dragon. Besides, he normally only writes when I'm stuck with a story."

"Are you?"

"Hmm, maybe." He planed a hand. "I wasn't planning for my bears to be stranded on pack ice at the water's edge, but I think I've resolved that."

"How?"

"Not telling you. Wait and see."

"Howww?" she persisted, trying to persuade him with a peck on his lips.

At that moment the door swung open and a tall lean figure in jeans and a buckskin jacket looked in. “Hey, lovebirds.”

“Hey, Russ.” Zanna sat up, swinging a leg.

“I assure you, this is not what it looks like,” said David, feeling a rush of color to his cheeks. He patted Zanna’s hip, trying to move her off his lap.

She, true to form, stayed put.

Russ laughed and said, “If I was where you are, I’d be whistling, David.” He winked at Zanna and tipped his battered old cowboy hat. “Got a message from Anders. He’s been delayed a while longer, because of bad weather.”

“Is he stuck on the pack ice at the water’s edge?”

“Huh?”

“Ignore her,” said David. “It’s a dumb inside joke.”

“Whatever,” said Russ. “Anders wants a couple of the team to drive in to Chamberlain and grab some supplies. Naturally, I thought you swingers would be up for it.” He threw Zanna a set of keys.

“The pickup?” she whooped, looking out the

window at the long red truck parked across the compound, next to a pen of rusting oil barrels.

"Don't wreck it," said Russ. "There's a big bad desert called the tundra out there, packed with potholes and killer lemmings. Stick to the road and take it slow. Weather flips quicker than a dime up here. If the wind kicks in from the north, it'll be just like driving through icing sugar. You get stuck, you buzz in on the com, OK?"

"No problem," said David, pressing his fingertips together in excitement.

"Here's a list," said Russ, handing him one. "There's a trading post in the center of town. You can't miss it. Sells everything you need from a button to a beaver." He took out his wallet. "Here's two hundred bucks. Put it in a pocket without a hole."

Zanna leaped off David's lap. "How long can we stay?"

"I want the both of you back in the base before seven, or I'll have Tootega feed your butts to the huskies."

"If we get lost," Zanna said, big-eyed, "will you come and rescue us in your chopper?"

David groaned and slapped a hand across his face in embarrassment.

Russ pointed a serious finger. "This is a treat, girl. Don't mess up." He opened the door and backed into the lab.

"Russ?" David called him back.

"Yup?"

"Any chance we'll see a bear?"

The pilot rolled a piece of gum against his cheek. "Maybe, though most should be up on the headland by now. You know the drill, right?"

Zanna laid her face against her steepled fingers. "Lie down and play dead."

"Takes a lot of bottle to do that, honey. Better to drop an item of clothing. Bears are curious by nature; they'll stop to check it out. Back off real slow and keep dropping if you have to, till you reach the nearest house. There's an unwritten law in Chamberlain that folks don't lock their doors. No one's gonna thank you for bringing home a bear, but they won't turn you away either."

"What if you run out of clothing?" Zanna asked.

Russ laughed and tipped his hat at her again. "Better to arrive butt naked than dead. Never run or look a bear straight in the eye. Makes 'em kinda testy. My advice is, you steer good and clear of those boys. If you're gonna go sightseeing, shy away from the rocks on the shores of the bay. High season, the bears hang out around there. You wouldn't be the first to be surprised by a sleepy male dreaming of his next seal supper. You copy that, David?"

"Sure," he said, fingering the polar bear's tooth around his neck.

"OK. Get wrapped. It's like the arctic out there."

"Cool," said Zanna.

"You'd better believe it," said Russ. "Don't forget the toilet paper or the beans."

Strange Goings-On

Meanwhile, back in Wayward Crescent, something odd was happening in the Dragon's Den. The stained-glass ornament which hung in the window behind Liz's workbench suddenly twirled on its string, and this was followed by a gentle fall of soot down the chimney. Gruffen, who was over by the door as always, sitting on his book of dragon procedures and dozing (because Lucy had forgotten to alert him), shook himself awake and went to investigate. The fireplace seemed to be largely undisturbed. Even so, he flew up it a ways, straining his violet eyes into the gloom. There was nothing to see. And when the atmosphere of filth began to irritate his nostrils, he went back to his perch and fell soundly asleep.

But unbeknownst to him and every other dragon

present, something solid had landed in the grate. When it was sure it would not be detected, it flew silently across the room, invisible except for the flecks of soot that were tracing its outline and flicking off its wings. It landed on the workbench. On tiptoes it approached the stone dragon, Grockle. It tilted its head in a sympathetic manner, placing a paw on the edge of the basket as if it would like to rock Grockle in his sleep. It did not touch the cold gray scales, but waved its paw in a circular movement over Grockle's head as though it was trying to break the cruel spell that had seen the poor creature born without fire. Grockle did not respond and the visiting dragon showed no sign of expectation that he would. Instead, it now walked across the table, leaving nothing but the faintest black prints on the wood. Then it carefully and cleverly opened David's letter. Now it faced a more difficult task, for its mission was to tear out Zanna's blood spot. But this it did, making barely a sound. Then it flew across the room and landed next to Gretel's cage. Sensing a presence, she drew toward the bars.

The invisible dragon stretched out its paw and dropped the blood spot and a small white flower inside the cage.

Gretel, no stranger to magics and spells, having once been a cohort of the sibyl, Gwilanna, showed admirable composure when these objects mysteriously appeared at her feet. She glanced at the sleeping Gruffen, then secreted the items away. On silent lips, she asked the dragon its name.

On the quietest of whispers it told her: Groyne.

Then it was gone, back to the chimney.

And no one, especially not Gruffen, had seen it.

For a short time after this strange encounter, Gretel did nothing but sit and think. Then she picked up the blood spot and warmed it in her paw, until the paper was crumbling in on itself and the tiniest prick of her mistress Zanna's blood had liquefied, ready to evaporate. With expert timing, she let it drip into the center of the flower. Its petals turned from white to a stormy shade of purple.

Then she began to cough.

Gruffen was awake in an instant. He saw Gretel tottering, holding her throat, a dark flower clasped between her stout front paws. The potions dragon. With a flower! How?

He zipped to her cage and peered warily in. Gretel, spluttering smoke from her nostrils and ears, seemed for all the world to be choking. Gruffen gripped the bars, completely taken in. As he put his snout close and asked what he could do, Gretel said, "sleep," and wafted the flower. The guard dragon jolted. His sparkling eyes stilled. He turned nine-tenths of a circle and fell.

Password, hurred Gretel.

In his flower-giddy state, poor Gruffen was helpless to resist. *Hrr-rr-aar-re-rurrr,* he murmured. The door clicked open and Gretel walked free.

Dragons around the room began to clamor with alarm, but Gretel, completely unmoved by the fuss, flew, posthaste, to Grockle's basket.

By now, Liz and Lucy were hurrying up the stairs, with Gadzooks flying on and G'reth just behind him. Calmly, Gretel made her move. She placed the newly darkened flower in the straw by Grockle's snout, stroked his head, and breathed in deep, making fire in the back of her throat. And with one quick jet of blue-white flame, she set the straw and the basket alight. . . .

On the Road to Chamberlain

This is *awesome,*" said Zanna, clinging hard to the pickup's steering wheel as they swept through clouds of onrushing snow. "If the weather on the pack ice is anything like this, I'd tell your bears to build a nice warm den and park their furry butts for a while." She smudged a gloved hand across the misting windshield and cranked up the speed of the wiper blades. A fan-shaped view of the road appeared, gray and straight, rolling with white spray blown off the surface of the neighboring tundra. "How're you getting them across the water, then? Come on, you know you want to tell me, really."

David, hunched inside a bottle green parka, pulled on the earflaps of his moose-fur hat. "When they wake, it will still be dark and the star will be reflecting across the ocean. Everywhere its light falls, an ice floe will form."

"To make stepping stones?"

"Yep."

"Neat. I like it. So this star is kind of magical, then?"

David glanced through the window at the ice-pocked wasteland, punctured here and there by tufts of grass. "Not sure yet. The story's still developing. All I know is, the star is what holds it all together. This place is phenomenal. Look at the trees."

"What trees?" said Zanna. As far as she could tell the ground was flat for miles around.

David pointed to some stunted firs. "See how they only branch on one side? The wind must have stripped them clean. Amazing."

"On the whole, I prefer the library gardens," she said, dipping her lights as a battered old Chevy came cruising past.

David broke open a packet of gum and folded a

clean stick against his tongue. "When we first arrived, I asked Bergstrom how I could describe the tundra. 'The unshaved face of God,' he called it."

The truck took a slight uneven bounce. "Well, next time you see Our Lord in Heaven, tell him to shave more often," said Zanna. "Hey, there's a thought."

"What? God shaving?"

"No, just God. There's a capital *G* if ever there was."

David flicked his gaze sideways at her. "God? A dragon?"

"Could be," she said.

The wind buffeted the side of the truck. David placed his feet against the dash for support. "I was joking."

"Naturally. You'd have to be."

"Why?"

"God's a woman. Any sensible person — and sensitive guy — knows that. Interesting, though. There are loads of creation myths involving dragons."

"Hmm," David grunted, trying to sound as though he wasn't really paying attention. Inside his sweater, he touched the tooth on its thin leather strip, letting his fingers run over its curves till his thumb was caressing the sharpened tip. The temptation to reveal what he knew about Gawain and his connection with the Arctic ice cap was immense. But Bergstrom had warned him if he spoke of these things in the presence of the tooth, the spirit of Ragnar would be unleashed. Although he wasn't fully certain what that meant, David sure as heck didn't want to find out here. "Woman?" he said, as a gender-challenged afterthought.

"Actually, in Inuit folklore, the world was made by a raven."

"What?" David almost lurched from his seat.

"You OK?" said Zanna, glancing across.

"Lost my footing. Raven, you said?"

"Mmm. Can't remember exactly how it goes. It creates the Earth, then night and day. It can do all the usual stuff: turn itself into things; animals; humans."

"Man or a woman?"

"Both, I guess."

David chewed his lip.

"Why?"

"Oh, nothing."

"Come on," she said, "spill."

He interlocked his fingers. How much dare he tell her? "There's a raven in my story. It sends Ingavar into Chamberlain."

"To the vet's?" she joked.

"No, to steal this." He dangled the tooth on its leather strip.

Now Zanna's dark eyes narrowed to a point. "I thought he was coming to have his shoulder healed?"

"Yeah, that's the deal. If he succeeds, she'll —"

"She?" Zanna said. She brought the truck to a halt beside a tall wooden sign which read:

WELCOME TO CHAMBERLAIN
POLAR BEAR CAPITAL OF THE WORLD

Farther ahead lay a cluster of single-story cabins, dressed overhead by telephone cables.

David pulled on his gloves. "Slip of the tongue. Come on, drive in. Let's find the store."

Zanna thought for a moment, then yanked on the hand brake. "What 'deal'? She who?"

Me and my big mouth, David thought. He steepled his fingers around his nose. "Gwilanna," he confessed. "She's in the story."

The Flower and G'reth

Mom!" squealed Lucy. "Hurry up! Quick! Gretel's escaped and she's trying to kill Grockle!"

Liz burst breathlessly into the den. She glanced at the cage and Gruffen's dizzied body, then placed a staying hand on Lucy's arm. G'reth and Gadzooks both landed on the bench, one on either side of the hissing Gretel.

"The fire," Lucy wailed as the flames began to lick around Grockle's ears.

"It's all right," Liz whispered. "Fire can't hurt him."

"But what if the house burns down!"

Gadzooks seemed to take this view as well. Hooking up his ridges to protect his eyes, he dipped forward to fight the flames. Gretel spiked her tail and forced him back. A shred of crackling, burning wicker broke off from the basket in which Grockle lay. Nearby stood a jam jar full of brushes, their hairs soaking in methylated spirits.

"Gretel." Liz spoke to her in soothing dragontongue.

The potions dragon flexed her claws.

"We have to put the fire out," Liz said calmly. "I promise you, no harm will come to you. But if we don't stop this, we'll have nowhere to live."

Gretel mantled her wings and stared keenly at the flames. One or two more seconds was all she needed. The petals of the flower were almost consumed. Once they went up, then —

Hrraaarr! Gadzooks dived forward again.

Instantly, he and Gretel locked jaws, wings whipping, tails thrashing, claws fully out.

Lucy squealed and covered her face. In all the eleven or so years of her life she had never seen her mother's dragons fighting before. The noise, the aggression, the *smoke* was terrifying. "Mom, make it stop," she cried.

That was also G'reth's intention. If he quenched the fire, there would be nothing to fight about. With Gretel distracted, he quickly swept in. In one deep breath he sucked at the blaze and took every last flicker of flame into his throat.

Gretel, hearing the deep inbreath, threw Gadzooks aside and turned to look. Charred straw. Rising smoke. Purple flower gone.

She roared and went for G'reth.

But by now Liz was there and clamping her wings. "Gretel, it's over. Don't struggle. Calm down. I don't want to have to use dragonsong on you."

Stupid Pennykettle dragons! Gretel hurred, catching G'reth with a spark of hot spittle. He staggered away, into the shadows beneath the wooden turntable where Liz modeled most of her dragons.

"*You're* a Pennykettle," Liz reminded Gretel. "Made by my hand. Cooled by it, if necessary." She took a chance and let her loose.

Lucy's eyes grew round with terror.

But Gretel did no more than slump by Grockle's snout, stroking the ashes off his blackened nose and singing dragon lullabies into his ear.

Gadzooks, by now recovered from the brawl (a sore foot where she'd spiked him; a chipped scale where she'd bitten) approached with caution. *Hrrr?* he said. A simple question: Why?

"How did she get out in the first place?" said Lucy. She went and got Gruffen. He was shaking all over and his eyes were swimming.

"Well?" asked Liz, crouching down beside the bench.

There was a dragon, said Gretel with a spiteful hurr.

Dozens of scaly ears pricked up. Gretel told them faithfully what had happened.

"Invisible?" gasped Lucy, running to the fireplace and peering up the stack.

Liz made a guttural sound in dragontongue to calm the nerves of the onlooking dragons. "Why was it here, Gretel? What did it want?"

Gretel shrugged. Truthfully, she did not know.

"Who sent it?" asked Lucy.

Gretel snorted in frustration and stomped her feet. *I was just about to find that out!* she hurred. *When the foolish wishing dragon stuck his fat snout in!*

"So . . . you weren't trying to give Grockle fire?" asked Lucy.

The potions dragon looked away, sullenly.

"Why set fire to his basket?" asked Liz.

A spark or two flew from Gretel's nostrils as she tossed her head like a petulant puppy. *Because the straw burned fast and the potion was fading. Breathing it in fire was the way to know its source.*

Liz lengthened her gaze to seek out G'reth. He was still under the table, whimpering slightly. "What effect would it have on a wishing dragon?"

Almost at once, G'reth let out a bone-chilling whine and fell back, writhing, tossing his head.

"What's happening?" Lucy gasped, rushing to the bench.

Her mother moved her quickly aside and cradled the wishing dragon close to her breast. Supporting his wings in the cup of her hands, she tried urgently to calm him with dragonsong. G'reth's eyes were fixed on a point in space, and it didn't look as though they were about to return. Liz lifted his spiky head, making the dragon splutter and cough. "He's having some kind of fit," she said. "Go to the bathroom and bring me a towel. I want to wrap him up to protect him."

Lucy ran from the room as if she'd chartered a jet.

She was halfway along the landing, when she heard her mother give a startled yell. She paused at once, unsure of what to do. "Mom, what's the matter?"

"Come quickly," cried Liz. Lucy pounded back, in time to see G'reth hovering in midair, held by a force that had cloaked his body in a blaze of blue light.

On the shelves, the dragons shuddered in fear. Gadzooks tried to fly to his brother dragon's aid, but Liz cried, "No!" and pulled him back.

It was just as well she did. Suddenly, the den was flooded with light. Violet eyes fast became ultraviolet, blinded by the sheer intensity of the beam. Then it was done. The light returned to its source in the heavens, and barring the stained glass clinking at the window, the room returned to normal.

With one exception.

The wishing dragon had completely disappeared.

At the Trading Post

"You're writing about *Gwilanna*?"

David shuffled uncomfortably in his seat, finding all the old springs in the fading upholstery. He presented one foot to the dashboard again and retied the yellow-flecked laces of his boot. The wipers sawed. The engine throbbed like a panting dog. Below the hood, a cooling fan kicked in. There was no such relief for Suzanna Martindale. Her heated disbelief was rising up in waves.

"It's just the way it came to me, Zanna. Sometimes when I'm writing, the story takes over. I let it run because it felt like the right thing to do."

Zanna dragged her bobble hat off her hair, making spiderweb veils of the static-charged ends. "What's her role?"

"She's evil."

"Yeah, tell me something I *don't* know, David. What does she want with your polar bear tooth?"

"It's a book, Zanna. A work of fiction. I can't answer that question, 'cause I don't know what the plot is. I haven't gone that far into it yet."

Zanna frowned and tapped her foot against the throttle. The engine responded with an irritated rev. "Did Gadzooks send you any of this?"

"No. He's had no input whatsoever — apart from the *G* I told you about."

She blew a deep sigh and shook her head. "This is spooky, David."

"It's just a story," he said.

"Yeah, right. David's answer for everything. 'It's just a *story,* Zanna.' Just a lie, you mean." She dropped the parking brake and gunned the truck forward. Its rear wheels squealed as they bit the road. Snowflakes as large as lemons hit the screen and were quickly swept aside into a layer of slush. Zanna shifted her gaze to the east. Out toward open water, surrounded by dirt stacks and rusting junked machinery, lay the moody hulk of the grain elevator, a large white ocean liner of a building, blackened with smoke from a nearby chimney, splashed against the bleak gray Manitoba sky. For eight months of the year, when the bay was clear of ice, Chamberlain fed the north with grain. The sight of it reminded her why they'd come. "Got your list?"

David unflapped a pocket.

"Why'd you do it?" she muttered.

"It's just a story," he repeated.

"David, don't be dumb. You found out when you were writing *Snigger* what a fine line there is between what you imagine and what you create. Something's going on here. I can feel it in my blood. That witch is up to something."

David folded his arms and turned to watch the scenery. As Zanna had remarked, it was all pretty bleak. The romantic in him had wanted to see a bygone time of people in furs outside their igloos, chewing skins and dressing kayaks. But the latter-day reality wasn't even close. The "igloos" were rows of painted wooden buildings, mostly squat residential cabins. The only suggestion of a native heritage was a parka-clad figure attending a dog team. The man had a cigarette hanging off his lip and two curtains of black hair sprouting shabbily from under his cap. The dogs, despite the unflagging cold, seemed as happy as a small flock of sheep in a summer field.

As they turned into the center of the town, David was reminded that one of the principal attractions of Chamberlain was its tourist industry. People came here to photograph bears. There were several gift shops testifying to it, plus an Inuit museum he'd heard Russ and Dr. Bergstrom talk about. On its wall was a sign declaring, FIVE CITIZENS FOR EVERY BEAR. He took this to mean that the town's population was approximately one thousand, as he knew from his studies that somewhere around two hundred bears passed through Chamberlain annually. Yellow warning signs were everywhere, reminding people of it.

BE ALERT!
POLAR BEAR SEASON
October thru November
Memorize this number

The number in question was the polar bear "police." If any bad guys lumbered in, Chamberlain, it seemed, was ready to run them out of town.

The trading post, when they found it, didn't quite match David's expectations either. He'd been hoping to see an old log cabin hanging with pelts and a pig's tail of black smoke curling out of a tilting iron chimney. Instead, they found a stocky, modern building, more a warehouse than a trapper's retreat. Wide and gray, with double-glazed windows, thick brown eaves, and a double gable front, it reminded him of the mobile homes he'd seen carried on huge transporters back in America.

Zanna parked out front behind a Cherokee jeep. "Don't think you're off the hook," she groused. "I'll talk to you later about Gwilanna. For now, let's go trade."

Collars up, they climbed a short flight of steps to a fenced-off landing, before opening the door on a room warmly lit by two clusters of spotlights. A jangle of wind chimes followed them in as their footsteps echoed off the polished wooden floors, answering high into the heavy beamed ceiling. The cloying smell of worked leather hung in the air.

"Wow," went Zanna, immediately entranced. She turned a full circle, gazing in awe at the Inuit wall-hangings and other forms of traditional artwork. "Aw, look, mukluks," she said, and shot into a side room where a large assortment of the arctic boots were on display on a tier of shelves.

Typical, thought David. *You bring a woman to the last store before the North Pole and what does she do? Heads straight for the shoes.*

"Howdy," said a voice.

From behind a counter stacked with candies, tobacco, and smoked arctic char, stepped a middle-aged man with ash-white hair. He was wearing a red-check lumberjack shirt and heavy blue jeans, turned up at the ankle. "Where you from?" he asked, with a welcoming smile.

"The research base just down the road," said David.

The man nodded freely, shaking hands. "Yar, shoulda guessed. You look kinda sharp. You up here long?"

"A few weeks, that's all. We're on a college trip."

"Oh yar," the man crooned, picking up a soft broom and sweeping the floor. He spoke in the happy, laid-back accent that some of the workers at the base possessed.

David brandished his list. "We've been sent here to buy a few regular supplies, but I can't see any of the stuff I need."

"O-kaay, let's see what you got." The man took the list and ran a finger check down it, reading off the items one by one. "Yar, we can give you all of that. We got general goods farther back, beyond the pelts. Why don't you take a look around here, buy your pretty girl some boots, maybe. I'll have this bagged up and put in your truck."

"Really?"

"Sure thing. Or I'm not Albert Walbert the third. That your pickup, right there?"

"The red one, yeah."

"On the way," he said. He disappeared, whistling, into the rear of the store.

David went to seek out Zanna. "Result. I traded with Albert the third."

"These are cool," she said, not hearing a word. She pulled on a pair of beige colored mukluks with bearded insteps and fox-fur trim.

"Two hundred and forty-five dollars?" said David, somewhat alarmed by the size of the price tag.

"Rich daddy," she reminded him. "And I have plastic. Besides, the fun is in the trying on."

David glanced at the shelves. There were thirty pairs or more, plus mittens for later. Zanna was on her fifth and not coming up for air. "Gonna have a look at the carvings," he said, and drifted back into the main craft area, toward a velvet-covered table arrayed with an assortment of soapstone figures.

There were several of bears and other arctic animals,

but the one which caught his eye was of the sea goddess, Sedna. She was sculpted in the shape of a common mermaid and made from the black variety of the stone. The detail was impressive. Her body shape flowed in graceful lines, but her face was twisted and tormented with grief. David turned the figure over to read the inscription on the green onyx base. Legend had it that Sedna had married a hunter, who had really been a raven and taken her to his nest. She had cried to her father to save her. He had rescued her and paddled her away in a kayak. But the raven and many seabirds had followed, raising the waves until the father feared the boat would capsize and he would drown. So he had thrown his daughter overboard to save himself. When Sedna clung to onc side of the boat, her father had cruelly cut off her fingers and thrown them in the sea, where they became —

"Seal," said a voice.

Startled, David almost let the carving drop. He turned to his right and found his way blocked by a short dark man with a face like crumpled leather.

"Seal, walrus, whale, and fish." The man flicked up a stubby finger for each.

"Tootega, what are you doing here?"

"Trade," said the Inuk. He nodded at a small clutch of furs on the counter, then at the carving in David's hands. "You buy?"

David put the figure back. "No, just looking."

"Um," Tootega grunted. "You ever see raven?"

Hairs rose all over David's body. "What?" he said.

"Raven. Bad spirit. Angry bird. Evil. He fool Sedna. Make her marry. You buy. She protect against harmful ravens."

"I don't need any protection, thanks."

Tootega spat on the floor. "Why you got a bear's tooth 'round your neck?"

This rattled David more than the talk about ravens. In all this time, he had no idea Tootega knew about the tooth. He zipped his parka up to the chin. "Gotta go. See you."

"Where's the girl?" Tootega put a hand on his chest.

David felt his stomach muscles tighten. Somewhere

in the hidden depths of his mind, the spirit of the great bear Ragnar roared. "Let me go," he said.

And the Inuk backed away. But though his movements were jerky and filled with apprehension, they did not seem related to the tone in David's voice. When David looked at him again, Tootega was staring wildly at the door.

"He is come," he said, in a voice rasping fear from the bottom of his lungs.

"Who?" said David. The outer door was closed.

Tootega stepped backward, shaking his head. He bumped against a table full of woven baskets, spilling them.

Outside, a dull thump started up.

"We only got the blue cheese," Albert announced. He came in, tucking a pencil behind his ear. His gaze suddenly fixed on the far bay window. "Oh jeez. Just when you thought it was safe to walk the streets." He dipped behind the counter and came up with a rifle.

In the road, with its paws raised, pounding the tail of the pickup, was a bear.

An Unwelcome Surprise

Gadzooks immediately flew to the window and spread his paws against the cold, dark night. The stars were out and winking faintly. He must record their pattern. He must. G'reth might be lost forever if he failed. He reached for his faithful pencil and pad, realizing with some bother that he'd left them on the windowsill in David's room. No matter. He would count instead, carefully record the pattern in his head, and check it against the others for the delicate changes that might indicate where G'reth had gone. His gaze panned left. One, two, three, four . . . sixteen . . . twenty . . . thirty-one, was that? He rubbed the glass clean and tried again. One, two . . . The dots began to blur. On his third attempt, he let out such a cry of frustration that

Lucy felt a tear trickle down her cheek. She reached for her mother. Liz was shaking and speechless. She patted Lucy's hand and went to Gadzooks.

"Come away," she said, and gathered him to her.

Hrr-ruur, he protested, and struggled to go back.

Hrrr, Liz sang, sending him gently to sleep in her hands. She laid him on the workbench near to Gretel. Even her wings were shaking lightly. Her eyes kept rolling toward the window. Outside now, all seemed calm.

Lucy drew up to the window and stared into the night. "Mom, what happened?"

Still numb with shock, Liz sank into her chair. "He's a wishing dragon, connected to the universe. He can move, theoretically, through time and space."

"Mom, something *took* him. He didn't want to go!"

Liz sighed and tapped her fingertips together in thought.

"Ask *her*," snapped Lucy, stamping toward Gretel.

"Lucy, stop it. This is none of Gretel's doing."

"But she escaped!"

"She was *released*. There's a big difference. Something

is trying to unsettle us. But I don't know why and I don't know what. I'm not entirely sure it's malevolent, even."

"M —? What?" queried Lucy.

"Evil. Wicked. I'm not convinced it's bad. If it were, it could have done a lot more damage."

"But we nearly had a fire! And G'reth's been stolen! How are we going to get him back?"

Liz dropped her hands against her thighs. "Whatever force took G'reth is impossible for us to fight."

"Well, at least put Gretel back into her cage!"

The potions dragon snorted and ground her teeth. All this shouting was hurting her head. She needed lavender, to clear the ache. With a snap of her wings, she flew across the room to a potpourri sachet and split it wide open, spilling dried flowers everywhere.

"She's as confused as we are," said Liz. "Besides, whatever set her free could just as easily do so again. Gretel, I was wrong to cage you. Will you help us to understand what's going on?"

Hrrr, she snorted grudgingly, meaning she would.

"Bring the phone," said Liz. "Now I *will* talk to David."

Lucy, though unhappy with her mother's decision, nevertheless ran for the cordless handset. She was about to press the TALK button to bring it into life when she paused, hearing movement in the house next door.

Liz looked at the calendar on the wall above the bench. "Sounds like Henry, back a day early."

Lucy gave an indifferent grunt. But Liz was secretly pleased to have him back. Henry Bacon, while not the most ideal neighbor, did represent some degree of normality.

Lucy hit a memory button on the phone. "It's ringing." She gave it to her mother, then placed herself close so she could hear every word.

A charming Scandinavian accent spoke back: *Hello, you have reached the office of Dr. Anders Bergstrom at the Polar Research Base, Manitoba, Canada. There is no one to take your call right now. Please leave a message after the tone.*

Beep.

"Dr. Bergstrom, this is Elizabeth Pennykettle, calling from America with a message for David."

"An urgent message," Lucy whispered.

Liz flapped her quiet. "Could you ask him to call me back as soon as he can. It's to do with his publishers. Thank you. Good-bye."

"His publishers?"

"I don't want to alarm him, Luce — or have other people knowing our business."

"S'pose not," she muttered, distracted by the sound of Gadzooks waking up. "Can't we send a message from him?"

"Yes," Liz agreed, "that's a good idea. He can reach David quickly on a deeper level." She put out her hand. Gadzooks fluttered onto it. "Can you do that?" she said, running her finger down his ear. "I know we shouldn't use you as a postal service, but this is important."

Hrrr, said Gadzooks.

"Quite," said Liz. She found a piece of paper and a lightweight brush. "I want you to send him this." And she drew as faithfully as she could remember the shape of the lines Gwilanna had made on the publisher's contract, the same shape the sibyl had scratched on Zanna's arm, the shape David called "the mark of Oomara."

The writing dragon twisted his snout and shivered.

"It means something to you, doesn't it?" Liz said.

It's in the David's story, Gadzooks confirmed.

"His story?" gasped Lucy.

Liz blinked in thought. "Then he either knew of this mark already or Gwilanna is pricking his subconscious mind with it. Zookie, go and bring your pad."

As he zipped away, Liz heard the flick of a switch next door. "That's definitely Henry. Go and invite him for a cup of tea."

"Now?" said Lucy.

Hrrr? went Gretel, in agreement with the girl. She didn't want to pretend she was a lump of clay at such a disturbing time as this.

But Liz insisted. "It's a neighborly thing to do. And it will hopefully take our minds off G'reth."

Lucy sighed heavily and clumped downstairs. She

was halfway through the door when Gadzooks came past her on his way back to the den. She thought nothing of it and continued on her way. If she had known that he had gone whizzing back to report that his pad and pencil had both been stolen, she would have hung around, no doubt. But instead she went to Henry's and rang the bell. Its trill reached far into the pitch-black house. That was odd, she thought. Why hadn't Henry put the hall light on? Stranger still, why was the door ajar? She slipped inside. The lounge was lit by nothing but the deep blue glow of the fish tank. "Mr. Bacon, are you there?"

"About time," a harsh voice grated.

A chair swiveled around. In it was a woman in a two-piece suit.

"You!" cried Lucy.

"Yes, me," said the woman. "I've been expecting you, child."

Zanna in Danger

With a quick *snap-snap,* Albert cocked the rifle and opened the door of the trading post. A cloud of snowflakes billowed in, blowing across the stained wet boards.

"Wait!" cried David, grabbing his arm. "You're not going to shoot it?"

"Son, that's a polar bear denting your truck. He's not here to trade, he steals for a living. I don't want him near my store. Now take your hand off my arm and stay outta the way." He stepped onto the landing of the outer stairs shouting, "Hey! Vamoose!" A bullet cracked the air. David, watching from the safety of the window, saw the bear leap back unharmed.

"What's happening?" asked Zanna, rushing to his side.

"There's a bear," he whispered.

"Oh my God. Where?"

"Behind the pickup."

Zanna skipped sideways to the next window along. "Where? I can't see him."

"Come on out!" Albert called. Another shot ripped out of the rifle. Across the windswept road, a group of people had gathered, pointing, shouting, training a light. But there was still no movement behind the truck.

"Did he hit him?" shouted Zanna, moving to another section of the window.

"No, he fired over him," David replied.

Albert, toting his gun at waist height, began to make his way down the outer stairs.

A moment later, a white-haired woman dressed, like Albert, in heavyweight jeans and a red check shirt, came hurrying through from the back of the store. She put an arm around Zanna's shoulder. "Aw jeez, is it a bear?"

"Apparently," said Zanna, not shifting her gaze.

The woman hurried to the counter and picked up a phone. Within seconds, she had a connection. "Oh, hiya, Andy. It's Margie, at the store. Yar, I'm doin' fine. Yar, I think so. Sounds like we got ourselves a bear sniffing 'round. Haven't seen it, no. Albert's out shootin'. O-kaay, I will. Come soon, now. Gotcha."

She put the phone down. "You see him yet, honey?"

Zanna wiped the window clean. The arms of the people shouting warnings to Albert seemed to indicate the bear was lying low. But the wind was up, almost blanking them out. "It's hard to tell," she shouted. "You see anything, David?"

"David? Who's David?" Margie asked.

Zanna's blood froze. She jerked her head back and saw the door swinging free. "DAVID!" she screamed, and burst through the door and onto the landing. Through the swirling snowstorm, the body of the pickup was still half-visible. But not the men. Zanna took a step down, slightly losing her footing on the gathering snow.

"Hey, get back here!" Margie called from the safe warm amber glow of the store.

"David!" Zanna pleaded, and reversed onto the landing. She ran to the far end. Clinging to the rail, she shouted again. It was then, just ahead, she saw a faint yellow light, drilling a well through the drifting flakes. It pooled like a spotlight in the middle of the road. At its center, sitting calmly, paws tight together, staring deep into her eyes, was a bear.

"David! I see it! It's there!" she hollered.

"Honey, get inside!" Margie shouted again.

"It's OK, it's OK, it's up the road," Zanna said, plucking snowladen hair from her mouth. Hearing garbled voices on the far side of the truck, she turned to direct them to the bear's location. But her eye was taken by a movement hard below: a fluid white shape, squeezing out from underneath the near side of the pickup.

Speechless with terror, she watched another bear raise its head toward the light. "Oh my God, there are two! One of them is here, right by the stairs!" The bear reared and pounded the fascia by her feet. The boards snapped and splintered like matchwood. With a sickly creak, the nearest support pillar broke in two and the landing dropped with a sudden jolt. Zanna pitched forward over the rail and fell eight feet to the earth below.

The bear swept around, snowflakes gyrating on its breath like moths circling an outdoor lamp.

Zanna, forgetting everything she'd been taught, turned onto her back and began to scramble for the jeep, hoping she might slide under it.

But as the bear padded forward, snorting at her, she suddenly stopped moving and looked into its eyes. The bear stopped also, angling its head to squint at the ripped sleeve of her parka. For half a second, there seemed to be a kind of recognition. Then the animal raised a paw.

At that moment, several things happened. From the far side of the pickup came a squeal of brakes. Doors opened and slammed. Bright white searchlights flooded the road.

David appeared at Zanna's back crying, "Don't let him touch you! He mustn't touch you!" He bent down to hook his hands into her armpits, intending to drag her away to safety. The bear hissed and coiled back, readying to strike, when — *whap!* — it was struck in the shoulder by a plank of wood, wielded by the Inuit guide, Tootega.

The bear howled in agony and crashed onto his side.

Albert skidded forward, aiming his rifle between the bear's eyes.

"No!" David screamed, and pushed him into the broken staircase.

A shot pinged off the cold gray tarmac.

"All of you! Get back NOW!" yelled a voice.

Another gunman had appeared, ten feet from the stricken bear's rump. He was dressed in a black badged jacket and hat.

"Don't kill him," panted David.

"Move, boy, or I'll shoot you first!"

"No!" he pleaded, as Tootega's rough hand took him by the collar and pulled him clear.

The gun cracked.

"His shoulder! Look at his shoulder!" David cried. He broke free and stood over the bear again.

Blood from an earlier wound was pouring down the ice bear's foreleg.

And his great brown eyes were closed.

As Above, So Below

"It's no use trying to run, child."

Even as Lucy turned to flee, she felt her muscles lock and her legs turn stiff. Rocking helplessly, she fell onto Henry's leather sofa, all the while trying to scream for her mother.

"Foolish girl," Gwilanna chided. With a twist of her hand, she sent a spell which turned Lucy's words to feathers.

Lucy coughed them away and tried again. This time bubbles of soap left her mouth.

"Once more and I'll make you speak nettles," said Gwilanna.

Lucy, defeated, pulled her lips inward.

"Good. Now speak quietly and above all *politely*. I am your aunt, after all."

"What do you want?" Lucy hissed, not at all polite.

Gwilanna brushed some dust off her skirt. "All in good time, child. All in good time. First, have you heard from the boy?"

"David's in Canada."

"I know that, girl. Don't test my patience. Has he spoken to you recently?"

"He wrote a letter. Why?"

"Hmm," went Gwilanna, stroking her chin. "Did he mention his story?"

Lucy shook her head.

"Pity. Then you won't know what's about to happen."

"What do you mean?" asked Lucy, wriggling her legs.

"Oh, stop fidgeting," Gwilanna chided, and turned the girl's lower half into a fish tail.

Lucy's heart nearly leaped from her chest. She whined

so much that Gwilanna was forced to restore the girl's shape lest her ancient eardrums should implode. "There. Now, behave yourself and listen. Your tenant is a nuisance, but an interesting nuisance. He has no bloodline to the olden ways, yet he and that peculiar dragon of his have abilities well beyond human expectation."

"Gadzooks just helps him write stories," said Lucy.

"Oh, he does more than that," said her aunt. "Between them, they can shape the future."

Lucy put her head back, looking puzzled.

"Remember this?" Gwilanna asked. From the shadows beside her chair, she brought forth a square-shaped wicker basket. A small lithe figure was darting around inside it.

"Snigger!" gasped Lucy.

Gwilanna raised a frown. "Is that what he called it? How dreadfully quaint."

Chuk, went the squirrel, standing on its hind legs and clinging to the wicker, doing its best to gnaw through the weave.

Lucy balled her fists. "What are you doing with him?!"

"He's a hostage," smirked the sibyl, and her face grew dark, "to make sure you do exactly as you're told. If you even *think* about squealing for your mother I'll turn this rodent into a pair of flea-bitten socks." She poked a finger at the cage, then reeled back sharply as Snigger tried to sink his teeth into her flesh. "I discovered — during my 'stay' with you — that when the boy wrote his story about this tree rat, he was ahead of time."

Lucy pulled a face. "What do you mean?"

"He could predict things, child; what he wrote came true, though the gap between the two only covered a few seconds."

Lucy puzzled over this but didn't reply.

"He, of course, was bewildered by it, just as you are now. His minute brain did not possess the intellect to understand that time does not truly exist."

Lucy glanced at the carriage clock on Henry's mantelpiece. "Why do we have clocks, then?"

The sibyl gave out an irritated sigh. "So we can glimpse different aspects of the present. Oh, never mind. Just take it from me, your tenant can do it. What's more, his ability is growing stronger."

Lucy pushed her hands between her thighs and shuddered. She didn't like the sound of this. "How do you know?"

Gwilanna stood up and paced the room. She dropped the basket onto the fireside rug, causing Snigger to tumble like a hamster on its wheel. "I decided to watch him. I left a calling card on that silly little contract he made with his publishers."

"I saw it," said Lucy, lurching forward. "Three squiggles — like on Zanna's arm."

"Squiggles!" Gwilanna's screech rattled the windows. "Don't be so insolent, girl. That sign is feared throughout the far north."

"Sorry," said Lucy, though she wasn't at all. Her mind was working fast. It had just occurred to her how to attract her mother's attention — if not that of a listening dragon. Gwilanna's last shrill burst would have been heard in every corner of the living room next door. If she could be made to shriek upstairs, it would easily be detected in the Dragon's Den.

"Where was I?" snapped the sibyl.

"I can't remember. Can I go to the toilet, please?"

"No, you may not. We were talking about the boy. Through magics, I have followed his latest saga. Did you know I feature in it?"

Lucy shook her head very slowly indeed. Gwilanna, in David's Arctic story? What could he be *thinking* of?

"Yes, child, I was astonished as well. But then the boy is a strange enigma. When he writes, it seems his auma is driven by the need to engineer his fate. He is creating the circumstances for — well, you will discover that in time. Look out of the window. What do you see?"

"Nothing." It was pitch-black outside.

"Stars, girl. Can't you see the stars?"

Not really, thought Lucy. One or two were winking gently, but . . . wait, here was her chance: "They'll be easier to see from Mr. Bacon's study window . . . upstairs."

"No doubt," said Gwilanna, not taking the bait.

Lucy clamped her fingers around her thumb and sighed.

"What do you *know* about stars?" Gwilanna pressed.

Lucy folded her arms. This was all she needed: a science lesson. "They're a long way off. Our sun is a star and the Earth revolves around it."

Gwilanna raised a half-impressed eyebrow. "Elementary, but correct. Now, let me teach you something else. Every object you see in the sky, every twinkling celestial body, exerts an influence on our lives. You and I, this house, this idiot squirrel," she kicked the basket, making Snigger squeak, "were created from stardust."

"How?" asked Lucy.

"Never mind, girl. Be quiet and pay attention. There is a significant alignment forming in the heavens, the same pattern that was present when dragons were first introduced to this Earth. As above, so below. Do you understand?"

Lucy was still a sentence back. "*Dragons?*" she queried, beginning to sound interested.

Gwilanna's gaze shifted back to the window. "There is a fire star coming, signaling a time of new beginnings. A time for dragons to rise again."

Lucy leaned forward, her mouth popping like a peapod trying to shed its seed. "You mean, proper *big* dragons?"

"Yes," said the sibyl. "And one in particular."

Lucy's skin turned cold. For she knew, without knowing, that her aunt was referring to the last true dragon the world had ever known.

Gawain.

Dressing Down

"Do you know how powerful a polar bear is?"

Anders Bergstrom folded his arms and sat back in his office chair surveying the two students standing in front of him. Neither ventured to answer his question.

"From the report I've been given by the Chamberlain Bear Patrol, the male you encountered is as big as anything I have ever seen. That means he weighs close to six hundred kilos, over half a ton. On its hind legs, such an animal would stand almost sixteen feet high and have an attack speed of approximately twenty-five miles per hour. It has the strength to lift an adult seal out of water, throw it onto level ice, and rip a hole in its belly as easily as you or I would tear open an envelope. It could take a man's head off with one swift blow, using roughly the same amount of energy that the man would exert to nip a flower off its stem. It is universally acknowledged as the most formidable predator on this planet. Am I beginning to frighten you yet?"

David looked down at his shuffling feet. "I didn't want to see it killed, that's all."

"Jeez," said a voice from across the room. Russ thumped his fist against the filing cabinet and pushed his hat way back off his forehead. "One person mauled in Chamberlain in the past thirty years. You two are here for less than a month and you almost triple the stats. Why didn't you just stay in the trading post? You didn't even get the supplies!"

"Ask him about his story," muttered Zanna.

"Story?" said Russ, his freckled brow concentrating into lines.

From a chair in the corner, Tootega glared at the girl and muttered something darkly under his breath.

"Don't worry, you're probably in it, too," she said.

David clenched his teeth. "Zanna, shut up."

"Don't you tell me to zip it!" she growled, whacking

a hand across his chest. She stared doggedly at Bergstrom. "Ask him about Gwilanna and the tooth."

Russ pointed a finger at his temple. "This a private conversation or can anyone join in?"

"It's on the laptop," she said, holding Dr. Bergstrom's gaze.

The scientist ran his knuckles down the blond hairs of his beard and swung his chair toward the pilot and the guide. He tilted his head in the direction of the door.

"You're the boss." Russ sighed, and both men started to leave.

Tootega paused briefly at David's back. "That bear. He remember you — her as well. Next time, you won't have chance to play dead."

The door closed. "What did he mean, 'next time'?" Zanna snapped.

Bergstrom's deep blue eyes pooled into her. "The bear was shot with a fast-acting tranquilizer. A new development we've made in the past year or two. It was taken immediately to a steel holding pen, commonly referred to as the polar bear jail. It will be operated on for a bullet wound to the shoulder."

Zanna winced and looked away.

"So he'll survive," said David, staring into the misted windows and whatever, in his mind's eye, lay beyond.

"He was lucky," Bergstrom said, smoothing his palms. "The bullet had touched his lung but the injury was more impediment than fatal. It will heal quickly. When it does, we'll fly him north and let him go."

"This is just too spooky," said Zanna. "Read the story, Dr. Bergstrom. *Now.*"

Bergstrom glanced at the open laptop, weaving colored pipework on its flat gray screen.

"No, I'm destroying it," David said. He stepped forward and moved the mouse. Bergstrom immediately clamped his arm.

"You have a contract, remember?"

David looked into the scientist's eyes. It wasn't clear whether Bergstrom was referring to Apple Tree Publishing or the personal promise David had made him to keep on writing about the Arctic. Even so, David said, "I'm wiping it." And he dragged the file into the computer's trash can and emptied it.

This was still not enough for Zanna. "Defrag the disk."

"*What?*"

"I don't want it in memory, even in bits. Run a defrag over it. Now."

"But —?"

"Just *do it,* David."

"Be my guest," said Bergstrom, wheeling his chair away.

Silently furious, David ran the program that would rearrange the disk so all the files were contiguous and any scraps of deleted files were eliminated. "There. Happy now?"

"No, not really," she said. "First you keep secrets about Gwilanna, then you won't tell me *why* I'm not supposed to touch that bear, and now you're trying to act like you're some kind of hero. Well, you're not.

You could have died out there! Oh, and do you want the *really* bad news?"

"What?"

"We're finished."

And then she was gone, leaving David and the door frame shuddering in her wake.

TAKEN

How?" demanded Lucy. "How will you make Gawain come back to life? You'd need his fire tear. You'd need —"

"Be quiet," snapped Gwilanna. "I know what I need. Everything is in motion, child."

Lucy's gaze dropped to a furious squint. "That's why you set Gretel free, isn't it?"

"What?" said her aunt.

"Don't lie," Lucy said. "I know you sent Groyne."

"Groyne?" said Gwilanna, and it was clear then, and somewhat frightening to Lucy, that her aunt had no idea about that dragon.

"He was invisible," Lucy muttered. "He gave Gretel

a flower and G'reth —" Here she stopped, realizing that what Gwilanna didn't know, she should not be told. That could mean more fish tails or feathers.

But Gwilanna merely turned away deep in thought. "Interesting. So the girl must be at work."

"Girl? You mean Zanna?"

Gwilanna breathed in deeply. "Gretel has gone over to her, has she not? The girl must have sensed her powers and been active."

Lucy thought about this. It did make sense. Zanna had been devastated when Grockle had turned to stone. But if Zanna was involved in setting Gretel free, why had Gretel not confessed to this?

"No matter," said Gwilanna, wheeling away. "Her abilities are useless compared to mine. Without guidance, she is like a poor, lost sparrow. In time, she will grovel just to do my bidding, and so will your foolish unfaithful mother."

"What's Mom done to you?"

Gwilanna loomed up close. "She has put aside her

duty to the ancient ways and sided with this boy. But when the star looms bright in the February chill, she will come back to me, to her true kind."

"February?"

"Three months. We must prepare."

"We?"

"You and I."

"Are you staying again?"

Gwilanna laughed and her features began to change. Her hands grew thin and her face became gnarled. With a tapering finger, she made a vertical, shimmering fissure in the air, as though she had torn through the fabric of the universe.

"W-what's happening?" said Lucy, pulling her knees up under her chin.

In his basket, Snigger turned circles of fear.

"Come," said Gwilanna. She put out a hand and the air around Lucy rushed toward it, pulling her toward the sibyl's grip.

"Mom!" she screamed, without hesitancy now.

"Come," Gwilanna snapped, "you have a date with destiny. Come, child, or the squirrel dies!"

"Where are we going?" Lucy cried, squirming off the sofa. "I don't want to go! Where are you taking me?" She was shaking her head, but already their fingers were interlocking.

Gwilanna pulled her toward the rip.

And in a flash there was nothing left behind but dust motes skirting the inrush of air and a squirrel fretting in the corner of his cage.

Groyne Returns

David put his face into his hands. "What's going on, Dr. Bergstrom?"

Bergstrom turned his chair square to his desk and began to flip through a file of notes. "I won't be taking any action about what happened in Chamberlain, though the incident will be logged by the police up there. Your decision to confront a bear, after all you've been taught, was highly irresponsible. This episode won't reflect well on the base. From now on, you'd be well advised to keep a low profile."

"That's not what I meant, and you know it."

"Then explain yourself, David. I have a lot to catch up on, including all your latest data to read through. Your beryllium results are really rather good."

David shook his head in disbelief. "How can you be so casual about this? Zanna stands here ranting about Gwilanna and you act as if nothing is happening. You haven't even asked me about the story."

"The story is deleted. You'll write something new."

"Is that *it*?"

"No, not quite. While you were trying to get yourself killed you had a call from America, from Elizabeth. She wants to speak to you, urgently. Something about your publisher."

David looked at the laptop and groaned.

"You have my permission to use the telephone in the next office. I want you back in here at ten tomorrow with a clear scientific head on your shoulders. Oh, and David, regarding you and Zanna, this is a small base, remember. Bad feelings between workers bring everyone down."

"Tell that to her! She was the one who did the dumping."

"I doubt her petulance will last that long. If you want my opinion it's not what you wrote that particularly concerns her, it's the fact that she nearly lost you up there. Go to her later, when she's calmed down. Now, if you would, I must get on." He gestured absently toward the door.

"I haven't finished," said David, hovering uneasily.

Bergstrom raised his head again.

"I lost the tooth."

The blue eyes narrowed.

"During the skirmish, the loop must have broken. The leather was thin and only loosely knotted. I didn't realize until we were back at the base. I don't know what to say — or what this means."

Bergstrom picked up a pen and continued to work. "That tooth was a charm, a ward against evil. You're fortunate to be alive. Perhaps its role is done."

"OK," David said, with a sigh, "explain this: Zanna saw another bear in the road."

"The police reported one. That's all I know."

"There were two in my story. A young one, injured by a gunshot to the shoulder; the second was wise, some kind of Teller. He knew about the stars. He was following a sign. It was you, wasn't it?"

Bergstrom breathed in low and deep. "Ten, tomorrow. Don't be late."

"But —"

"Tomorrow, David."

And the student, realizing he would gain nothing more, beat a fist against the wall and left the room.

A moment later, the air above Bergstrom's desk shimmered, and something small with a jagged white outline materialized on an upturned coffee mug. To a man's eye, the creature was almost invisible. But to Bergstrom's practiced squint it had the shape and features of a birdlike dragon.

"Well?"

The creature hopped down off the mug and placed a pencil and several small sheets of dotted paper in front of its master. One sheet had the letter *G* written upon it.

"Draw the rest," said Bergstrom.

The dragon found itself another (sharper) pencil and started joining dots on the other five sheets, until each one displayed a letter.

"You've done well," said Bergstrom. "They were

very close to knowing." He stared through the window at the yellow star pulsing low in the sky. "And that would have been three months too soon. What news of the wishing dragon?"

Hrrr, said Groyne, and took a large gulp of air.

"All the way back? To the very beginning?"

Groyne flicked his tail.

"Then he is special indeed," said Bergstrom. And closing the results file he had from David, he rearranged the sheets that Groyne had delivered, making a word that began with *G*.

The small dragon jerked in surprise.

Bergstrom ran a finger down its scales and smiled. He clicked his fingers and the creature changed into a piece of bone, etched with a variety of whirls and symbols. It fell into the scientist's hand and he put it away in a drawer of his desk. Then he reached behind his printer and lifted some twenty sheets of paper from its tray. The first had a heading which said, *The Shooting.*

"In the beginning was the auma," he whispered, and

laid the manuscript over the word on his desk until the letters had burned in like a watermark.

And the word that was written there was this:

GODITH

Part Two

Gretel Does Her Part

"What have you told Henry?" David said.

Through a crumpled tissue pressed tight against her nose, Liz replied, "That she's gone to stay with her Aunty Gwyneth."

"Did you put any kind of time frame on it?"

Liz moved her head slowly from side to side.

A-row, mewed Bonnington, on the floor by her feet. His wide copper eyes were like a universe expanding. He rose up and placed a paw against her thigh.

David reached out across the kitchen table. His palms, warm from the mug of tea he'd been cradling, covered and comforted his landlady's hands. "Whatever it takes, I'll find her. I promise."

Liz blew her nose and threw the tissue in the bin. "I'm so glad you're home. Was Dr. Bergstrom annoyed?"

"No. He arranged the flights and everything. He's as keen as I am to see that Lucy's safe. I'll e-mail him when we've talked things through."

"And poor Zanna. She must be so disappointed."

"She was fine," said David, rubbing her hand, giving no hint of the fallout in Chamberlain. "She'll come here as soon as she gets back to America. Now, tell me again what happened. You heard Lucy screaming and you ran next door."

"Yes. I was just too late. I didn't see them disappearing, but I felt the shift."

David threw her a quizzical look.

"Gwilanna is able to pass through time and space. The movement leaves a ripple. It makes you dizzy for a second."

"You're certain it was her?"

Liz smiled and pulled another tissue from the box. "There aren't many people with such a talent, David."

He sat back, making the chair legs creak. "And she

left no note, no ransom demands? Nothing to say why she'd taken Lucy?"

"Nothing. All I found was the squirrel." Liz nodded at the empty wicker cage on the tabletop. "I set him free in the garden. It didn't seem right to keep him cooped up."

A-row, went Bonnington, dribbling slightly from the side of his mouth. He padded across the kitchen and leaped onto the drainer. And there he sat, as he often did, watching the garden world go by.

David fiddled with a place mat, as if putting it in alignment with the table edge might induce the answers he was seeking. "Was it Snigger?"

"I couldn't tell. I'm sorry."

"But why catch a squirrel? What have they got to do with it?"

Liz touched her fingers lightly to her temples, stretching the skin into worried ridges. "Why steal Gadzooks's pad? Who set Gretel free? What's happened to G'reth? I don't know, David. Something strange is going on and I'm very, very confused."

It didn't help that the doorbell rang just then. Liz jumped and sat back with a hand across her heart. David pushed aside the place mat and went to answer.

The caller was a healthy-looking Henry Bacon, who had not long returned from his sunshine cruise. "Stand aside, boy, need to speak to Mrs. P."

"Henry, not now. Liz isn't feeling good."

But by then Mr. Bacon was halfway down the hall, leaving fine, sooty footprints on the dark green carpet. "Bird down the chimney," he was saying to Liz, as David made it into the kitchen.

"Bird?" Liz repeated.

"Could be bats, bird more likely. Probably a pigeon. Stupid creatures. Worse than squirrels."

"In the chimney?" asked David.

"That's what I said, boy. Or have you turned deaf again? Having breakfast this morning. Sudden fall of soot. Dust all over my scrambled eggs. Need to sweep it, Mrs. P. Anything your side?"

"I'll check upstairs," said David, gesturing to her, "in case we've, erm, any . . . unwanted visitors." He clicked his fingers at the listening dragon. A slightly baffled Henry turned to look. But in the blink of a human eye, the listener had sent an alert call to Gruffen and also adopted its solid state.

David ascended the stairs in silence. On the way, he picked up a fishing net that Lucy always kept in the umbrella stand in the hall. As he crept on tiptoe into the den, Gruffen pointed a wing toward the chimney. Something was coming down the inside of the stack. David edged closer. A shower of soot fell. There was a scrape, then an object fluttered in the grate.

"Got you," David said, and netted it in an instant. The creature twisted and hissed and sent a fine jet of blue-white fire from its throat. It was blackened with soot from head to toe, but its violet eyes were blazing. And it was carrying what appeared to be a bunch of flower heads.

Gretel.

Gruffen gulped and jerked back. The potions dragon was not a happy being. Gretel punched her wings outward to tear through the netting, all the while huffing and stomping her feet and warning that if the flowers were damaged, then the stupid human only had himself to blame.

"All right, all right, calm down," he said, trying to lift her out of the grate.

She spiked his hand and flew to the workbench.

Immediately four guard dragons (pressed into service by Gruffen) closed around Grockle to protect him from attack.

Hrrr! went Gretel, saying something unkind about the hopelessness of Pennykettle dragons in general. She shook herself down, blinding half the guards with a shower of soot, then proceeded to dust the flower petals clean, spitting angrily at David for each one that broke from the head of the flower.

Sucking his hand, he knelt down to her level. "Gretel, what are you doing?"

"Learning," she hurred. "Flowers hear."

David looked at the chimney they shared with Henry. "Words, you mean? People talking?"

Gretel raised an eye ridge. "Bring the listener."

"Watch her," David whispered to Gruffen, and he hurried downstairs and slipped into the kitchen. Henry Bacon turned to him at once. "Well, boy? Any problem?"

"Nothing we can't handle. Need this," he said to Liz, grabbing the listener off the top of the fridge.

Henry's facial muscles swelled with disbelief. "What the deuce are you up to now?"

A question mirrored in Liz's face.

"And why are you back so early from the north?"

"Too chilly," David said. "Didn't like the cold." He hugged himself, then shot up the stairs. By now, Gretel had cleaned the petals to a satisfactory state and was busy flicking droplets of water over them.

The listener struggled free from David's hands and landed on the workbench beside the potions dragon. There was a brief and rapid exchange of dragontongue while Gretel arranged several flowers in her paws. Then she began to sing. It was a lullaby, not unlike the kind of thing Liz would use to calm a restless dragon into sleep. To David's amazement, the flower petals bristled, then turned toward the sound. Gretel gestured at the listener, who cocked one large and fragile ear, wrapping it close to the centers of the flowers. After a while, its eyes began to open in sheer amazement.

"Well?" asked David.

Ssss! went Gretel.

The listener listened. And listened. And listened. With each revelation, it seemed to grow ever more bewildered and shocked.

"What's it telling him?" David pressed.

The flowers faded and the listener pulled away. It took off its spectacles and gave them a polish. Then with a jitter, it related what it had heard. It came in broken phrases, some more revealing than others.

"Fire star?" muttered David.

"Gawain?" hurred Gretel. She dropped back onto her haunches, looking slightly frightened.

David bolted downstairs again.

He found Liz in the hall, waving Henry good-bye. "What was all that with the listener?" she asked.

"Go and sit in the living room. We need another cup of tea."

She caught his arm. "I'd like to know now."

"Gretel has 'interrogated' Henry's pot plants. Gwilanna is going to try to raise Gawain. I think she's taken Lucy to the Tooth of Ragnar."

Return to Chamberlain

"Going somewhere?"

As he turned to see Zanna, leaning back against the outer wall of the base, idly brushing snow off her flawless mukluks, what startled Tootega the most was the stealth she had used to creep up on him. Here she was, a mere girl, a *kabluna*, inexperienced in the ways of the hunter. And yet she had stalked him as easily as a bear might ambush a fat and witless seal. It was twenty-five yards to the nearest door and the snow was solid enough to crunch when it broke. How had she closed the gap and made no sound? And even if his ears were bemired with blubber, why had the team of dogs not stirred?

"Nice woofers," she said, and pushed away from the wall.

Tootega did not understand these words, but his instincts warned him he was being scorned. He hissed at her through broken yellow teeth as she moved among the thirteen panting huskies. Showing no fear, she crouched by the handsome lead dog, Orak, looking deep into his eyes as she gripped the thick fur around his neck and roughed his head back and forth like a doll. Orak growled, but did not snap or bite.

"Good boy," she said, and held out her glove.

Frightened to see the animal sniffing it, Tootega stepped forward, halfheartedly flicking a sealskin whip. "You go. Leave here."

"We talk," said Zanna, using such a mordant edge to her voice that the leather-faced Inuk shuddered and fell back, almost toppling onto his sled.

Zanna stood up, testing the tautness of the ropes that bound furs and tarpaulins over a bundle of hidden possessions. "Heavy load. Doesn't look like a quick scoot round the bay. Moving igloo, are we?"

Tootega swore at her and spat between her feet.

"Nice," she said, toeing the stain into the snow.

"First you try talismans to scare me away, now your foul smelling, whiskey soaked phlegm." She pulled off a glove and pushed back her sleeve. "What does this mean, Inuk?"

"He can tell you on the way up to Chamberlain," said a voice. And there was Bergstrom, walking steadily toward them in a billowing blue windbreaker that rustled at every step.

Tootega whistled the dogs to their feet. "We go now."

"No," said Bergstrom, looking absently across the bay. "You take Zanna in the pickup to Chamberlain." He leveled his blue-eyed gaze at the Inuk. Tootega nodded and backed down instantly.

Zanna dropped her sleeve. "What's happening in Chamberlain?"

"The bear is ready for release," said Bergstrom, grimacing against the low, sharp sunlight.

Tootega grunted in his native tongue.

The two men exchanged a short babble of Inuit words, then Bergstrom spoke in English again. "Russ is up there, waiting for you. He'll fly you to the pack ice where you'll set the bear free. Enjoy it, Zanna. David would envy you for this."

Zanna pulled off her bobble hat and tied back her hair. "David quit," she said. "Let's roll."

For the first five minutes on the road to Chamberlain, Zanna said nothing, knowing this would irritate Tootega even more. His anxiety levels, already visible in the whiteness of his knuckles as his hands steered the straight gray road ever north, were at a maximum when she eventually said, "The Inuit, they like stories, right?"

Tootega breathed in deeply. His narrow black eyes remained fixed on the road.

Zanna smiled and folded her arms, shuffling herself into the angle of the seat and the rattling door. "On the flight over, David told me one — set here, in the north, thousands of years ago. He's not sure how it came to him, but what does that matter? Stories float around like snowflakes, don't they? They settle on the ears of anyone who'll listen. It's about a time when polar bears — nine of them — ruled the ice, lived in packs, and outnumbered men. Sounds corny, right? But then all myths do. Except, David doesn't think this *is* a myth. He wouldn't say so, to your face, but in his heart he believes every word of it is true. He started to write about it while he was up here. Good yarn. Wanna hear it? Gotta pass the time somehow."

Tootega muttered something under his breath.

"Fine. I'll take that as a yes," said Zanna. "So, we're in this Inuit settlement called Savalik. It's a small place, somewhere in the Canadian High Arctic. More teeth in a man's head than occupants, you know? It's been a bad year for weather, even worse for seals, and the main guy, some hunter — David calls him Oomara — comes back from a hunting trip empty-handed to find his kid, a boy of ten, dead from starvation. So Oomara builds some kind of ceremonial shrine and lays the kid out in it, wrapped in furs. Now this is where it starts to get a bit creepy, 'cause a day or so later a bear wanders by — not a daddy bear — a cub, and he's starving, too. He sniffs out the corpse and starts to eat, until all that's left of the kid is bones. But Oomara discovers it and he's filled with rage. So he goes to the shaman of the settlement who says, 'Kill the cub. Take back what the bears have taken from you.' But Oomara's afraid, really afraid. Bears rule the ice. They're fierce and powerful, their spirits even more so — but then working around Bergstrom, you'd know that, wouldn't you?"

The pickup wobbled a fraction off course. Tootega, desperate not to look at the girl, ground his teeth and babbled out a litany of blasphemies — or prayers — while he swung the spikes of his lank black hair back and forth across the pits of his sunken cheeks.

Unrepentant, Zanna continued: "So Oomara goes back to the shaman and says, 'How? How do I do this, without bringing the soul of the bear into my house?' And the shaman says, 'Take a bone of your dead son's body and strike the bear cub once in the forehead —' "

"You stop now," yelled Tootega, slapping a hand against the steering wheel. Sweat beads rolled across his creased dark brow and dripped into the fur around the hood of his parka.

"But this is the interesting bit," said Zanna, leaning forward and tapping her sleeve. "The blow Oomara inflicted on the cub left a mark in its head like the one on my arm. *Identical*, I think, to the one on my arm. I didn't want to believe it till we came up here last time and had our little encounter with —"

"We see bear. Let him go. Come home," snapped the Inuk. "Then you and I . . ." He slashed his fingers across his throat.

Zanna smirked and pointed a toe of her boot. Idling a finger in a patch of condensation at the edge of the misty windshield she said, "Oh yeah, I sure plan to see Ingavar again. I'll say one thing for David, he's a talented bunny, drawing characters to him just by writing about them. Hey, do you think the bear *will* remember me?" She sat up suddenly, forcing Tootega to punch the brakes. The cab filled with the smell of burnt rubber as the tires locked onto available tarmac. The truck skidded to a halt, steam rising from the hood.

"Nice driving," Zanna drawled, setting herself straight.

Tootega looked away from her face to the dribbling mark of Oomara in the windshield. "What you want?" he spat, eyes wild with fear.

She knuckled the screen. "To know what this means. Am I cursed or blessed? I need an answer, because I know now I'm related to her."

"Who?" the Inuk grunted.

"You know who," Zanna sneered back. "The shaman of Savalik, the priestess, the sibyl, the legendary 'wise' woman who forced the simpleheaded Oomara to murder a bear and so turned the laws of the north on their head. To you, she's something unpronounceable, no doubt. I call her by her western name, Gwilanna."

"We see bear," Tootega repeated, flaring his nostrils till the soft hairs inside were glistening with dew. "I do what Bergstrom say." He started the truck again and roared away.

"Oh yeah, Bergstrom," Zanna said, nodding. "Champion of bears and keeper of mysteries. Wow, you must have seen some shamans in your time, but never one quite like him, eh? Thing is, anyone can bang a drum and claim to speak with spirits, but transfiguration . . . that's something else, isn't it? Changing yourself into an animal — and back. Ever seen it happen? Ever seen the good doctor do the magic?"

"You should be dead," the Inuk growled as they sped on, blurring past the tall town sign. "I pray to bear, eat you up and spit your bones." He lurched the truck left, heading west beyond the houses for a piece of open ground, dominated by the outline of an orange and white helicopter.

"Not this bear," Zanna grunted, mimicking the Inuk's soupy accent. "Ingavar, my friend. He talked to me. He got the mark of Oomara on his head."

"You lie," Tootega shouted, stopping the truck again. He pulled a knife and jabbed it at her.

"Oh, that's *really* smart," she said, looking down, unperturbed, and laughing. "How are you gonna explain that to the Chamberlain police — and Russ?"

Tootega glanced ahead. Some fifty yards away, the pilot was standing over the body of a prostrate bear.

One of the uniformed policemen beside him gave the pickup a salute of recognition.

"You so much as glint a light on me," said Zanna, running her finger down the flat of the blade, "and I'll call the sibyl down from that tin can there."

Tootega swallowed hard and stared again. Perched on top of a cylindrical steel holding pen that was used to jail unruly bears was a large raven.

Zanna moved her eyes toward the men. All three were staring in confusion at the pickup. "They're beginning to wonder what the holdup is. If I were you, I'd drive."

Tootega bundled the knife away and slammed the truck into gear again. Within seconds, they were pulling up by the bear.

"Hey, cowboy," Zanna said, jumping out before the wheels had fully stopped turning.

"Hey," said Russ, glancing at the cab. "Why the wait? Everything OK?" He nodded at Tootega, sitting motionless with his hands on the wheel.

"Freaked by the blackbird," Zanna said, laughing. She pointed at the raven and walked on by. "How's the baby?" she said to one of the policemen, a middle-aged guy with full red cheeks. He was spreading out a large rope net beside the bear.

"Kinda sleepy," he replied.

"Can I touch him?"

"Oh yar. He ain't gonna bite. Any minute now we're gonna roll him up in this big old net and take him for a long ride outta town."

Zanna smiled and hunkered down. Through half-closed lids, the bear's dark brown eyes stared vacantly at her. "Hello, Ingavar," she whispered, and taking off her glove she ran her hand over the fur of his neck and upwards to cup his ear in her palm.

On the roof of the holding pen, the raven squawked.

"Beauty, isn't he?" Russ came to crouch beside her.

"The best," she said. "What's with the blood on his lip?"

Russ knelt forward and opened the bear's mouth. Its thick black tongue lolled sideways, into its upper palate.

"We took a tooth," he said, showing off a gap in the lower jaw. "Messy, but it'll heal all right."

"Tooth?" said Zanna, looking up at the bird.

"Umm," Russ grunted, laying the head flat. "Every year, they add a new layer of enamel. If you section through it you can count the layers, just like you can with the growth rings in a tree. Easiest way to age them. This guy's about twelve. In his prime. It would have been a travesty if the goon that shot him had finished the job."

Zanna pursed her lips and made her straight hair dance. "I think he's got a really big future, this bear."

"He's got a big journey, that's for sure," said Russ. "Fifty miles, up the coast." He stood up and patted her shoulder. "Come on, we need to get this package wrapped. It took a lot of dizzy juice to knock this guy out. He's strong. He won't be asleep for long. Tootega, lend a hand, here."

With a shuffle of feet, the Inuk stepped forward. Zanna immediately stood up and faced him.

"The bird knows," she said quietly. "You'd better

give it back." She rubbed her fingertips together, guiding a smear of blood across her skin.

"Tootega, come on, take a paw," Russ called.

But the Inuk was watching in horror as Zanna pushed her hand inside her sleeve and carried the blood of the ice bear, Ingavar, to the scratches on her arm. With a lurch, he stumbled past her and helped the other men roll the bear onto the netting.

"OK, have it your way," Zanna whispered and raised her dark-eyed gaze once more.

The bird extended its sleek black wings.

"To the ice," said Zanna.

Caaark! went the bird, and flew away.

North.

What to Do About Lucy

She can't raise Gawain. That's impossible," said Liz. She put aside the tapestry cushion she was clutching as David handed her a cup of strong tea. He put a plate of cookies on the sofa arm beside her.

"Well, Gwilanna obviously believes she can. And in three months' time, she's going to give it a try."

"But it's ridiculous. She'd need his fire tear for that. How can she revive him when he's locked in stone?"

David sat down, focusing on the space between his knees. "We'll talk about the tear in a minute. Tell me what you know about this star."

"Nothing. I've never heard of it before."

"You don't know how dragons came to be?"

"There are myths," Liz said, "about a dragon called Godith."

"Oh? You've never mentioned him before."

"Her," Liz corrected. "Godith was supposed to have created the world with one gigantic outgoing breath, making dragons in her image — as you would."

Hrrr, went the Pennykettle dragons in turn, who had gathered as a group on the mantelpiece.

David scratched the side of his neck. He looked at Gadzooks, Gretel, Gruffen. All of them had their ears cocked forward. "I thought dragons were created from clay and their fire was born from the center of the Earth?"

"They are," said Liz, "but something had to kick the process off. It's like saying how did *we* get here? How far back can you go? No one truly knows. Actually, Henry's very knowledgeable on this subject."

"The birth of dragons?"

"No, cosmology. If you're looking for a connection with this so-called fire star, he might be able to identify it for you. He's got dozens of books on the subject."

David nodded and broke a cookie in half. "What about Lucy, then? Why would Gwilanna take her away?"

On the floor at Liz's feet, Bonnington mewed. Liz widened her arms to let him jump onto her lap. The cat sniffed at the cookies and drew his nose away. He circled twice, then settled down and started to groom his paws. Liz stroked him gently as she spokc. "It was always going to happen that Lucy would have to spend a while with Gwilanna. As you know, Gwilanna is always present at the birth of a dragon child. She takes it upon herself to instruct us in the old ways. I was taught by her myself, like all the descendants of Guinevere before me."

"This is different," said David, crossing his arms. "She snatched Lucy without your permission. She hasn't gone to school, Liz. She's being held hostage on an island in the Arctic."

"You don't know that for certain."

"It's a pretty safe bet. Gawain turned to stone on the Tooth of Ragnar. It's seems sensible, therefore, to think that's where Gwilanna will take her."

Liz put her tea on a coaster by a lamp and broke a

cookie in half herself, showering Bonnington with oaty crumbs. "She won't harm her. Lucy's far too precious. She's the youngest living relation to Guinevere, the woman who caught Gawain's fire, remember. She's a princess to the throne of dragonkind. Gwilanna will want to preserve all that."

David blew a sigh and dunked his cookie. "I know you have this grudging respect for Gwilanna; I saw it when Grockle was born. I do understand how important she is to you, but she's selfish, Liz, and hungry for power. Frankly, I'm worried about Lucy. Call me weird, but my fairytale imagination keeps reminding me that 'princesses' are traditionally despised by their wicked godmothers. I have this unpleasant notion running through my head that the 'godmother' in this case might need the blood of a Pennykettle 'princess' to carry out some kind of resurrection ritual."

There the dialogue was brought to a halt by a stiff *hrrr* or two from the dragons on the mantelpiece.

"Shush," Liz said, soothing them with a note or two of dragonsong. She looked at David and shook her head. "Hair," she said. "If she takes anything from Lucy, it will be her hair. This . . ." she fingered her own red locks, ". . . was always part of the Guinevere legend. Remember I told you how Gwilanna burned a lock of it to join Gawain and Guinevere in fire?"

David tightened his lips. "Lucy's got fair hair."

"Not for much longer. If you'd looked at her closely on her last birthday you'd have seen the first strands of red appearing. We go through a change around the age of eleven. We start to develop ability with the clay — which you saw when she made G'reth — and our hair changes color . . . and so do our eyes. By February, she will be as redhaired as I am, with sharp green eyes. And that may be another reason Gwilanna wants her present at the raising of Gawain. The sight of . . ."

"A Guinevere clone?"

". . . yes, might calm him when he wakes."

David took his cookie — half his cookie — from his tea. "Then why take her so early? What 'preparations' does she need to make? And let's say you're right, that she stands in waiting when Gawain is raised. She's a child, Liz, somewhat small in stature compared to a dragon. He's only got to stretch a wing and bang, good-bye, Lucy. This is always assuming she's not crushed by the rockfall that's going to ensue when — or rather if — he stirs from the grave."

Liz winced and pushed a loose lock of hair behind her ear. "He'll know Lucy's there. Dragons have a very keen sense of smell."

"After thousands of years locked away in stone? I wake with two gummy nostrils every morning and sometimes struggle to get a whiff of Bonnington."

Hrrr, went Gretel, though it might have been *urrrgh.*

Liz ran her hand down Bonnington's back, producing an appreciative purr from his throat. "Trust me, he'll know. If Gwilanna is going to succeed, I'd rather be in Lucy's shoes than hers."

"Yeah, well, that's where the ifs and buts come to an end."

Liz lifted an eyebrow. "Meaning?"

"She's not going to succeed. I won't allow it. I know what became of Gawain's fire tear. If Gwilanna was to restore it to him, she could end up destroying the world as we know it."

An unsettled *hrrr* rumbled off the mantelpiece. Even Bonnington stirred and raised his head.

"You found out where it's hidden?"

David nodded. "I'm concerned that Gwilanna has learned that I know and plans to use Lucy as a ransom demand."

"Like Gwendolen," Liz muttered, letting her green eyes slowly defocus as if she was looking back through time. "Like the redhaired daughter she promised Guinevere in exchange for Gawain's fire. She's running it again."

"Maybe," said David. "Only this time, it's Lucy, not Gwendolen, for the fire. That's the choice I'm worried she'll present us with: your daughter's life — or the rest of mankind. . . ."

At the Tundra's Edge

There!" Russ shouted, raising his voice over the drubbing revolutions of the helicopter blades. He pointed left and down, toward a wide expanse of flat, white ground just to the west of the body of sea ice.

Zanna nodded and put up her thumb. "Isn't that tundra?" she shouted back.

Russ pushed his headphones back a little, freeing his ears so he might hear more clearly. "Yeah," he replied, starting the chopper on a decline toward it.

"Thought you were letting him go on the ice?"

"Too dangerous," he said, mouthing the words carefully. At this volume, repetition was hard on the throat. "The ice is newly formed. Can't trust the surfaces. Too broken up to risk putting us down there.

The bear will have enough to walk or swim across, but there are too many pockets of water for the chopper."

Zanna peered down at the blue-white jigsaw, glistening in the sweep of the pale yellow sun. It was hard to tell precisely where the join between ocean and continent lay, but where the flow of the water had been stopped by cold, the ice had stacked into long, uneven ridges, as if a giant hand had forced it against the barrier of land, making it pile up and heave off dozens of blocks, all caught in a chilled and motionless froth. Between these compressed, marshmallowlike regions were flatter areas, pebbled with smaller lumps of wreckage or long blue gashes of thinly iced water. They reminded Zanna of a transparency Bergstrom had shown the students when they had first arrived at the Polar Research Base, of ice floes and the water around them looking, according to the enigmatic lecturer, like wounds in the chest of a slumbering white giant.

"Tega, we're ready, get the hatch," Russ shouted.

Zanna watched the Inuk move, sullen-faced, toward the doors in the belly of the helicopter. He threw a clamp and slid them open, making hardly any sound against the throb of the engines. Cold air rushed in, pulling his normally flat black hair out into an inch-high rippled fringe.

"Can I watch?" Zanna shouted.

"Wait," Russ said, looking at his instruments. He skillfully adjusted altitude, turning them sweetly into the wind as the helicopter yawed crablike to its left. When it was hovering still, he said, "All right, scoot. But be careful, OK?"

Zanna smiled and unclipped her belts. She joined Tootega at the open hatch. The Inuk gave her a sour-faced glance, then tipped his body forward to gauge the distance to the specked white tundra. The helicopter's slightly elongated shadow could just be seen beneath the drugged and netted body of the bear. Zanna guessed they were some twenty feet off the ground.

Tootega stretched an arm back and tipped his fingers, to indicate that Russ should take them down farther. The helicopter dropped like a well-oiled elevator. The vortex of its blades stirred the ground below, blowing loose snow aside and flattening the dark green tufts of sedge that were brave enough to poke through the ever-present permafrost.

"Good," Tootega yelled.

The 'copter paused, pitching its nose no more than a degree. Zanna saw the netting crumple and noted the curve in the slackening cable. Tootega released the hook and threw the loose cable onto the ground, taking care to aim it away from their cargo. The bear had landed.

"Done!" Zanna called.

"Hold tight," Russ shouted. The helicopter jerked again, cruising forward some twenty yards, before turning tight through ninety degrees and settling down with hardly a bump.

Russ killed the engine, bringing the blades to a puttering halt.

"Can I take this off now?" Zanna asked, already unstrapping the yellow crash helmet she'd been forced to wear throughout the flight. "Doesn't do much for a girl's image."

Russ laughed and banged his door open, kicking out

a folding flight of steps. “Come on down when you’re presentable, Miss Martindale.” Leaving the radio channel open, he took off the enormous set of headphones he’d been wearing, then removed his baseball cap as well, replacing it, as always, with his cowboy hat. With one foot on the doorsill, he missed the steps entirely and jumped the short drop onto the snowcaked ground.

Zanna dropped her helmet onto a seat. “Now’s your chance, Inuk.”

Tootega stared back darkly at her.

“Give me the tooth. Don’t make this awkward.”

From outside Russ called, “C’mon, guys, let’s do this.”

A crowcall cracked the morning air.

Tootega jumped as if the sound had pierced his heart.

“Hand it over,” Zanna said. “I know you stole it.”

“Go home,” said Tootega, and kicked his door open.

And once again Zanna had to bite her tongue.

By the time she had rejoined the men, Russ had the net untied and spread. “Take a tug while we shuffle him,” he said to Zanna.

She picked up her side of it and took the strain. With Tootega at the hind legs and Russ at the front, they rolled the bear over onto his back, then heaved him with a twisting motion off the net.

"He's a big one," Russ exclaimed, ungritting his teeth. He let go and the bear flopped onto his side, staring drunkenly at the horizon, his pelt quilted into squares by the ropes. Then, with a flicker that made Zanna jolt, his eyes took a snapshot of the shallow landscape.

"He blinked," she said.

Tootega snorted at her ignorance and started to gather in the cable and net.

Russ crouched down and thumbed the eye wide open. "Just the drug wearing off. Another half hour and he'll be padding around like he owns the place again. Do you want to cradle his head for me? I need to put him into the recovery position."

Zanna got into place and looked at him doubtfully. "What, so we're doing first aid now?"

Russ gave her a grin as wide as Texas. Leaning over, he grabbed two handfuls of blubber and pulled the bear straight, then stretched its left leg forward and out, bringing the paw up to pillow the snout. "When he wakes, it's important that the first thing he smells is his own scent, not ours. Or he might panic."

Zanna nodded, settling the black nose into the scarred, but creamy, white fur. She stroked the bear's head, noting with amusement that Tootega shuddered. "Aw, he'll be OK," she said. "Not the sort to be easily fazed, are you, Nanuk?"

Russ spluttered with laughter and tipped back his hat, squinting as the sunlight caught his eyes. He was about to pass comment when the radio crackled. "Tega, you wanna get that?"

The Inuk, who was closest to the aircraft, didn't move.

Russ leveled his hat. "What is it with you today?"

Zanna twisted around, making her parka crunch. On the tip of the nearest rotor blade sat the great black raven. "Followed us here from Chamberlain," she said.

The bird crowed loudly and mantled its wings.

Tootega stumbled back a pace, mumbling in terror.

"OK, OK, I'll see to it," Russ said. He stood up and patted Tootega on the shoulder, then walked on, calling to the bird to flee.

The raven daggered its small, sharp beak, darkening the ice with its malevolent stare.

"You get it yet?" Zanna said, brushing down her clothes. She stood up, threatening the Inuk with her eyes. "She's not gonna let you go. That machine's doomed unless you give up Ragnar's tooth."

"What you do with it?" he snarled, turning on her.

She dipped a finger. "Give it back to them."

Tootega gave a shriek of disbelief and shook his head.

On the rotor blade, the bird gave an agitated call.

The bear for which David had written the name Ingavar tightened his claws and blinked three times.

"Last chance, Inuk. It belongs to them. *Give it.*"

Tootega stood back again, breaking sweat. As his hand went limply to a pocket of his parka, a sharp wind tugged at Zanna's hair, making her turn her head to the north. "Well, what do you know? The boys are back in town. . . ."

On the sea ice, in a mirage of gray mist and sunlight, three enormous bears were approaching.

David Takes Stock

I have a solution."

"You do?" Liz said. She lowered the kitchen blind and opened the door. Bonnington tripped in and leaped onto a stool, where he sat with a look of casual absenteeism as if he was practicing yoga for cats.

David, who was munching on a piece of toast, bumped back against the countertop and stared into the same space that seemed to be absorbing Bonnington's gaze. It was ten o'clock at night and he was weary and pale, jet-lagged from his long flight home. "My writing," he said. "My writing is the key."

Liz stacked some plates into a cupboard.

"Gwilanna was right about that time-lapse effect. I often felt when I was writing *Snigger* that the scenes were being mirrored in real life. That might also be why she snatched him from the library gardens, to see if it was him who had the gift, or me."

"David, you're tired. Go to bed," Liz said, making no effort to hide the suggestion that he might be talking gibberish — the last sentence at least. "All day long you've been raking over this, pacing up and down, taking stock. Give yourself a rest. There's nothing you can do."

"But there is," he said. "If the stories I create are somehow coming true, then all I have to do is write Lucy back here and deal with Gwilanna at the same time. The end."

Liz took off her apron and hung it by the fridge. She nodded at Gadzooks, who was sitting on the table blowing smoke rings for Bonnington. Gretel, whose paws were unoccupied for once, blew a finer wisp of smoke into Bonnington's ear, then flew around his head to see if it appeared on the other side. It didn't, but the cat did burble and twitch his ears in an amusing manner.

"I don't mean this unkindly," said Liz (ticking Gretel off for being mean), "but I think you'd struggle without Gadzooks. Whoever sent Groyne to steal Zookie's pad and pencil knows he's your source of inspiration. That's probably why they disabled him: to stop you interfering in the way you suggest. Either that, or they've plans of their own." She opened the bread bin and put away the loaf that David had sawn through rather than sliced. Crumbs were everywhere, on the countertop, on the floor. She swept the excess into her palm, then opened the door again to throw them onto the patio for the birds.

"How can that *be,* though?" David said, his face contorted by agonized thought waves. "Very few people know about Gadzooks. I can't believe Zanna would do a thing like that."

"I agree," said Liz, cutting Gretel off before she could sound a disapproving *hurr.* "She's not developed enough. Gwilanna's got that wrong."

"Then it must be Bergstrom."

"Must it?"

"Who else is there? He knows about Gawain and he's capable of . . . well, all sorts of things."

Liz, still on her domestic tour, paused by a vase of flowers to rearrange the stalks and pluck out any dying ones. Gwillan, who was polishing the glass with his paw, flicked his tail and said hello. "I don't doubt that Dr. Bergstrom is involved," Liz said. "The Arctic is his domain. But I think you should be thinking in wider terms than him."

David looked at her with questioning eyes.

She threw some rotten stalks into the bin, fluffed the spray of flowers, and came to sit down. "When I made Gadzooks, I constructed his shape and poured my love and know-how into him, much as I do with any dragon. But something far greater inspired me to make his pencil and pad, something in the universe that knew more than I did what he had to be. It was the same when Lucy made G'reth. At her age, she should not have been capable of making a wishing dragon anything as effective as him."

"So what are you trying to tell me, that this whole

situation is being engineered by . . . a ‘force’ that’s beyond our control?”

Liz glided a knuckle down Bonnington’s ear, encouraging the cat to nuzzle her hand. “In truth, I don’t know what’s going on. Since you went to the Arctic and that contract was mailed, everything has been so topsy-turvy. Lucy is my daughter and I’d die for her, you know that. I want her back just as much as you. But I’m convinced that we should follow our faith and intuition rather than engage in an up-and-at-’em fight against Gwilanna — though it might still come to that.”

“But we can’t just sit back and wait for things to happen.”

“No, I agree. But we can’t rush headlong into anything either. Like you, I’ve had a bit of time to think, and I keep coming back to G’reth. Something very powerful took him away. Something deep in the heavens, where your fire star is. That’s where I think you . . . we . . . should concentrate our efforts.”

Hrrraar-rr-ruuw, Nanuk, said Gadzooks.

Furff? went Gretel.

"Quite. I didn't get it either," said Liz.

"It's a line from my novel," David explained. "You and I and all that we are, came from the center of these lights, Nanuk. A polar bear called Thoran — who may or may not have a strange association with the mysterious Dr. Bergstrom — says it to another bear while they're following a star across the ice."

Liz nodded and raised her thin dark eyebrows. "Then that's what you should be doing as well. Following this star, learning about it. You're speaking to yourself, David, through your writing. I have a theory that the wish you made, to know about Gawain and the secret of his fire tear, is still not done. Find G'reth, by whatever means possible, and I think you'll have the key to outwitting Gwilanna."

David blew a sigh and put his palms against his forehead. Find a little dragon, among billions of stars? It would be easier to tape clouds together. He put the thought away and picked up Gadzooks. "Can't you just make him a new pencil and pad?"

Liz smiled sympathetically and shook her head. "The German language has a word called 'zeitgeist,' which roughly translated means 'the spirit of the time.' The creation of Zookie and all that he stands for was unique to the time you moved into this house. I can't possibly recapture that moment. The only way you'll restore him is to find his missing pieces, to see this through."

"That's going to please Dilys Whutton when she calls."

"You can still write, David, just maybe not as animatedly without him. It sounds like your novel is taking shape anyway."

"It was — or would have been — had I not destroyed it."

"Destroyed it? Whatever for?"

"Gwilanna was in it. You might as well know that Zanna and I argued about it and she made me erase it from Bergstrom's laptop — just before she ended our relationship."

"Oh, David."

"It gets worse," he said. "Remember my polar bear tooth? The charm I was given to protect me against Gwilanna's magics?"

"Yes."

"I lost it during the skirmish in Chamberlain. I don't know what happened, but it somehow came loose. In my story, I wrote that Zanna would somehow be involved in its theft and that Gwilanna was sending a bear to kill me, to make sure of it."

"Then I'm very glad you're here in Scrubbley," Liz said.

David put Gadzooks into her hands. "I'm going to bed. I'll talk to Henry about stars and stuff in the morning, see if it throws up any new leads. Don't look so frightened. I ditched the story, honestly. It can't come true."

"No," she said, and brushed his arm lightly as he left the room.

She waited for his door to close, then raised her gaze to the listener on the fridge. "When he goes to Henry's, call a meeting. I want to see all the special dragons in the den."

Hrrr? asked Gadzooks, meaning "why?"

A slight tear ran down Elizabeth's cheek, making Gadzooks rattle every scale he had. The auma of a human burned brightly in their tears, just as much as it ever did in a dragon. "We have to protect him," she whispered closely. "His writing, once created, can't be destroyed. You remember it, don't you, every word?"

Gadzooks gulped. Sometimes a special dragon's role was hard.

"I want you and the others to get together and do anything you can to keep him safe," said Liz.

"Anything?" hurred Gretel, flying onto Liz's shoulder.

"Anything," said Liz. And she took a pair of scissors from the table drawer and cut off a lock of her wavy red hair. She gave it to Gretel. "Absolutely anything."

INGAVAR WAKES

"TEGA! ZANNA! GET BACK HERE! NOW!" Russ was calling out a warning from the helicopter cabin, pointing urgently toward the oncoming bears. He fired the engines, rupturing the stillness. As the blades began to whirr and shred the air once more, the raven took off and circled low. Zanna laughed and opened her arms, welcoming the spiraling mist of snowflakes the bird was magically creating with its flight.

"Aye-yee," wailed Tootega, who could take no more. He threw the tooth at her (it bounced onto the ice), then ran for the safety of the waiting aircraft.

"ZANNA!" Russ called out again.

But the girl ignored him, or possibly couldn't hear him, for she was kneeling down now, removing her glove. She picked up the tooth and squeezed it tightly in the center of her palm. Instantly, her head jerked back and she cried out to the shifting sky. The auma of countless generations of bears spread through her clenched fist and up along her veins. In her ears a man was shouting and a raven was screeching and somewhere on the none-too-distant horizon, paws were thudding against frozen water. But all that Zanna saw were pictures in her mind, of a time when bears and men had warred, when the Inuk, Oomara, and the pack leader, Ragnar, had both been consumed in a blaze of white fire, until . . . "David," she whispered, falling forward. "David, I know what has to happen. Forgive me." And though her conscious mind queried the wisdom of her actions, she could not seem to prevent herself from placing Ragnar's long-lost tooth under the tongue of his latter-day descendant.

Immediately, the tooth found a life of its own and rooted itself in Ingavar's jaw.

With a surge of power, he woke and rose.

"God in heaven," breathed Russ, skidding to a halt. He had come to haul Zanna away. Now he found himself unarmed, within ten yards of a bear, and caught in the midst of a freak snowstorm.

The bear, still groggy, steadied himself and focused his gaze into a menacing squint. A long low hiss issued out of his throat, drowned by the irritating hum of machinery. He shook his head freely and stamped both forepaws, blowing the heat from his freshly worked lungs in wisps of fast-disappearing steam.

"Zanna, can you hear me?" Russ said evenly. No response. She was on her side, curled up, not moving, just behind the ice bear's massive bulk. He took a pace back, praying that the girl was simply playing dead.

With a yap more akin to a dog than a bear, Ingavar dashed his paw against the ice, tilling the surface with strands of his fur. Taking heed of the warning, Russ backed off farther, slowly removing his cowboy hat. He waved it like a stick, raising glints of curiosity in the bear's eyes, then growled the word "fetch" as he tossed it aside.

Ingavar looked disdainfully at it.

"That hat cost me sixty bucks," Russ said. "You could at least trample it. Move or die, you crazy lump."

Ingavar stood his ground and scented. The north wind spoke of bears approaching. They were close. Very close. One of them he recognized. An old male. Thoran.

A shot rang out. Ingavar yowled and swayed his head in anger. He had not been hit, but the sound of the bullet had scorched his eardrum, sharply reminding him of all that he had been through. He roared and swung a paw at the man in front of him, but he still did not move away from Zanna.

Russ was jumping back before the paw came out and was never in danger of being mauled. He could not believe Tootega had missed, and this irked him for a moment till the second shot exploded by the ice bear's paw, spraying its chest with dirt and snow. Then he saw Tootega's logic. Killing the animal outright might mean it falling across Zanna's body. And even if the half-ton weight didn't crush her, she would be badly pinned down. One man could not move a large bear alone, especially when three others were fast approaching.

So in desperation Russ retaliated in kind, leaping forward, screaming, gesturing rage. He'd heard stories of hunters throwing punches at bears, and he was drawing back his fist to do just that when his reach was shortened by a squealing tangle of feathers and claws. The raven was in his face. The bird squawked and rained down a multitude of wingbeats, its talons seeking flesh, its beak tugging hair. Russ crossed his forearms to protect his eyes, and never did know what happened next. But he felt the ground shudder and the north wind blow and he fell back helpless, praying for a miracle.

It came, but not in the way he had hoped.

Suddenly, all the clamor died down and the raven, for reasons only it knew, flew away to become a shrinking thunder cloud in the sky. Russ scrambled to his feet and hurried through the whiteout toward the droning helicopter.

There he found Tootega, seated, in shock, staring back at the place where the bear had been. The rifle had slipped through his trembling hands and was lying inert on the floor of the cabin. Russ shook the Inuk's knee but he did not move. Around the seat was a strong smell of urine.

"I'll be back," Russ panted, and grabbed the gun. "Zanna!" he called out. "Zanna! Zanna!"

He went on like that for the next five minutes, sweeping back and forth across the tundra, searching for any sign of the girl.

All he found was a favorite item of her clothing: a rainbow-colored bobble hat. It was wet with snow and trodden hard into a paw print amongst the sedge.

One soggy woolen hat.

Zanna, and the bears that had come for her, were gone.

The Pictures on the Wall

Bears!" squawked Gwilanna as she landed with a flap inside the mouth of the cave, scattering snow and loose earth ahead of her.

Lucy, her knees drawn up to her chin, gave a little start as the large black raven clattered in, crashing through the mouth-shaped window of light which looked out onto the frozen ocean. Her hand closed around a small, sharp rock. It felt warm against her skin. The whole cave did. She had never stopped thanking Gawain for that. His body, though petrified in this island and robbed of its rightful dragon fire, nevertheless radiated something of his warmth. She gritted her teeth, playing the rock through her fragile fingers. How many times had she prayed to the dragon to give her the courage to draw warm blood from Gwilanna's head? One good throw or blow might do it. But how would she cope in the aftermath? Alone. Lost. Starving. A killer. And, of course, she might well miss. . . .

"I hate bears!" Gwilanna squawked again, preferring to strut around in circles for a moment rather than change into her sibyl form. "Interfering, paddle-pawed lumps. They're beginning to make me just a little bit *peeved.*"

"Well, I like them," Lucy snapped defiantly, scratching a line into the smoke-charred wall to remind herself of how many days she'd been here. Three so far. Three too many. She threw a twig onto the small fire guttering by her feet, her best source of light this deep into the cave. "What have they done to you?"

"He came, with his *Teller,"* said Gwilanna, treading her claws in a pathetic little gesture of birdbrained fury.

"Who?" asked Lucy, sensing a possible glimmer of hope. Every day, she prayed for a rescuer to come. Her mother. Her dragons. Her hero, David.

"Thoran," said her aunt, at last growing into her

human features. "That irritating lump of shaggy gristle they deign to call a shaman."

Lucy sighed and gripped the rock hard, tempted to throw it out of sheer frustration. Thoran? Who was Thoran? And why did Gwilanna always have to speak as if people were supposed to read her mind? "I don't care what happened," she said in a huff. Though of course she did. For in this lonely hermitagelike existence the only comforts she received were the warmth from Gawain, the glistening beauty of the Arctic ice (and at night, the iridescent lights in the sky), and these useless, if irritating, dialogues with the sibyl. At least they carried news of the world outside, and reminded her she still had a tongue to exercise. One day, she might need to scream for help.

"Be silent," said Gwilanna, "I need to think." She ripped up a handful of the mossy black weeds that grew limply out of the cracks in the rockface, pushed the stalks roughly into her mouth, and chewed them till saliva was trickling down her chin. Lucy sank her head between her knees in disgust. Weeds, berries, all manner of wild-growing mushrooms (peeled), stale birds' eggs, and saltless fish formed her daily diet now. What she wouldn't give for a chicken drumstick or one of her mother's custard tarts.

"They are trying to take the tooth back," said Gwilanna, still muttering at Lucy as if she were a mirror.

This did cause Lucy to raise her head. "You mean the island?" she asked, pointing upward.

The sibyl's response was unusually calm. Instead of the raging fizzle of anger that typically surfaced when Lucy asked a question, Gwilanna spoke in a measured hiss. "In a way, yes. The girl has fallen under their spell and that conniving Ingavar has tried to double-cross me. I had to save his woolly-haired bones again to keep him from taking the tooth to his grave. They think by planting it in his jaw that I will not be able to have it. Arrogant, squinty-eyed, waddling fools. When the fire star comes, he will carry the charm here and then he will die. The dragon will swat him like the insect that he is. It will spare me the need to do it myself."

Lucy gave out another aggravated sigh. She was, by now, lost as to which tooth was which and would have given up her questions entirely had it not been for the mention of a "girl." "Do you mean Zanna?"

Gwilanna gave a snort of deep contempt.

Lucy knew then she had guessed this correctly. She sat up, shouting, "What have you done to her?"

"Nothing, you fool. The *bears* took her."

"What? Where?"

"Don't screech, child. Your squeaky little voice is enough to make the dragon shed every scale he's got!"

On cue, there came a rumble from deep within the mountain and Lucy felt the bedrock beneath her shudder. A silt of dust and very fine grit sieved its way through the fissures in the cave roof, most of it falling into her hair. "What *happened*?" she insisted, shaking it out.

Gwilanna waved an idle hand. "She picked up the tooth your tenant was given to protect him against . . . well, against me — and seemed to have a reaction to it."

"What does that mean?"

"She fell over!"

"Is she —?" Lucy was shaking so much she could not bring herself to say it.

"Dead?" said her aunt. "It wouldn't be much of a loss, but I doubt it. No, they carried her away, under cover of *my* storm!"

"B-but," Lucy spluttered, "that doesn't happen. Bears don't take humans away."

"Hmph," went Gwilanna and rubbed her fingers over the aged wall of the cave. The surface cleared as if a window had been wiped. There, etched out, in what appeared to be charcoal, or the burnt end of a stick, was a tableau of primitive drawings.

Lucy picked up a firestick and went to look. "That's a bear," she said, pointing to a reasonable attempt at one. Faced by the flickering orange flame, the figures appeared to be almost dancing.

"Yes," said Gwilanna, with her usual intolerance. "And the erect figures are people, Inuit people, and this is the sun, and this is the moon, and this is your great, great next of kin."

Lucy looked at the picture of a human figure, a

woman (she could tell by the shape of her body and the long flowing hair) being hailed as some sort of goddess or spirit. "Who is she?" she asked.

Gwilanna sighed. "Has your mother taught you nothing?"

Lucy looked again. "Is it Guinevere?" she gulped.

"NO!" screeched Gwilanna, her voice echoing through the intestines of the mountain. More silt fell. The rocks grumbled again. The small fire flickered brightly and the flames fell flat. "Of course it's not Guinevere. She disappeared with the first white bear."

This was news to Lucy, but she didn't interrupt.

"She was *my* daughter," Gwilanna said bitterly, stabbing her finger at the drawings again. And Lucy was shocked to witness what appeared to be a pang of bereavement in her aunt. "I created her," the sibyl rattled on, "from Guinevere's hair and the scale of Gawain and the clay of the Earth and the blood of my womb. I delivered her into this world and she . . ."

But she would not say any more than that. She swept her hand across the wall again, returning it to its dark, damp state. "Eat," she said. "You need to stay strong and your hair must continue to change and grow." And taking another handful of weeds, she stalked away to the furs in the corner, rolled herself into them, and closed her eyes.

Lucy pulled at the knot at the back of her head and let her hair fall loosely about her shoulders. In the short time she had been here it had grown half the length of her ear and wasn't stopping. It was nowhere near as long as the woman's in the picture, but by February, when the fire star came, she was sure it would be. "I know who she is now," she said in a whisper. "She ran away, didn't she? To live with the bears." And Lucy finally understood why she felt such affinity for their kind, and why a bear had come to speak to her in person during the heavy snowfall in Scrubbley. They revered her distant ancestor. The redhaired child of legend: Gwendolen.

A Curious Void

Dust," said Henry Bacon, flicking some off his dining room table, then spraying the wood liberally with furniture polish and buffing it up with a soft yellow cloth.

"Dust?" David repeated doubtfully.

"That's where we came from. Cosmic stardust. All a bit beyond your simple brain. Takes more than the tumbleweed and windmills in your head to understand the origins of the universe, boy. Stand up, need to polish that chair."

David pushed himself out of his seat and moved to another on the far side of the table. "Henry," he asked rather tentatively, "do you have to wear an apron and disposable plastic gloves while you're cleaning? You're doing household duties, not forensic science."

Henry gave him a baleful look. "Paid sixty dollars for these pants, boy. Don't want them ruined by a lacquered finish." He gave the spray can a truculent squeeze. "If you took a bit more pride in your appearance you'd be half the man that I am, and that's saying something."

David glanced down at his pale blue jeans. Dare he confess that either leg of the factory-ripped denim was probably worth more than Henry's casual slacks? Maybe not. "OK, where did the stars themselves come from? What was there before we had stars?"

"A rather curious void," said Henry. "A vacuum containing no light or sound or time or space or matter. Have you spilled tomato soup on this chairback?"

"No," David pouted. "I put food in my mouth, not over my shoulder. Besides, I haven't eaten here for weeks."

This only made Henry wince with suspicion, as though the culprit could not possibly be him and therefore the stain had been in place for weeks. He exchanged his duster for a dampened cloth and cleaned the chair thoroughly, legs as well.

"A void," David repeated thoughtfully. "An emptiness. A nothing. How can all *this* grow from nothing?" He waved his hands to indicate the "this." "When you open a vacuum flask you don't see stars coming tumbling out. It's ridiculous. It doesn't make sense."

Henry gave an impatient sigh. "It's creation, boy. A miracle of design. It takes vast amounts of energy to make something out of nothing."

David wiggled his nose at that. "At school, in physics, they taught us you can't make something out of nothing."

"Quite. And therein lies the cosmic riddle. Only the creator knows how it happened."

"God, you mean?"

"Of course I mean God! It wasn't a caveman rubbing two sticks together, was it?"

"You believe in him, then?"

"I suppose you don't?"

David held his tongue. He didn't care to enter a religious debate, not with a stuffy old stick like Henry. But to tease him lightly he tried another angle: "Liz says a dragon called Godith made the world."

Mr. Bacon made a strange kind of whimpering noise. "You'll be telling me next that a squirrel knocked this table together from an oak tree. Wonderful woman, Mrs. P. Does have some fanciful notions, though. Ever studied Einstein?"

David shook his head.

Mr. Bacon gave a snort of despair. "Try reading something other than cereal boxes one day. Very profound and clever man, Einstein. Helped us understand how the universe works. Geniuses like him have allowed modern science to trace our origins back to one billionth of a trillionth of a second after the big bang."

David sat up brightly. "I've heard of that! So it all began with an explosion, then?"

"No."

"You just said it did! A bang is a bang. *Ker-poww. Ba-boom!*"

Henry shuddered manfully and took off his gloves as

though it was going to be an awfully long morning. "It was more of a rather large stretching out, like ripples on a pond, like God breathing."

"Or burping," said David. "That's more explosive."

"Don't be facetious," Henry said. "What you should be considering, boy, is why the scientists can't go all the way back to the 'bang,' but have to stop one billionth of a trillionth of a second after it."

"Yeah, so what's the answer?"

"No one knows."

"That's not an answer!"

"Of course it is. Read your Bible. *John: chapter one, verse one.* 'In the beginning was the Word, and the Word was with God, and the Word *was* God.'"

David sat forward, jostling his knees. "Well, here's the gospel according to David. In the beginning was the word and the word was . . . durr? You can't plant God in there just because it suits you. You have to prove it."

"Nonsense. Proof's all around you, boy. Air. Aquarium. Carpets. Rubber plant. All part of the grand plan. God put energy into the void. The void expanded, creating heat and simple elements: hydrogen and helium, giant clouds of gas. When the gases cooled, gravity condensed them into stars. Each star was a giant chemical factory, transforming the simple elements into far more complex ones, ninety-two in all. Those ninety-two bits combined together to make planets, worlds, all *life* as we know it."

"Even me?"

"Unfortunately, yes. And that's only the stuff we can see."

"Eh? We can see all of it, can't we?"

Henry flicked his duster. "No. And that's another godly conundrum. Only about ten percent of the known universe is visible. The other ninety is made up of dark matter."

"Dark matter?" said David, perking up. "What's that?"

"No one knows."

"*Whaaat?*"

"Don't squeak!" said Henry, tucking his elbows into his sides. "Makes my capped teeth grate."

"Well, don't keep dangling metaphysical carrots, then taking them away from me, then! Is there *anything* about the universe we know?"

Henry set his beady eye hard upon his neighbor. "The Lord made it, in his vast mysterious way, and for some unfathomable reason chose to include you. This is giving me a headache. I need a drink."

"Too right," said David. "What have you got?"

Henry opened the cabinet in his sideboard. "Sherry for me; orange juice, in the fridge, for you."

"Very generous. I'll pass, *thanks*. OK, let me get this straight: Everything we see is made from stardust?"

"In a manner of speaking, yes."

"What if a new star appeared? What would that mean?"

Henry knocked back his sherry and said, "Wouldn't see a new star forming, boy. More likely an old one, dying out. Supernova. Massively bright cosmological spectacle. Huge release of energy. Blast wave felt throughout interstellar space."

"You can see a star *dying*?" Was that what was happening with the fire star, David wondered? Somehow, that didn't feel right.

Henry popped the decanter and poured another drink. "Probably from thousands of years ago. Takes a long time for the light of the explosion to reach us."

"And when it does, what happens then?"

Henry gave a shrug. "Bit more stellar radiation passing through." He patted his tummy. "Get it all the time."

"So, it wouldn't have *any* effect on the Earth or any . . . creatures on the Earth?"

Henry wiggled his mustache, spraying a droplet or two of sherry. "Not in your lifetime, boy."

"Even if I'd seen one, in the Arctic?"

"Without a telescope?" Henry hooted loudly. "You probably saw a shooting star — or knowing you, lights from the alien mother ship."

"Very funny," David muttered, as the telephone rang.

Henry picked it up. "Bacon residence? Ah, Mrs. P. Yes, he's here." He passed the phone to David.

"Hi, Liz. It's me."

"Can you come home?" she said. "I need to talk to you."

"Sure. I'll be there in a minute. You OK?"

"I need to talk to you," she said again, after a pause. "Please don't be long." The telephone burred and David slowly lowered the handset.

"Everything all right, boy?" Henry said, easing the phone from the tenant's grasp and cleaning the mouth part thoroughly with his duster before replacing it on the cradle.

"Um, yeah," said David. "Thanks for the info. I need to go." And falsifying a smile, he walked away, gradually increasing the pace of his footsteps until he was outside and jogging across the driveway. He could sense that something wasn't right, for in the half-second gap between Liz ceasing speaking and hanging up the phone, he had clearly heard her sob.

Bad News for David

"What is it? What's the matter?" he asked, the moment he set foot in the Pennykettles' hall.

Liz waved a hand in front of her face as though speaking was just too much for her then. But in a breaking whisper she managed to say, "Come into the front." And taking his arm she guided him there, making him sit in his usual chair.

"Is it Lucy?" he asked, almost bouncing straight out of it.

"No." She motioned for him to sit again. Interlacing her fingers, she paced the floor twice. Finally, she found the wherewithal to speak. "I had a telephone call while you were out at Henry's."

David glanced suspiciously at the instrument, as if

he'd always suspected it of underhanded treachery. "Who from?"

"Your instructor. Dr. Bergstrom."

"Bergstrom?" A flicker of panic crossed David's face. He clicked his thumbnails one against the other. "What did he want?"

With one hand resting against her throat and the other picking at the sleeve of her cardigan, Liz said carefully, "There's been an accident in the Arctic. Zanna's gone missing."

Across the room, on the table that stood in the bay, there was a sudden clink of pottery and Gretel emerged from behind a shallow planter. She had been collecting pollen from the trumpetlike flowers of a Christmas cactus and her paws and snout were stained bright yellow. *Hrrr?* she queried, turning her violet eyes first on David, then on Liz.

"Answer her," said David. "What kind of accident?"

But Liz could say no more. With a short cascade of sobs, she broke down and openly started to cry. Gwillan, who'd been dusting the mantelpiece clock, flew with haste to the tissue box and returned with a handful of paper comfort.

David immediately picked up the phone and simultaneously pulled his wallet from his jeans. He flipped through it quickly and punched out the number on the scrap of paper next to his credit card.

"I'm so, so sorry," Liz wept.

He counted eight long rings, one for every five beats of his heart. "Pick up," he urged, and his prayer was answered. There was a crackle and a rugged male voice broke through: "Manitoba Polar Research Base."

David turned in his chair, pulling the base of the phone off its table, almost clouting Bonnington in his basket. "Russ? Russ, that you?"

"*David?* Jeez. Where are you calling from?"

"Home. America. I just heard about Zanna."

There was a flat, dead pause. The pilot said, "Oh."

A ripple of fear squeezed David's chest. "What's happened, Russ?"

"Didn't Anders call you?"

"He spoke to Liz, my landlady here. She says there's

been an accident, but she's too upset to tell me. What's going on? I need to know."

The pilot sighed, clouding the line for another few seconds. He muttered something that seemed to strengthen his courage, then in a solid voice he said, "OK. This morning, Zanna came out with me and Tootega to transport the bear you rumbled with in Chamberlain to a safe zone north of the town. We got caught in this . . . freak whiteout, and three more big ones came to party."

"Three bears? *Together?*"

"Straight off the sea ice. Almost as if they'd been waiting for us. In sixteen years of working with these animals, I've never seen anything like it."

David swallowed hard and looked across at Liz. A fretful Gwillan was perched on her shoulder, desperately trying to stem her tears. Gretel appeared to have flown from the room and Bonnington had gone back to sleep in his basket.

"You still there?" asked Russ.

David gave an involuntary nod. "Was she mauled? Is she —?"

"She disappeared, David. That's the best I can tell you."

"*Disappeared?* How?"

"Like I said, there was a storm; I couldn't search on foot. By the time I could get the chopper in the air there was hardly a trace of Zanna or the bears. I did a fifty-mile sweep, but —"

"They *took* her?"

Russ gave out an anguished sigh.

"They *took* her?" David repeated angrily. "Why didn't you *shoot* them?"

"It was Tootega's call. He fired a couple of rounds, trying to scare them off. Then he just . . . I dunno . . . he just froze."

David shook his head. "No, Russ. You've gotta do better than that. If Zanna was in danger, why didn't you pull the trigger and keep on pulling? I thought that's what you were trained to do?"

A defeated silence connected the miles. "Something went wrong. That's all I can tell you. Tootega peed his pants. He was out of his wits when I got to him. He saw something that totally freaked him out."

"Like *what?*"

"I don't know," said the pilot, on a taut and troubled rein. "He hasn't said a word since we came back to base. And before you ask why I didn't shoot, I had a raven in my face."

Raven? David tugged at the phone cord as if he'd like to drag the entire Arctic continent down the wire and into his fist. "Where's Bergstrom?" he asked through tightly clenched teeth.

"Heading for Toronto. He's flying to the US — to see Zanna's parents."

David's heart lurched. "No," he said. "He knows what happened. Bergstrom always knows."

"David, how could he? He was nowhere near."

And though he was aware that his voice was breaking and tears were channeling down his cheeks, David said, "No. That can't happen. Not Zanna. She can't be gone."

The phone crackled and Russ said, "I'm sorry, David. I know how much you loved her. We all did, fella. But the chances of us finding her alive are —"

"No!" David cried, from a place deep within, a place he had hardly ever dared reach into. "She's not gone. She's not gone. She *can't* be gone." He felt Liz's warm arms closing around him and fell sideways into them, dropping the phone.

"Shush," she whispered, singing sweet dragonsong into his ear.

Russ's disembodied voice spoke out near the floor.

"I want her back," David wailed to Liz.

"I know," she said, and hung up the phone. "Listen," she whispered. "Listen to me now." And she sang him a lullaby that could have calmed a dragon.

And long before she was finished, he was still.

A Close Encounter of the Dragon Kind

It was the best show on Earth. Except he wasn't on Earth. He was flying among the stars. And seeing wonders.

G'reth stretched out his paws as far as they would reach, as though to catch every passing atom. So much beauty in so much darkness. It was just like being a piece of fluff, dancing on the breeze through a garden filled with spectacular flowers. Every time he spiraled, a new cluster of lights came into view. Galaxies, billions of miles away. Turning, glistening, radiating life. If he lifted his paw in front of his snout, his thumb could blot them out as if they were salt grains. So close, and yet so far away. The universe. The playground of a wishing dragon.

For an unknown time, over an unknown distance, on an unknown winding path he traveled.

Then one day, if days there could be, the force that had gathered him brought him to a halt on the orbit of the fire star shining back to Earth.

The wisher quietly beat his wings, for he was treading space now, neither here, nor there, nor anywhere in between. And though the star was burning brightly, casting its yellow heat over his scales, it was a different kind of warmth that touched his mind.

Somewhere close was a special kind of auma.

He pushed a paw forward. Space rippled. He pulled his paw back. Space flattened out.

His wingbeats quickened. His tail flicked. He was on the edge of something. Something new. Something that did not seem to exist. Something invisible from where he was hovering. Something dark to a dragon's eye.

I wish I knew the secret of Gawain's fire tear.

He closed his paws and put the wish out to the universe once more.

And right there, in front of him, a hole opened. A

hole that had gathered sufficient light to give its perimeter a soft, fuzzy edge.

G'reth looked in. Saw nothing. Heard nothing. And yet felt . . . drawn.

He flicked his wing tips and drifted through.

He had a startling impression of emptiness now. No light. No color. No temperature. No smell. And yet he *sensed* he was not alone.

He was not.

He felt it enter through the tip of his tail, lift the scales along his spine, and whisper through the tunnels of his spiky ears. Intelligence, finding its level, like water. A youthful, happy being, fusing with his auma.

What are you? it said, tickling his thoughts.

What are *you*? G'reth asked it.

I am Fain, it said. *Shall we commingle?*

Hrrr! G'reth gave out a breath of surprise as the being opened his eyes from within. And in that one momentous second, the darkness cleared and G'reth could see. Not land, not water, not sky, not stars, but a different world: a world of *possibilities*.

You are in the image of Godith, said the Fain. *Will you stay with me? I will teach you things.*

But G'reth, as taken as he was by this marvel, shook his head gently and repeated his wish.

The being moved to his paws and closed them. *Then, let me go with you,* it said.

The hole reopened and drew them through.

And G'reth returned to the known universe, enlightened, inspired, and more *aware* than ever.

But even he, for all his newfound sentience, could not have known just then that when a being looks into the mirror of his dreams, something in the mirror is always looking back. . . .

A Challenge for David

When David woke, he was lying on his back on the floor of the living room with his head supported by a large, fluffy cushion. Gretel was sitting in the center of his chest.

"Welcome back," said Liz. She knelt down beside him and wiped his brow. David angled his head. The curtains were drawn. "How long have I been out?"

"Long enough," she said.

Bonnington padded up and touched his nose to the tenant's cheek. Chicken-flavored Chunky Chunks. "Lovely," said David.

Nyeh, went the cat, and padded away.

With some difficulty, David focused on Gretel. She

had her paws behind her back and was tapping her foot. "What does she want?"

Gretel, who like any living creature resented being spoken about, rather than to, snorted and spiked him once with her tail.

"Ow!"

"She wants to give you something. They all do," Liz said.

David widened the scope of his vision. On the chairs, the sofa, the coffee table, the mantelpiece — on every available surface, in fact, sat one of Liz's special dragons. "Zanna," he said, suddenly remembering, suddenly filled with a rush of grief.

"Later," she soothed him. "We'll talk about her later. Right now, stay with the dragons. They've found G'reth — or rather, he's found them."

"Really?" David tried to push up, only to be spiked by Gretel again. "*Ow-ww!* Will you please stop *doing* that! Where is he?"

"Out there," Liz said. She gestured with her hands

to nowhere in particular. "They made contact with him through Gadzooks. He's got a kind of plan. Something he wants you to do."

With a flutter of wings, Gadzooks landed awkwardly on David's chest. He, too, had his paws tucked away behind his back.

"What are they hiding?" David asked, caution in his voice. "What exactly do they want to give me?"

Liz nodded at Gretel, who showed him her paws. In them was a lump of clay. She laid it in the hollow of David's chest. Gadzooks leaned forward and did the same. Then Gruffen. Then Gwillan. Then the listener from the kitchen. Every special dragon in turn.

"OK, what am I s'posed to do with *that*?" There was now a sizeable mound of clay staining one of David's favorite shirts.

"Make a dragon," Liz said, playing with the ends of her wavy red hair.

"Pardon? Are you kidding?"

"No," she said. "That was the message. G'reth wants *you* to make a dragon."

The Call of Gwendolen

Lucy loved her mother. Of course she did. She missed her from the moment she woke in the morning till the time she fell asleep through the long Arctic night. For the first few days of her life as a hostage on the Tooth of Ragnar, the floor of the cave was so wet from her tears that Gwilanna complained she could smell black mold growing in the damp rock. Lucy, by reply, would turn her back and cry into the musty, sealskin furs, hoping that Gwilanna would catch a chill when next she rolled up in them. But the sibyl never did. And the molds never grew. And in time the crying slowed, until the day came when Lucy did not weep at all. That day, she made a pact with herself. She knew by now she could do little of practical use to escape the clutches of her so-called "aunt." So she resolved to make the most of her strange predicament. One morning, after breakfasting on double-stewed lemming (the remains of "dinner" from the previous night) she lifted her head and said, "May I go for a walk?"

Gwilanna's reply was tainted with scorn. "Are you planning to consort with bears?"

"I'm bored!" snapped Lucy, rocking forward, her unwashed hair lying thick around her cheeks. "I'm fed up of sitting around watching my hair grow!" She pulled her furs about her. "And where's the sun gone? I hate this darkness. What am I doing here?"

"You are becoming attuned to the dragon," said Gwilanna. "When the fire star moves into its rightful position, you will aid Gawain to rise."

"How?"

"*How?* By being what you are. It's in your blood, girl. You are a child of Guinevere's line. You will act because you have no choice. The call of the dragon will be all there is."

"Then what?" Lucy said with a frown.

"That is for me to know and the idiots of mankind to discover," snapped Gwilanna. "Now, no more prattle. You will stay in the cave until I say otherwise. The Arctic winter is closing in. There will be permanent darkness for a time . . ." she paused as the rocks beneath them shuddered, ". . . but the island will be lit by the fire star's auma, and when it reaches the very top . . ."

"I hope Gawain chews your head off," said Lucy.

"Clear the slops," growled Gwilanna. She kicked the stew pot over, making Lucy squeal.

With a show of defiance Lucy kicked it back, making it crack against a nearby boulder. The pot split into two clean halves. They separated away like the husk around a horse chestnut seed.

The sea of darkness within Gwilanna's cruel eyes boiled. "Well, child, now you have something to keep you from idleness. While I'm gone today, you will make another pot."

"How?"

"With your hands and the dirt and dust you see around you. You are a Pennykettle. Find clay. Shape it. Or else."

The "else" made Lucy shudder. For there were times when she imagined that, while it might be preferable for Gwilanna to have a descendant of Guinevere present when the last dragon in the world was raised, it was not completely essential. It frightened her to think she was probably dispensable, but, determined not to show it, she hit straight back. "Why don't you teach me something? You're always complaining that I don't know things."

"And what, child, would you like to learn?"

"Magics," said Lucy, surprising herself. Though terrified by Gwilanna's powers, she envied the sibyl as well. Once or twice she'd caught herself snapping her fingers at the embers of the fire, trying, without luck, to make them dance. Gwilanna commanded such elements with ease.

The sibyl gave an unkind hoot of laughter. "Guinevere's line couldn't charm a flea. You have too little of Gwendolen in you. You're not capable of any form of enchantment."

"Mom is. She made Gadzooks — and Gretel."

"Hmph, with the aid of the shaman bear. Without

the icefire, your mother's pathetic creations would be no more use than doorstops or bookends."

"That's not true!"

Gwilanna waved her away. "I have work to do," she snapped, and shrank into a dark-eyed raven again. She stretched her wings and flapped them twice, creating a widespread blanket of dust.

Lucy pressed herself tight up against the wall. Even now, these transformations made her start. "Where are you going?"

"To find the girl."

Zanna. Lucy's hopes of company rose. "Are you bringing her here?"

"No," the bird spat. "I'm going to observe her. She's dangerous. She is —"

"Like you," said Lucy. "A sibyl. I know. She's one of us, isn't she? Is she my sister?"

"She is the youngest of Gwendolen's line," said the raven, "and therefore your part-sister. She is a natural born. She has a human father. Somehow, despite these . . . impurities, she has a remarkable degree of untouched power. . . ."

"Don't you hurt her," said Lucy, curling her fingers.

"When the time of the dragon comes," said Gwilanna, rolling her blue-black eyes fully forward, "the girl will wish she had died on the tundra."

She stretched her wings for flight.

"What about Gwendolen?" Lucy said suddenly, forcing the raven to abandon its takeoff.

"What about her?" it screeched.

"She lived with you. Did you teach *her* things?"

The mountain rumbled, rocking the bird from side to side. "Everything," it said, with bittersweet resentment. "I taught her everything." And away it flew, a dwindling black line in the oval of the cavemouth.

Like the slow, pendulous tick of a clock, the heart of the mountain moved on another beat. The broken pot clinked. Silage fell from the high dark places. Bored, frustrated, tired of being showered, Lucy picked up a firestick and decided she would change her position yet again. She had done this several times already in her search for the safest, warmest spot to sit. It had not been a very fruitful endeavor. Fear of the unknown (strange creepy crawlies, if she was honest) had forced her to roost in the open, by the firelight, even though this was the worst place for debris. But there were several unexplored areas of the cave. Many cheerless alcoves, for instance, most of them barely a superficial notch in the jagged wall of stone that faced the cavemouth. But there were deeper cuts, too, all of which Lucy had so far avoided. They had as much appeal as a lonely alley or a bottomless well. Nevertheless, she did approach one, pushing her timid carnation of fire into the eye of the island's secrets. Almost immediately, the rocks groaned again and released a genielike wind around her ankles. Lucy shivered and the furs slipped off her shoulders, leaving her in sneakers, jeans, and sweater. And how incongruous a sight was that? A sweet young girl, used to all the comforts that a modern life could offer, standing in the throat of an Arctic island, bravely trying to reassure herself that she had an inherited right to be there. She rested her hand on the smooth dry wall and with a gulp she said, "It's all right. I'm your friend." It was not the first time she had spoken to Gawain, but it was the first time she had thought to use dragontongue — and the first time she received a reply.

From somewhere deep within the belly of the island, she heard a whistling moan.

"Who's there?!" she gasped, and jumped away.

No reply.

Her firestick went out.

Frightened, she ran back to her sleeping area for another. But by the time she had returned, she had no need of it. A new and beautiful light was shining. Starlight. Falling through the mouth of the cave.

Lucy traced it back into the open air. The sky glittered. Beneath it floated the parchment of sea ice, faintly reflecting the night like a bruise. On the horizon, low down like a setting sun, one bright yellow star was throwing its radiance onto the island. Lucy put out her hand and let its magic stream over her, watching it weave through the furrows of her palm. Then she turned and ran back into the cave again, to see what the light of the star wished to show her.

At first, nothing but a plain slab of granite, set back a little like a recessed door. Or was it a plugged-up tunnel, Lucy wondered? She raised her firestick and thought she could see a chink or a vent on the uppermost surface. Wedging the light into a crevice, she scrambled over a loose mound of boulders, put her hands into the chink, and pulled with all her might. Hardly a pebble came away. She tried again and again, but the barrier would not budge. Frustrated, she hit it with the heel of one hand. There was the faintest of cracks, but something definitely moved. She hit the wall again, with both hands this time, and the whole structure collapsed inward, carrying her forward and down.

With a squeal of terror, she rolled to a halt and found herself looking back the way she'd come, up a dimly lit tunnel that was roughly the diameter of a very large washing machine drum. She leaped to her feet and squealed again, as her hair caught on a frozen spike of rock. There was just enough light from the treacherous star (for that was how she thought of it now) to show her she was in some kind of den. Its depth was barely double its height, and the walls — what she could see of them — were slightly rounded, scooped out like a Halloween pumpkin. She took a pace forward, crushing something underfoot. With a gasp she halted, not daring to look down, wondering what ghost she might have disturbed. When no specter materialized, she bent her knees and felt warily around the floor. Straightaway, something dry and powdery came into contact with her trembling fingers. Courageously, she closed her fingers around it, long enough to work out its structure and shape. It was a bone. She had stood on and crushed a piece of bone.

Out of that hole, like a hare, she went. She sat among the furs for a timeless time, quaking with fear and humming sweet dragonsong. And maybe it was that which soothed her mind and told her she should not be afraid to go back, because surely only the living could hurt her and nothing *dead* had come to haunt her. Or perhaps it had something to do with the fact that she now knew something about this island that Gwilanna did not. For the sibyl had never spoken of a tomb. But who would have the arrogance to rot away here, overshadowed by the petrified remains of a dragon?

She slithered back in with a good, strong light. It was indeed a tomb, for there were two complete skeletons laid out in the center. One was small and clearly human. The other, lying nearby, was enormous. She guessed it was the carcass of a polar bear. At first she came to think that the bear must have caught a careless human hunter and brought it here to eat, then been trapped by a landslide. But she soon realized this could not be so. Both sets of bones were in perfect order, not scattered as the human ones would have been if the body had been torn apart. So had the person come here to die, she wondered, with the bear lying down beside them, like a guardian? These thoughts brought a lump to her throat and moved her closer to the human frame. Just below the skull lay a necklace of charms: teeth, a bear claw, hanks of fur, and several small carvings made from a stone Lucy did not recognize. She raised it from the shreds of rotted clothing, severing through the crumbling neck bones. "Sorry," she whispered to the staring skull. "It's beautiful. May I keep it?" The bones did not reply. So Lucy slipped the necklace over her head, gathering it softly against her chest. Then she noticed something else. In the skeleton's hand was a small stone vessel. It was the height and shape of a slim tea mug and had a bound, hinged top made from some kind of animal hide. Lucy prized it from the grasping bones. The binding snagged and all but disintegrated. Around the walls of the cave, a wind from another world began to blow. Lucy opened the lid and tipped out the contents. Two objects fell into the palm of her hand. The first was a braid of red and cream tresses (human hair and the fur of a bear, forever intertwined). The second was a small triangular piece of matter that most people would have mistaken for leather or a tough chunk of peel from a tropical fruit. But Lucy knew right away it was precious. The first moment it touched her skin she felt its power race along her veins and set fire to her youthful, quivering heart. She was holding a piece of dragon scale. The only part of the beast she had ever heard her mother give a proper name to. The *isoscele*. The very tip of the spiky tail.

What Tootega Saw

He told no one he was leaving the base. Two days after the incident with Zanna, with the omnipresent threat of an arctic winter keeping the sun pressed low in the sky, Tootega harnessed his dogs to his sled, drove them, tails high, out onto the frozen crust of the bay, and followed the unadorned coastline north. He knew this land. Every hump and hollow and curve of the earth was written in the vessels on his retinal membranes, every pattern in the snow was a message from the wind. After five long days spent pushing the dogs to the edge of their endurance, roaring in defiance at the whirling blizzards, his dark brown eyes took in the headland he'd been waiting for: Seal Point. On the far side of those pregnant cliffs lay the Inuit village of Savalik.

A modern settlement of twenty or thirty large wooden houses, it mirrored Chamberlain in all but size. It was snowbound on three sides, the houses huddled in a cloistered heap like Christmas presents on a large white armchair. Tootega, when he saw it this time, was reminded of something David Rain had said about Inuit settlements looking like a room that you forgot to clean. Anything an Inuk did not need, any broken-down appliance or unused item, he would cast away — but not very far. So it was in Savalik. An incongruous mix of brightly painted roofs and overhanging wires and old oil barrels and junked bent metal and columns of steam. But it was home, and the dogs knew it, too. Their noses lifted at the first scent of seal meat warming in a pot. Their tails wagged. Their paws spent less time in contact with the ice. Orak, the lead dog, whose mapping was every bit as sensitive as his master's, was tugging his comrades toward the colony long before the whip was up.

"Yai!" cried Tootega. The seal skin cracked the air twice before its tongue was muted by a fast buzzing engine. In the distance, a figure dressed in a dark blue parka and large purple sunglasses was bumping a snowmobile across the ice.

Tootega pulled the team to a halt as the snowmobile, smelling of diesel fumes, swung around beside them. The rider's mouth twitched. "Welcome, brother, we've been expecting you."

"How is this?" said Tootega, though he knew in his heart that Bergstrom would have worked out where he was going. Had the scientist sent word ahead? Was he here, perhaps?

"Grandfather always knows," said the rider. He leaned back, gunning the snowmobile's throttle. Its bull nose lifted. The skis on which it sat tap-danced on the ice.

With the rear of his glove, Tootega wiped the frost off his upper lip. "I must speak with him, Apak."

The younger man nodded. The halo of fur around the hood of his coat glistened in the rays of a deep orange sun. "A good time to be home. Just before Sedna closes her eye." He smiled a familiar gap-toothed smile.

"Ayah," said Tootega, and whipped the team onward.

He released the dogs and tethered them beside an old refrigerator, using the snowmobile to lug the sled up the slope toward their grandfather's house. While Apak secured it to a post, Tootega looked around. His arrival had not gone unnoticed. Everywhere, people were watching. He waved at Peter Amitak, who was standing by his boat with a young child whom Tootega did not recognize. He called out a greeting. Peter Amitak waved. The child stared as though it had seen a great spirit. "What's the matter with them?" Tootega asked Apak. "Why don't they speak?"

"You have been away a long time," Apak replied.

But Tootega sensed there was more to their distance than unrenewed acquaintance. They seemed wary of his presence here. Frightened, perhaps.

He stepped inside the house and was glad of its warmth. The oily scent of seal meat and drying arctic char turned his belly and made it speak.

Apak laughed and clapped his brother's shoulder. "What has become of your hunting skills that you should make your innards complain so, brother?" He clapped his hands and called out, "Nauja!"

A door opened and a young woman came to greet them.

"My wife will feed you," Apak said, grinning.

"You —?" Tootega gaped at them both in amazement. The last time he had seen the little "seagull," Nauja, she had still been his baby cousin. The brothers laughed and hugged and Nauja, though pleased to see them in happy spirits, bade them be quiet for their grandfather's sake.

"Is he sleeping?" asked Tootega, blowing air at the door to the old man's room.

A voice weathered by age and cold croaked out, "Why does my grandson not come to greet me?"

Nauja tilted her head.

Tootega went in, bowing his head. The old man, famed throughout the north as a healer and shaman, commanded great respect within the community and even more esteem at home. He gave a thin cry of joy to see his firstborn grandson and called out to Nauja, *Mattak! Mattak!* meaning she should bring them whale meat to chew. Tootega crossed the floor, surprised to find a woolen rug under his feet. It dismayed him every time he came to this house to see his grandfather a little more absorbed by southern culture. This room, with its wardrobes and lampshades and remote-controlled television, was a painful affliction of the disease called progress. Tootega could readily remember a time when this proud and happy man, now lying in a bed that had drawers in the mattress and propped up loosely on a cluster of pillows, would have been surrounded by furs and harpoons and a seal oil lamp, with blood and blubber stains under his feet. On the wall above the bed, slightly tilted at an angle, was a framed embroidered picture saying "Home, Sweet Home" in the Inuit language. To see it made Tootega want to empty his gut.

He reached out and took his grandfather's hand, reeling himself into a firm embrace. "Your arm is strong," he said, though it clearly was not. But it brought a dentured smile to the wrinkled face. His grandfather's name, Taliriktug, meant "strong arm." With a fragile cough, he waved his visitor into a chair, clouding the space between them with smoke. He put a flimsy cigarette into an ashtray. There were burn holes in the patterned pink eiderdown. *How many more,* Tootega wondered, *in the old man's withering lungs?*

Apak, resting himself against the windowsill, said, "Have they released you from the base?"

Tootega shook his head.

"Then you have heard what has happened here? Is that what brought you?"

Tootega raised his shoulders in confusion. He was about to speak when his grandfather took a rattling breath, looked up to the ceiling, and gave a short wail. "My grandson has the scent of bears about him."

Tootega cracked his knuckles and stared down between his knees.

"Is this true?" asked Apak. "Only —"

"Let him speak," the old shaman commanded. "He has fled across the ice to tell us what he knows." His eyes closed and he began to rock back and forth, singing and begging the souls of the dead not to allow any bad thing in.

Apak raised a thin black eyebrow at his brother.

"Taliriktug looks into my soul," said Tootega, making a fist at his mouth as he spoke. "I have been with Nanuk. I have seen . . . strange things."

The old man softly moaned.

Apak said quietly, "Tell us your tale."

"I was releasing a bear on the tundra," said Tootega. "It woke before it should have, threatening a young *kabluna*, a girl. I was in the helicopter, answering the radio. When I saw what was happening I took up my rifle and shot at Nanuk's ears to make him run. But he stood, bravely. Then others came."

Apak crossed his arms. "He was walking with cubs?"

Tootega shook his head, angry that his brother should think such a thing. His face stretched with fear as he brought the scene back. "It was a male, not a mother. Other males came to join it. Two sat between me and the girl. The other . . ." He stopped and pressed his palms to his temple.

Apak knelt before him. "What did you see?"

"Aiyee. Aiyee," Tootega wailed.

Taliriktug, meanwhile, raised three fingers and clawed a sign in the air in front of him. A current of air struck the windowpanes, trying to shake them out of their frames.

"I am cursed," said Tootega, clutching at the very roots of his hair.

"What did you see?" Apak said again. "Who has come?"

"Oomara," their grandfather said, in a voice too deep to belong to his throat. Suddenly, his body jack-knifed forward and his eyes rolled up like hard white eggs. The ashtray and its contents spilled to the floor. Outside, the pack dogs howled. The light in the room began to flicker.

Apak cried out, "What do you see?" For the old man could travel far beyond his body and reach out into the underworld of life.

"Spirits, flying," Taliriktug hissed.

"They were on his shoulders," Tootega panted, clinging tight to his brother's arms. "Spirits, like birds, with fire in their mouths."

The door opened. Tootega did not hear it, but saw a pair of feet, in mukluks, come toward him. Apak moved aside. The visitor, a young woman, knelt down in his place. "Did one of them have paws like this?" she asked. She curled her fingers slightly and stretched them as far apart as she could.

With a scream of terror, Tootega leapt backward out of his chair, crashing it against the wardrobe door.

"Thanks. I missed you, too," the woman said. She rose up and backed toward Apak and the door. "He saw dragons," she informed him. "The servants of the universe. Bring him to me when his head reassures him that the sibyl, Zanna, is alive — and doing well."

Well, Golly . . . Gosh!

This is silly," said David, rocking back in his chair. He crossed his arms firmly and stretched his long legs across the kitchen floor. On a wooden board on the table in front of him sat the chunk of clay the dragons had donated. Knives and brushes lay alongside, plus a paint-stained jar of methylated spirits. Ranged behind the clay stood the Pennykettle high command: Gadzooks, Gretel, Gruffen, etc. Behind them, in a chair, sat his landlady, Liz.

"Just pick up the clay and work it," she said.

"There's no point," David replied, tartly. "I'm absolutely useless with it. I tried it at school, once. We were told to make a personalized teacup, in Art. Mine came out warped, like an oven-baked ashtray. If Salvador

Dalí had painted it as still life, he'd have made a small fortune."

"Salvador *who*?" someone hurred to Gruffen.

Gruffen checked in his book of dragon instructions. Nothing appropriate came up under *S*.

"He was an artist," said Liz, "and all artists start somewhere. So can you, David."

"But why? What's the point?" he argued back.

Gretel tapped a foot and hurred impatiently.

"I don't know," said Liz, her green eyes flaring. "But right now, we don't have a better option. If G'reth wanted this, then you should do it. He's part of you, and part of Lucy, too. For both your sakes, I'd like to see what happens. Now, take the clay. In both hands. Come on."

Reluctantly, David wriggled upright in his seat and closed his hands around the chunk, working it silkily through his fingers. "Don't blame me if it comes out like a pudding. What do you start with? Head or body?"

"Either. Body is usually easiest. Break it up until you think you've got the right amount."

David tore the clay apart and selected a chunk. "Now what?"

Hrrrr, went Gretel, puffing smoke. She made a few model poses, sarcastically suggesting David should copy one.

He tried. He really did. For a good ninety seconds he molded the clay as best he could. His final effort came out resembling a pear.

The dragons ground their teeth in disappointment.

The tenant threw up his hands in defeat. "There. See? Told you I was useless."

"That's it," said Liz, snapping her fingers. "Seeing. You're seeing too much. Trying too hard. You should be following your heart, not your head. Close your eyes."

"What?"

Is this wise? Gruffen hurred to the rest of the group, pointing to a few spots of clay on the ceiling, the result of David's gesture of failure.

Bonnington, pushing his food around his bowl, gave up and hid behind the ironing board. If clay was going to fly, he was taking no chances.

"Close your eyes," Liz repeated.

David muttered, "This is dumb." All the same, he did as he was told.

"Now, dream it," said Liz. "Let your hands move to the dragon that comes to you, not how you think the average dragon ought to look."

David waited several seconds, then sighed and drummed his fingers. "Can't see one."

"*Dream* one. Think about G'reth. Think about Gawain. Let it just appear at the front of your mind."

So David let his fingers knead and squeeze. It wasn't long before he heard a hurr of modest astonishment and guessed he must be doing something right.

The dragon in his mind's eye stretched its wings. They were as fragile as butterflies and shaped like harps. David let his thumbs describe their form, then fumbled around and pressed them to the body. Feet followed. Quick and graceful feet. And a handsome head, with less flare in the snout than Liz would have given to one of her creations. (David thought he heard Gretel give a kind of whistle, and guessed he might be making a young male dragon.) The tail he gave an upward curving sweep, finishing off with a perfect little triangle at the tip. Lastly came the arms. These proved tricky, for the dragon kept moving them about such a lot. Yet, somehow, David tuned his fingers to the movements, as if the dragon was helping to make itself. Light flooded his mind and the image disappeared. David sat back and rubbed his eyes (leaving clay on the ridges of his cheekbones).

"Jeez," he gasped as he took away his fists. "Did I do that?"

There, on the board, stood a wondrous replica of the dragon in his mind. It was gray, of course, and had no eyes or patterns for its scales, but it was *there*. A clay figure. A work of art.

"Well, well," said Liz, her green eyes sparkling slightly violet. "He's quite . . . fascinating."

"Is it a 'he'? How can you tell?"

Liz smiled, but didn't reply.

Gretel, who had circled the dragon twice by now, hooded her eyes and pointed to a blob in the creature's right paw. *What's it holding?* she hurred.

David shrugged. "In the dream, I couldn't tell."

"It doesn't matter," said Liz. "It'll be clear when we kiln him. Do you want to name him now?"

David shook his head. "Later. Is he going to be . . . y'know, special? Don't you have to use the icefire for that?"

Liz touched the dragon's back with her little finger. "That depends on the maker, David. Do you feel you need to use it?"

"Dunno. Not especially."

"Then we won't. Here, draw his eyes." She handed him a stick.

He put it straight down. "Can't. Didn't see them."

He had no eyes? the crowd of dragons hurred.

"Yes, he had eyes," David reassured them. "I just didn't see him open them, that's all."

Liz was at a loss to understand this, but knowing better than to question the workings of the universe, she patiently helped David to reconstruct the face, as if they were building a police sketch. She also showed him how to score the surface of the body, making an unusual pattern of scales that in Gretel's opinion was completely unfashionable.

And thus it was that the dragon was born. "He needs kilning now," said Liz. "Wave good-bye. It will be about two days before you can see him next."

"Can't I come and watch?"

"No," she said emphatically and, calling all the special dragons to her, she took the new creation down the hall and disappeared with it into the Dragon's Den.

Those two days seemed to be the longest of David's life. While he waited, he couldn't help but think of Zanna, and that drew him down into a spiral of dejection. Not even the sight of bright white snowflakes falling past his window could lift his spirits. In fact, it made them worse. For snow meant ice, and ice meant the Arctic, and that meant polar bears and that meant sorrow.

On the second day, he put on his overcoat and boots, cleared an inch of snow off the garden bench, and sat outside, hoping he might see Snigger. That was one thing he couldn't work out. What purpose could the young gray squirrel have in this?

A quick sharp screech cut across the garden.

Or, for that matter, a crow?

Sitting on Mr. Bacon's fence was Caractacus, the crow they had once done battle with to save the life of a squirrel known as Conker. David stared at the bird and thought about his story.

Caark, it went again, as if it might have news for him.

"Fly north," David whispered. "Find her for me. Tell her I love her."

The bird tilted its head.

Then it caarked again and spread its wings, disappearing into the glare of the morning.

On the third day, David was back in the kitchen, unshaven, unwashed, and drifting around aimlessly in his pajamas, when Liz and her posse returned with the new dragon.

"Wow," he managed when she handed it to him. "Why is it so light?"

"I don't know," said Liz. "I don't know why its scales are silver-blue either, or why its eyes are closed . . . and I still don't know what this is for." She bent down a little and touched the small object in the dragon's paw.

"Looks like a toolbox," David said.

"Mmm," Liz nodded. "He's yours now. Time to name him."

David whistled. "Gosh," he said, "I —" He paused. The dragon had blinked its eyes.

Is that it? Gretel hurred, flying up to the fridge to confer with the listener. *Gosh?*

"That was an exclamation of surprise." David sighed.

"Seemed to do the trick all the same," Liz said.

David wrinkled his nose. "I can't call him Gosh!"

The dragon blinked again.

The other dragons murmured among themselves. Gadzooks was dispatched to David's shoulder, where he whispered another suggestion.

"Or Gollygosh," said David, frowning at him.

The new dragon yawned and spread its wings.

Every Pennykettle dragon gasped in awe. The newcomer's wings were completely *translucent*.

"Name him, officially. Now," Liz insisted.

David brought the dragon up to eye level. Its eyes were blue, the same shade as his. "OK, I name you . . . Gollygosh Golightly — until I can think of something better."

This started a *real* rumble. Gruffen was urged to consult his book to see if a dragon might have a double name, even if they did both begin with a *G*. Gruffen checked, but could find nothing to the contrary. So the listener duly recorded the new dragon as Gollygosh Golightly. "Golly" for short.

"Do you speak dragontongue?" David asked him (using the dialect of hurrs and growls).

Gollygosh blew a smoke ring and nodded.

"You seem restless," David said a little warily, feeling the claws pricking into his palm. No one knew, yet, what this dragon could do.

Golly's eyes slid sideways. He turned his head and looked at the toaster.

"That's a toaster," David said, trying to be helpful. "It scorches bread — at least it does when it works."

The dragon flew to it and picked up the plug.

"What's he doing?" David muttered, as every dragon present craned its neck to see.

Golly frowned thoughtfully and put down his toolbox. It opened automatically with a cantilever action and an asterisk of light seemed to jump straight out of it and into his paw. Something resembling a screwdriver appeared there.

"What *is* he doing?" David repeated, watching his creation unscrew the plug and lift out the fuse. The dragon held it, ends on, between his paws. Within seconds, a spark of light had zipped along its length, giving out a faint electrical crackle. The dragon, looking rather pleased with its efforts, quickly fitted the plug back together and plugged the toaster in. A hot red glow began to seep from its elements.

"Oh my, what *have* you done?" gasped Liz.

"It would appear I've made a do-it-yourself dragon," said David.

"Oh no. You've done more than that. I never thought I'd see one. Not in my lifetime."

"One what?" said David. "What does he do — besides home improvements?"

Liz called to Gollygosh, who turned and flew to her. *"He* is very special *indeed*," she said, running her fingers over his spine. "You've made a natural healing dragon."

A Bay of Stars

"She came two days ago," Apak said, lobbing a pebble into the snow. He was sitting on an upturned *umiak*, a wide-bottomed boat, trying to hit the pebble that his brother, Tootega, had already thrown. It was a game they had played many times as boys, but never before without laughter in their hearts. Apak's pebble came to rest just beyond his brother's throw. Tootega, standing solemnly beside the boat, threw another stone and also missed.

Apak took aim again. "It happened in the middle of the night. Peter Amitak said he was woken from his sleep by a spirit calling out to him across the ocean. He rose from his bed, put on his boots and a fur covering, and opened the door to his house. The moon had spread her light across the bay and he could see the ridges in the ice very clearly. With his hunter's eye, he noticed a movement. One of the ridges was growing in size, swelling at its summit and then becoming still. He knew, as any Inuk would, that a bear had climbed to the top of the ridge and was sitting there staring back into his soul. Peter Amitak went inside for his spyglass. What he saw is still being spoken of in whispers."

He threw his pebble. It broke the crust of the snow, lodging close to the target stone, but still not touching.

Tootega turned his head and looked across the vast and shadowed landscape. The dark kiss of winter, collecting in speckled frost all around the fur of his parka hood, had stopped out all but the largest features. But he did not doubt Peter Amitak's story. He bade his brother, Apak, tell the rest.

The younger Inuk beat a fist against his heart. Although he respected the ways of the elders, he had never lived by their primitive traditions or taken shelter among their beliefs. And yet when he spoke there were tremors in his voice, a quiet fear coming from a distant time, deep beyond his thirty-three years. "Peter Amitak says Nanuk was waiting for their eyes to meet. When he focused the spyglass, the bear was looking straight at him, he says. He saw the white fire burning in its eyes and the mark of Oomara clearly on its head."

"Ayah," Tootega muttered through his teeth, hurling his remaining stones away. One hit the rusting wing of a snowmobile, wedged in a drift like a bright red wafer. The others scattered like dead black seeds, waiting, as all things did, for the thaw.

Apak, knowing the game was over, merely put his pebbles aside. "Peter Amitak called to his wife. 'Kimalu, come see! Quickly, woman! The spirit of our ancestors is here among us!' Kimalu came and put the glass to her eye. She tells how Nanuk opened his mouth and a bay of stars poured out of him. He breathed them wide across the ocean and they turned into a blizzard of burning snow. By the time the last ashes were resting on the surface, Nanuk had gone and the ice was still. Peter Amitak rode his Ski-Doo down the hill, shaking the wits into the rest of the village. Andrew Irniq and others raced after him, crying, 'What is happening? What is happening?' I was among them. At the foot of the ridge where the bear had been, we found the girl.

"Her skin was blue and she was taking in no more air than a bird. Her eyes were half-open, but seeing nothing. Peter Amitak fell to his knees, saying she was Sedna come to eat our fingers. Andrew Irniq said he had the brains of a dog and sent him away to chew on a bone. We wrapped the girl and I carried her here, to grandfather's house. He called her 'Qannialaaq,' falling snow, and said she was the one he had seen in his journeys."

Tootega gave his brother a questioning look.

Apak pointed into the dusk. "Taliriktug has been traveling among the spirits. He says there is a yellow star shining in the sky. This star, he says, is a sign that Oomara will appear among us again. Others are saying it must be so, for how else could this pale white girl have survived the jaws of the ice and the bear? And now here are you, telling stories of Oomara with spirits on his shoulders. What did you really see there, brother?"

Tootega stared ahead, as if the cold had reached

inside his skull and frozen his brain and eyes from within. "I saw Oomara take off his coat. He was shaped like Nanuk, and then he was a man. In this form, he lifted the girl from the ice. Then the blizzard came down and I saw no more."

Apak stretched his fingers inside his mittens. "People are saying this girl is a goddess, resting on human bones. Grandfather is guiding her in the old ways."

"How?" Tootega grunted scornfully. "Taliriktug speaks as much English as this boat."

Apak shrugged. "She uses Inuktitut, in a tongue only a shaman like him would understand. She has a name for it. She calls it dragontongue."

From above them, suddenly, they heard a sharp croak. A dark bird was circling under the clouds.

Tootega reached inside his coat for a knife.

Apak clicked his tongue. "Slay a raven, you bring death upon us all."

"It follows me," Tootega said, spitting phlegm.

Apak watched the bird seep into the underbelly of a cloud. "So many signs," he said. "People fear a change is coming. They say the ice is about to burn. Some say the world will be consumed by it. Grandfather says Qannialaaq has come to save us from these things."

"A-yah," growled Tootega and dismissed it with a wave.

"He says you will be there to see it," Apak added, but these quiet words dissolved into the crunching snow as Tootega stomped away to the old man's house.

He found them, Taliriktug and Zanna, in the room in which Nauja accepted visitors. They were sitting cross-legged on the bare wooden floor, facing each other just a few feet apart. The furniture had all been pushed aside and a blind had been drawn across the window. A seal oil lamp was flickering its light near Taliriktug's elbow. The air was thick with the jarring smell of incense. The wooden walls rattled to the song of the wind.

"Tootega is with us," Zanna said, even though her head was down and her face was hidden by her falling hair.

The hand of fear squeezed the Inuk's heart. His

brother was right. The girl *could* speak a broad Inuktitut. But the dialect was odd, guttural, like an animal. The words had formed in her throat, not on her tongue.

The old man said nothing to indicate displeasure. He was rocking gently back and forth, beating a thin drum against his thigh. He was almost in a trance, Tootega knew. Soon he would be traveling to the ocean or the stars.

Zanna, who was dressed from head to toe in furs, passed her hand over a line of small rocks, laid out in a shallow arc before her. To his astonishment, Tootega saw the stones wobble and knew she had crossed them with a stroke of magic. She lifted her head and shook her hair proudly. Feathers and beads had been sewn into the strands. Her face was pale, like the coat of a seal pup. Black rings, mixed from charcoal and grease, were painted around her eyes. "We need to prepare," she said.

Tootega, not comprehending this, merely jutted his dimpled chin at her and said, "What do you want here, girl?"

Taliriktug beat his drum and wailed softly. The footsteps of the wind crept through the house, whistling where they found any weakness in the timbers. The seal lamp flickered but did not go out.

Zanna pointed to the far left stone. For a second or two, a faint light seemed to pulse from its surface, then it grew a head, four legs, and two wings.

Tootega stumbled back against the wall in fright.

"This was the beginning," Zanna said in dragontongue, touching the stone and turning it green. With her other hand, she pointed at the far right stone. "And this is the end." And that stone, too, made the shape of a dragon.

"Leave!" snapped Tootega. "Go back to the ocean!"

"I intend to," said Zanna, studying the stones, "and you will be coming with me, Inuk. We have a date on the Tooth of Ragnar."

Tootega half laughed. Was the girl insane?

"But that's not the next part of the story," she muttered, running her hands across the stones once more.

At the second pass, she paused by a flattish piece of rock. She picked it up and laid it in her palm.

Like the others, it began to alter its form. Tootega saw the developing shape and cursed it through his gritted teeth.

"It's an island," said Zanna, wonder and surprise creeping into her voice. "But where . . . ?"

But it did not look like an island to Tootega. He knew the shape well. Every Inuk did. Some gave it credence. Some did not. To him, it had always been a vague curiosity, another soapstone carving, nothing more. He had never found answers or comfort in its promises. Yet in some deep place it frightened him, because of the trust many white men placed in it. He formed spittle in his mouth, but swallowed instead. This girl. This dark, unwelcome witch, who could play games with solid stones. Why had she called that figure an island? No island he had ever seen was shaped like a cross.

Just then, Taliriktug let out a groan so unworldly that it might have been his last. He put back his head and stopped his breath. In that instant, the wind beat its cold fist against the house and the window blind tore itself away from its fastenings. Flapping behind the glass was a raven.

Tootega, half in, half out of his wits, picked up a piece of southern decadence — a boot scraper — and hurled it with all his strength through the glass. The bird squealed in alarm. In its panic, it was somehow sucked forward by the pressure, raking its talons against the cut edge of glass. A bead of blood rolled down the pane. The bird fluttered and dropped backward, mortally pierced by a shard of flying glass.

Tootega charged out of the house and found the raven laboring beneath the broken window, red stains seeping into the snow. The boot scraper lay among a nest of splintered glass. He lifted it again, intending to bring it down on the bird's head. What did he care if this evil thing died? But as he tried to strike, he felt his wrist gripped by Zanna's hand.

"No!" she snapped, and threw him aside with more force than her muscles ought by rights to have mustered.

She fell to her knees and cradled the bird, feeling its heartbeat slipping away. In its eye, she could see the mirror of its purpose. Dozens of reflections, one raven after another, running all the way back to a garden in America, where a young man sat on a bench in the drizzle, speaking to a crow he called Caractacus. *Tell her I love her.* "He sent you," Zanna said. "David sent you to find me." And she wept against the bird as it died in her hands.

"What is happening, here?" Apak came running. He gave a jolt of fear when he saw what he saw.

"Your brother killed a raven," Zanna said coldly. "He thought it was the sibyl, Gwilanna; he was wrong." She buried the bird and blessed it, then stood. "Get your things," she said to Apak's quaking brother. "We leave in one hour."

"Going where?" scoffed Apak. "We are on the crust of winter!"

"It's plenty warm enough where we're going," growled Zanna. "By the end of winter, your brother will have witnessed the birth of a dragon."

Good Night, Lucy

Sometimes it came down in beautiful flakes, or was blown across the cave in jeweled crystals when the wind skimmed the island's icy escarpments, but mostly the snow was diced by the wind into a biting blizzard that did little more than plug the mouth of the cave and shut out the rest of the natural world. When it started, it blew for days. Though "days" was really an approximate guess. Time was almost impossible to gauge when the precious moments of clear white light could be counted in minutes rather than hours and the sun preferred to hide on the horizon rather than struggle above it. But there were two fresh scratch marks on Lucy's wall anyway. Two days she reckoned she'd been left alone to fend for herself, living off a dwindling supply of lichens and that "treat of all treats," the boiled mushroom. If Gwilanna did not return soon, Lucy knew she would have to face the threat of starvation or the unknown dangers beyond the cave. Many people might have crumbled in such a situation, but the Pennykettle spirit, the dragon in her blood, merely made her more determined to overcome her captor and put what she knew about this place to some use.

She had done a lot of thinking in her time alone, projecting ahead to the month of February and wondering what was going to happen. The thought of seeing Gawain alive both terrified and excited her. The last true dragon. The Lord of the Skies. Would she fall down praying or scream and run for shelter? Her life would never be the same again. And yet, as she sat in the wake of the beast, listening to his great lungs grinding and shearing against the rocks, she could not help but remember her mother's words, that Gawain should be left to rest in peace and not freed into a world where dragons, in general, were loathed and feared and misunderstood. But to do that, Gwilanna must be stopped, and she, Lucy Pennykettle, daughter of Guinevere, part-sister to Gwendolen, was one of few people who might be capable of it.

A dragon's tailpiece and a double hank of hair. What could she do with them? How could they help her? They must be special. They must have power. Why else would Gwendolen take them to her grave? Lucy tried to focus her mind. Gwilanna, she remembered, had come to Scrubbley with a scale of Gawain locked up in a case. She had worked spells with it. Perhaps Lucy could, too?

So she tried. Over and over again. Once, during a break in the blizzards, she stood in the cavemouth and held the isoscele up to the stars. In dragontongue, she implored the Earth goddess, Gaia, to take her back to her mother in Scrubbley. But it did not work. Nothing worked. Neither the moon, nor the sea, the ice, nor the bears, the bones in the den, nor the spirit of Gwendolen (whose bones she was certain lay in there) made any amendment or impression. After some time, Lucy threw her finds down and collected herself into a huddle of dismay. She might just as well bind the scale onto a stick and use it as a spoon to stir the sibyl's stew!

Why could she not find magic in these relics? Why wouldn't the universe come to her aid?

Then one day she had a brain wave. While she was gouging out her usual scratch, she thought about the paintings on the wall. She had tried, without success, to restore the images Gwilanna had shown her, but these were not the ones she was thinking of. On the wall inside the den where she had found the remains, she remembered seeing some drawings untouched. Maybe she could find some clue in those? Lighting up a fire-stick, she hurried down into the hole to see.

It took several minutes to locate what she thought was the start of the drawings, for they were scratched all around the circle of the den, as if the story they depicted was never ending. She started with a clear illustration of a polar bear. It was small. She guessed it was a baby, a cub. Through the sediments of centuries she traced its story. It wasn't pleasant. It had fed on a child and been killed by a hunter. Then a bigger bear had come. The cub's mother, perhaps? Some people had fled. Others had fought it. The bear had lost. Lucy gulped at the picture of it feet up, speared like a large pincushion. Farther around was another bear, standing on its hind legs, roaring in anger. More fighting. Many stickmen spilled on the ground. A man crushed in the great bear's arms. Then a spooky drawing of the bear's head on the man's body, lit by a heavenly light from above, and stickpeople falling to their knees and praying. Lucy moved closer, flaring the light until the old rocks blushed with the desire to burn. There was something odd about this part of the story. Someone had drawn what looked like a hole, stretching through the sky, way into the stars. People seemed to be floating through it. At the end of the hole was a picture of a dragon, holding out its wings as though it were an angel. Something on its head caught Lucy's eye. A mark. It sparkled as she drew the flame nearer.

"That's the same as on Zanna's arm," she muttered and was stepping backward to gather her focus when, without warning, the firestick flickered and the flame went out.

With a frightened gasp, Lucy scrabbled up the tunnel

on her hands and knees, finding, more to her surprise than horror, that all the lights in the cave, including the embers of the fire, had been extinguished. What's more, she was not alone. She could sense a warm body and smell wet fur.

A bear had entered the cave.

Most people would have been mortally afraid to find themselves in such a predicament, for there was nowhere to run and no way to fight. The bear, if it desired, would have little reason not to kill her and eat her. But Lucy had encountered a spirit bear once and knew instinctively that this visitor was something out of the ordinary. Sure enough, as the north wind licked around the edges of the cave and the clouds outside were driven apart, a faint wash of light fell into the cave, picking out the bear's exact position. It was silhouetted right in the center of the floor, sitting, as bears and cats often do, with its front paws tucked between its widespread rear paws, waiting, it seemed, to be formally greeted. Awed, but not afraid, Lucy stood up and brushed down her furs.

"Hello," she said.

The bear snorted softly and shuffled its paws. "Child," it said, in perfect dragontongue. Then the most bizarre thing happened: It appeared to absorb all the light from beyond and spread it luminescently throughout its body, until it was glowing like a Christmas decoration. Before long, Lucy had a perfect view of it. It looked old and wise, but not at all doddery. It was a bear that had seen many things, she thought.

"Who are you?" she asked.

The bear tilted its head and squinted at her kindly. "I am all things to all men," it said. And the words seemed to wrap around Lucy's head, as if they were a wind from another world.

"Is this your cave?"

"Sometimes," it said.

"Have you come to save me?" She looked toward the cavemouth, wondering if her prayers had been heard, after all.

The bear pondered a moment, then shook its head. It raised itself and took a pace forward.

"Don't hurt me," Lucy gulped and clasped her hands to her chest.

The bear halted, then sat down once more. A second passed, then it lowered its head and the glimmer surrounding it grew more intense, until Lucy was almost blinded by the glow and lost sight of the animal in the brightness. She covered her eyes, but the light was quick to dim and when she looked again the bear had disappeared. In its place was a fair-skinned woman with flowing red hair and eyes of a pale, translucent pink.

"You!" she gasped.

"You remember me," the woman said, looking pleased.

"I prayed to you," said Lucy, and dipped her knee. "Zanna said you were the Earth mother, Gaia."

The woman smiled. "Sometimes," she said. "Look, child, I have something to show you." She opened her hands. In each sat a dragon.

"G'reth!" Lucy cried, making out the handsome wisher at once. He waved a big paw and flew into her hands. She raised him up, hardly able to believe it.

"Where did you go? Where have you been? And . . . oh, who's this?" The second dragon, an unusual-looking white creature, more the shape of a bird than a dragon, had landed on Lucy's shoulder. On his way, he had picked up the isoscele and hair.

"Give me those," she said, trying to snatch them from him. But he was quick, and buzzed to her other shoulder.

"Child," said the woman in a soothing voice. "Groyne does not want to steal your possessions. He merely wants to take a lock of your hair."

"Groyne?" queried Lucy. "But he was the one who —" She broke off suddenly to stare at G'reth, who was teasing out her hair between his wide front paws. There was a strange, bright glint in his oval eyes and their color was changing in merging swirls of violet and blue. At first, Lucy was frightened by it, for she thought that his fire tear was going to be shed. But then she recognized wonder, not sorrow, in his gaze and that, in a way, began to shake her even more. G'reth was studying her hair (which was longer and very much redder now) as if he had never seen it before. How could that be?

Groyne turned the isoscele deftly through his claws until the sharp tip was pointed away from him. Lucy caught the movement and was suddenly alert. "Why does he want my hair?"

"It will help you sleep," said the figure of Gaia.

The island rumbled. Lucy looked up at the roof of the cave. "Will Gawain *really* come alive again?"

"Always, child, in your dreams."

Then the isoscele flashed and a thick lock of hair was quickly cut free. Lucy immediately buckled at the knees and fell into a heap on the floor of the cave. Groyne handed the hair to G'reth.

"There, you have what you need," said Gaia. She looked at Groyne and said, "Twine the old strands around her wrist and place the isoscele in her hand."

Groyne did this, amazed to see Lucy's fingers curl around the age-old piece of dragon skin.

"She will be protected," the woman whispered, and pointed at the firesticks on the wall. All three of them flickered into flame once more. "Come, we have work to do." And with a pulse of collapsing light she resumed the shape of a polar bear and walked out into the swirling blizzard.

It was an hour before the second bear entered the cave. She was old and walked tiredly, hobbling against an arthritic knee. There were patches in her rumpled fur and signs in the creased black lids around her eyes that her life was now a burden, not a joy. She'd been coming to this cave on the Tooth of Ragnar every third year of her twenty-one seasons. In that time she had delivered five litters of cubs. This time she was barren and believed she was coming here to sleep her last winter. The last thing she'd expected to trouble her in death was the prostrate body of a sleeping manchild and the cave lit by orange fire.

She nudged the body. There was no response. She nudged again and this time her snout caught the scent of a bear, next to the manchild's skin. The old bear shuffled back and snorted in confusion. That was her *ancestors'* scent. How could this child be carrying a trace of the female, Sunasala, the fabled mate of Ragnar? That could not *be*.

The mountain spoke. The bear snorted back. She was used to the island's rumbling voice, but this groan had a hollow echo to it. A change of tone meant a change of shape. A new chamber must have opened somewhere.

So she hunted around and found what she knew to be a tunnel to a den. Deep within the dust of countless years, she found the scent of bones: human and bear.

She shook herself and looked at the girl again, remembering an old den story. A legend about a red-haired Inuk woman, who had walked with bears and devoted her life to them. A woman so respected by the Council of Nine, that when she had died a bear had been chosen to lay down beside her to protect her on her journey to the far side of the ice.

This was enough to convince the old bear that this child, too, should be protected. And so picking Lucy up between her jaws, she carried her carefully into the den. As her paws crunched through the ancient bones, she began to wonder at the wisdom of her actions, fearful of the creeping whistle of the wind, taunting her from the mouth of the tunnel. But it was done. She was committed. There was no turning back. She set the girl down in the center of the space and washed her face with long sweeps of her tongue, according to the way it had been in legend. Then she curled around the child and fell into a slumber, never knowing if the sun would rise for her again.

This was how Gwilanna, the sibyl, found them. "Well, child," she hissed, poking a firestick around the chamber, reading the drawings, taking them in, "you have surprised me yet again. Now you know a little more of our kind. Very well, lie down with your stinking bear, but remember: A child who sleeps with ghosts, sometimes wakes with them in her heart."

And she doused the flame and climbed out of the tunnel, leaving Lucy and the bear in darkness and dormancy. And that would be the way of it for three long months: until the fire star moved into place above the island.

A Healing Crisis

"I don't get this," said David, leaning back in his chair.

Liz looked up from her ironing. "Get what?"

"It's been three days since I made Gollygosh and all he's done is mend . . . trivial things."

Liz stood the iron on end. She folded Lucy's best pajamas and smoothed the last crease with a rub of her hand. "That depends on what you see as trivial," she said, stretching a T-shirt across the board. Lucy's favorite. *Save the red squirrel.* She paused a moment in contemplation. Gwillan, thinking this was a cue for action, warmed the flat surface of the iron with his breath. Liz thanked him and continued with her chores.

"I didn't mean to imply . . ."

"What?" she said, without looking up.

I didn't mean to imply that what you're doing is trivial, David thought. But he couldn't bring himself to say it. Every day he watched Liz going through the motions of being a good and caring mother, washing clothes for her daughter, tidying her room, setting a place for Lucy at breakfast. None of it mattered, in a physical sense. It was simply her way of filling up the emptiness. He cautioned himself to be careful what he said.

"Yesterday, for instance, he tuned my guitar. Gretel flew past it and made the strings hum. Golly magicked up a tuning fork from his toolbox, then put the guitar in tune by clutching the strings and changing their resonance. He didn't even need to turn the machine heads. It was amazing. I could make a small fortune out of him."

Liz sprayed a little water over the T-shirt. The excess caught Gwillan, making him sneeze. "He's not here to make you rich."

"I know that. But what is he here for? I made him at the dragons' request because that's what G'reth had told them we needed. I grant you, Golly is extremely talented. We can now get Channel five very clearly and my computer is completely free of viruses, but how is that helping us with Lucy or Zanna? Or Zookie even? When is something important going to happen?"

Liz pressed on the iron with added weight. "David, when are you going to learn? These dragons act when the universe moves them. You've seen what Golly does. He puts things right. In time, who knows what he'll do? Be patient, and proud; he's a wonderful creation. Have faith. We've yet to see the best of him, I think."

At that moment the cat flap rattled and Bonnington oozed in carrying a broken black feather in his mouth. He leaped up onto the kitchen table, leaving wet and muddy paw prints over the surface. He dropped the feather by David's hand.

"Thank you," said the tenant. "Didn't know you worked for Postman Pat?"

"Oh, Bonnington," Liz chided, turning for a cloth.

David picked up the feather and twiddled the shaft. "Where'd you get this?"

A-rowww, yowled Bonnington and shook himself

dry. It had been snowing since dawn and the big brown tabby was glistening with flakes.

"Oh, for goodness' sake!" Liz cried, as bullets of water patterned her ironing. "David, dry him off. Before he drowns us all."

David leaned backward and pulled several sheets of paper towel off the roll. Bonnington, who always enjoyed a good rub, purred like an overworked refrigerator pump while the tenant drew the dampness out of his fur. "This is strange," he said, nodding at the feather. "I wonder why he's brought me this and not secreted it away in the garden like he usually does?"

"Cats and snow don't mix," Liz said, checking through the pile of clothing for casualties. "Maybe it's a present from Snigger and Caractacus."

"Maybe it is," David muttered, leaning forward. "I saw Caractacus the other day. I asked him to go and find Zanna for me."

Liz paused and looked across the ironing board at him. "Well, maybe he's succeeded. Perhaps that's a sign to say she's alive. Put it under your pillow. Dream of her."

"I do. Every night."

Liz paused, then picked up her iron again.

David stroked Bonnington and changed the subject. "He's very matted again. Here, look, and here, around his back legs."

Liz frowned at the knotted, slightly tacky clumps of fur. "Hmm. I don't know what's the matter with him lately. He's not looking after himself like he should. He's spilling his food from his dish a lot as well. Might take him to the V-E-T for a checkup."

"Why don't we try an experiment instead?"

"This is a house, not a lab."

"I'm serious, with Golly. So far all we've done is sit back and watch him. Why don't we see if he does things to order?"

Before Liz could contest it, David had sent Gwillan to find the healing dragon. The little puffler zipped away down the hall and was back in twenty seconds, with Gollygosh and Gretel (who had not left Golly's side since the day he'd been kilned) in tow.

Golly landed on the ironing board (making Liz tut and plonk her hands on her hips).

"Bonnington's not well," David told him, without being too specific. He was keen to see if the healing dragon's powers of analysis worked as well with living creatures as they clearly seemed to do with inanimate objects.

Gollygosh pricked up his ears and looked acutely at Bonnington. He put down his toolbox, but for once it did not open.

"Off," Liz said, ushering Gretel and the healer off her board. Golly flew to the table and sat between David and the cat. Bonnington, who had never been entirely sure of the scaly little creatures which flew around his house, looked down his nose and twitched a whisker. Something in the dragon's gaze caused him to gulp, and he flexed his jaw awkwardly, dribbling saliva from the corner of his mouth.

Golly reached out and caught a drip.

"Ugh, don't drink that," David said parentally, as the dragon stared round-eyed at the drool. Then he saw what Golly could see and his mood changed completely: The spit was glowing purple.

"Hey, Liz, come and take a look at this."

She was folding some clothes, but turned back in time to see Gretel conversing with the healer, then the pair of them whizzing off up the hall. "What was that about?"

"I don't know," David said. "Something's up with Bonnington."

Liz wiped his chin. "He's slobbering a lot."

"The dragons took a sample. It was glowing — purple."

Liz sat down and pulled the tabby to her lap. "It must be the icefire he swallowed."

David thought back. During their battle with Gwilanna the cat had consumed a large amount of Liz's "special dragon ingredient." At the time, he had seemed unaffected by it. Now he was really bubbling with the stuff. "I don't think Golly healed him. You'd better call the vet."

"I'm not entirely certain he's ill," Liz said. "I'm more concerned about why those dragons wanted that sample. . . ."

The telephone rang, quickly ending her speculation. She let Bonnington go and picked up the cordless set. "Hello? Oh — yes. He is back from the Arctic. Slightly earlier than expected. Would you like to speak to him?"

Who is it? David mouthed.

Liz put the phone on mute. "Dilys Whutton, from Apple Tree Publishing."

David pulled a face. "Tell her I'm out."

"Da-vid?"

"Please, Liz. I'm not in the mood. Tell her I'll call her tomorrow. Please?"

Liz opened the airwaves again. "I'm sorry. He's not in his room. I think he's probably slipped out to college. Shall I ask him to call you —? Er, yes, you could try again later if you like. He's usually home around five. That's fine. I will. Thank you. Good-bye."

"Thanks, you're a hero."

"No, I'm a villain. *That* was very naughty, David."

"I know. I know. But she'll talk about bears and that's just going to remind me of Zanna." He stood up, turning the feather in his hands. "I'm going out, in case she calls back early."

"In this?" Liz gestured at the snowbound garden.

David put the feather in an old fruit bowl where Lucy collected pebbles and pinecones. "I could use a walk. Anyway, I'm s'posed to be in college, remember?"

Dr. Bergstrom Returns

The Geography department was practically deserted. Four students were playing pool in the lounge and the woman who ran the *Goodtime* snack bar was wheeling a rack of drinks and candy into a back room before locking up. Guessing that most of his friends were in a lecture, David clattered downstairs to the student pigeon holes. There was a small stack of mail for him: course notes and the regular flyers; a letter from home, which he slipped inside his jacket; an invitation to join the drama society (he scrunched that up); a reminder from the library regarding an overdue book; and two circulars wanting to sell him insurance. Then, sandwiched in between the junk, he found one of the dark green envelopes the college used for internal mail. Inside it was a short, handwritten note. *I'll be here Friday till 3 p.m., Room 441. Anders Bergstrom.*

Friday. Today. David dashed a look at the clock above the dining hall. Two thirty-five.

He hit the stairs.

Forty seconds later he was opening the door of 441 ahead of Bergstrom's casual, "Come in."

The room was cold and narrow, the atmosphere not helped by paintwork resembling the inside of an eggplant. Bookshelves filled the left-hand wall. An uninspiring beech-colored desk stood opposite. Bergstrom was sitting in a cheap, padded chair, his blue eyes fixed to a laptop screen. In profile, he seemed to look younger, David thought. His honey-blond hair fell in waves to his shoulder. Any eighteen-year-old guy with an eye for a girl would have paid good money to have half the stubble on the scientist's chin. He was dressed, as usual, in a light cotton shirt, open at the neck and rolled up at the sleeves. His shoes had been kicked aside, under the desk. All the extremities could breathe, it seemed. "I take it you got my note?" He waggled a finger at the only other chair, a standard-issue, salmon-colored, two blocks of foam job.

David stretched his fingers to their fullest extent, a technique that was supposed to release sudden tension. Supposed to. "Where's Zanna?" he demanded.

Bergstrom continued to type, his hands moving with surprising speed across a keyboard far too compact for them. "Have you come here to fight or to talk to me, David?"

"I want to know where my girlfriend is and when you intend to bring Lucy home from the Tooth of Ragnar."

Bergstrom made a few precise clicks with the mouse. In the window recess, an inkjet printer rattled awake and whisked its printhead from side to side. "Last night, I went to see Zanna's parents. I told them what you already know. Zanna is missing."

"That's a lie."

The padded chair swung through an even arc. Bergstrom stared at his wayward student with a gaze that would have mesmerized a lesser creature. "As far as they and the college are concerned, it's the only acceptable truth — and you will say nothing to the contrary."

"Are you *threatening* me?"

"No, I'm trying to save you from appearing foolish. I have two eyewitnesses who will testify to the fact that Suzanna Martindale was surrounded by polar bears and disappeared in a sudden whiteout. Any rational thinking person will come to the conclusion that the girl was savaged and dragged into the ocean. Anything else would be a miracle. And miracles don't happen to most people, David."

"Says the man who abducted her or probably arranged it. Where *is* she, Dr. Bergstrom? Tell me the truth."

The printer whirred. With a clatter of parts it pushed out a single sheet of paper. Bergstrom studied it as he spoke: "In an Inuit settlement, with Tootega."

David closed his eyes to shutter his relief; the accompanying anger was harder to stifle. "Doing what?"

"Preparing — for February, as you should be. Look at the screen."

There were graphs there. Complex scatterplots. David shook his head, too irritated to study them.

Bergstrom put the printed sheet into his hand. "This is the result of your research in Chamberlain. It's a graph predicting the effects on the polar ice cap of a three-degree rise in local temperature."

David glanced at it grudgingly and shrugged. "Total meltdown. This is old news. We already know this will happen if we don't stop destroying the ozone layer."

"Look at the timescale."

David steered the graph around to read the "y" axis. Where he expected to see years marked off in decades, he saw weeks. He shook his head again. "This doesn't make sense. We can't reach crisis greenhouse conditions in a period spanning four and a half weeks. What could possibly cause such a sudden, massive rise in temperature?"

"An influx of dragons," Bergstrom said.

There was an in-box on the desk. David dropped the graph into it. "*Dragons*?" he said, stressing the plural. "I thought our problems ended at Gawain?"

"So did I."

"What's that supposed to mean?"

Bergstrom closed the laptop down. "In mid-February, Gwilanna will attempt to raise Gawain from the Tooth of Ragnar. She must be stopped."

David bobbed his head. "Yeah, well, the sight of a dragon tearing through the clouds is going to freak a few people out, I guess."

"Gwilanna is thinking wider than that. I believe she is planning to use Gawain as a signal to attract more dragons back to Earth."

"Where from?" said David, with a skeptical frown.

"An invisible universe," Bergstrom said plainly, "governed by the laws of dark matter."

A fluorescent strip light flickered uncomfortably. David, struggling to take this in, managed to mumble, "How do you know this?"

"Through your wishing dragon."

"G'reth? He's been in contact with you?"

"He's been working with me. Our paths crossed during our search for understanding. G'reth has journeyed to the heart of the stars and made some incredible discoveries, David. He has validated the theories of quantum physics and returned with knowledge of the Earth's beginnings."

"And what's this got to do with invisible universes?"

"Everything," Bergstrom said. "This planet was once a seeding ground. A small, but significant, hatching place for dragons. Water at its surface, fire at its center, layers of clay and earth between. There were many such places across the universe, but this was one of the favored ones."

"Favored? Who by?"

"A transdimensional race called the Fain. G'reth made contact with a young Fain being and from it learned everything I'm teaching you now."

David couldn't help but splutter with laughter. "G'reth watches TV at home, Dr. Bergstrom. His favorite program is *Star Trek: Enterprise.* I know he can touch the shadows of the universe, but maybe he's gone too far? Too boldly?"

Bergstrom smiled but refused to submit. "According to G'reth, the Fain revere dragons. They believe that the world was created by one. Their homeworld was once a paradise for them, but they are dying out there, and G'reth could not establish why.

"Now, listen to me carefully, David, for this affects all that we do. According to G'reth, the Fain were here at the dawn of *Homo sapiens,* intending to colonize fully one day. But something went wrong. Some giant cosmological event disrupted space and closed the link, leaving a number of survivors behind. Gwilanna is one of them."

A chasm opened in David's chest. "You said the Fain were transdimensional. Gwilanna's got physical form."

"The body you see is not the Fain, merely the shell of the woman it invaded."

"They can *possess* you?"

"They commingle. G'reth's word, not mine. After centuries fusing with skin and bone, Gwilanna may have settled and become quite fixed. However, she has not lost sight of her ancestry and in February, on our planetary calendar, she will have the chance to make contact with her own."

"The fire star?"

"Yes. After millions of years, it has finally found alignment with the Earth again. When it reaches its zenith it will open a portal, a wormhole if you like, into the realm of dark matter, into the world of the Fain. Gwilanna could then do one of two things: travel through the portal to rejoin the Fain or call any number of dragons to Earth, using Gawain as a beacon or lure. We cannot take the risk of the latter option. If dragons breathe their fire across the Arctic again, the consequences will be catastrophic."

A flurry of snowflakes fluffed through the window, diverting David's attention for a second. He watched the flakes thaw against the warmth struggling out of an air-conditioning vent. If the Arctic ice cap was to do something similar, sea levels would rise and the time of the great white bear would be over. "I agree it's not desirable to have dragons causing global hysteria, but their fire would still be a pinprick in the atmosphere. No worse than a hot-air balloon going over. Why should that wreck the northern biome?"

The padded chair creaked as Bergstrom leaned back. "Your studies on beryllium 10 should have told you that thousands of years ago atmospheric conditions were far more stable than they are today. Back then, dragons could expel their fire without fear of causing environmental damage. Now, with the ozone layer badly weakened, the combination of heat and chemical elements would be cumulative and toxic."

"Then why are you allowing Gwilanna to meddle? Why don't you move in and stop this now?"

"Because I want to encourage her to leave this planet. Gwilanna is a powerful, malevolent nuisance. Her ambitions, though worthy, are outdated and dangerous. When that portal opens I want her to see there is no hope of reestablishing a dragon culture on this planet and that she would do better returning to the Fain.

There are three ways we can bring this about. One of them will see Gawain put to rest; one will retain his stasis in stone."

"And the other?"

"The other will end in his death. And if necessary, you will help me to achieve it."

Discussions

"No way," David said. "You're out of your mind."

Bergstrom took a swig of water from a bottle. "It's my duty to protect my bears and their habitat."

"Tell that to Liz; she'll never go along with murdering Gawain."

"The choice is between one petrified dragon and a disaster of global proportions, David."

"Not petrified. Flying. Big sharp claws. Neither you nor I could take out a dragon."

"No, but a pack of polar bears could. When he swoops to the ice, the bears will be waiting."

"Not an option," said David, sick inside at the thought of the clash. "Why can't we send Gawain through the portal? If the Fain revere dragons, why wouldn't they take him?"

"They probably would. But you're forgetting what happened to Gawain. If he wakes, he will sweep the ice and learn what became of his fire tear."

"How?"

"He's a dragon, David. A servant of the Earth. He knows, instinctively, about her structure. He'll destroy the ice trying to take it back. And that would be worse than a dragon invasion. Now do you appreciate how serious this situation is?"

David sighed and laced his fingers round the back of his head. "Why is this even happening, Doctor? When Zanna and I confronted Gwilanna we robbed her of the scale of Gawain she carried. You told me if that was returned to the island, Gawain would go peacefully back to the clay."

"And he would have," said Bergstrom, throwing his weight against his chair and rolling it back to the end of the bookshelves. He took a small silver key from a jacket hanging there. "But I have since discovered other pieces of the dragon are still extant. Without them, Gawain can never be at rest."

"Then you'd better get searching, fast. There's no way I'm going dragonslaying."

"I've accounted for all but one piece."

"Then let's find it, return it, and get this thing over with."

"If it was that simple," the scientist snarled, "don't you think I would have done so by now?"

The standoff produced a few seconds of silence. David turned away, adopting a slightly more submissive pose. "OK, so what's the problem?"

Bergstrom thrust the key into the desk drawer lock, pausing again as he twisted it. "It's hidden from me, protected by a force that even your wishing dragon can't track down."

"What, like someone's put a hex on it?"

"I'm not sure. Lucy has discovered Gawain's isoscele: the tip of his tail: one of the most potent talismans of dragonkind there is. There were no charms covering that."

"Lucy? With a talisman? Can she use it?"

"No, not as yet. But Lucy is going through rapid changes. She is related to the sibyl, Gwendolen, and may well inherit some of her powers."

"Where is this talisman?"

"With her, on the island."

"*With* her? What if Gwilanna finds it?"

"I'm confident she won't. Any vibration given off by the piece will be lost in the general auma of the island."

"Yeah, but Lucy can blab for America. She'll —"

"Lucy is in a hibernation state, protected by a female polar bear; Gwilanna will let her be for now, grateful that she does not have to cope with the girl through the coming months of darkness."

"And what happens when they wake?"

"If the final dragon piece is still not found, we could try to use Ingavar to block Gwilanna's power."

"*Ingavar?* My character?"

"He's real, David. You drew him into Chamberlain. The wounded bear who attacked you by the trading post is the one you encountered in your mind. You tapped into the universal auma of the north and from it latched onto a descendant of Ragnar. He is in possession of his ancestor's tooth. That makes him a very powerful ally. The island has a spiritual link with the bears. Ingavar should be able to monitor any movement of rock or dragon. He could yet turn out to be our savior."

The window rattled. More snowflakes melted sweetly on the glass. David shook his head, trying to take this in. Ingavar. Real, after all? "Why wouldn't you admit this back at the research base when you let me have it for being reckless?"

"You're a loose cannon, David. Sometimes, I have to rein you in. Discipline and patience are not your strengths."

That didn't make the student feel much better. He sighed and pouted and thought back to his story. "So Ingavar got the tooth after all?"

"Yes," said Bergstrom. "And his rise has been the

trigger for more movement. Bears loyal to the line of Ragnar are gathering from all over the Arctic. They will reach the island by the end of winter. You can follow their progress with these." He slid the drawer open and handed David a small brown envelope.

David split the seal. Inside were three items: a clay pencil and pad, and an unmarked floppy disk. He gave a nod of resignation. More reining in. "So it *was* you who took them. Groyne is yours?"

"Forgive me, I had no choice," said Bergstrom, shaking his blond hair off his collar. "Gwilanna was tracking your every move. I couldn't run the risk that you might give her too much information through your writing."

"And this?" David took out the disk.

"Your saga, reproduced from a printout in my office. As your instructor, I took the liberty of making corrections; you still have much to learn about the ice and the bears."

David dropped the disk back into the envelope. His gaze, for want of somewhere different to settle, focused on the spines of the nearest row of books. Bizarrely, he spotted the name "Lono" on one, as he had done once in Henry Bacon's study. "You want me to continue with the story?"

"It's what your publisher — and hopefully your public — would want."

"And you, Dr. Bergstrom? What do you want? What if I write that a bear called Thoran dies at the hand of an evil sibyl?"

With a stare as cool as glacial ice, Bergstrom replied, "You will write what comes to you. That's the way it is. I have no control over where your mind wanders, but there's something you ought to know about that. The Fain work in the realms of higher consciousness, creating events in much the same way that a writer makes real his imagination on the page. In that state, words, like thoughts, become living things."

"So be careful what you wish for, it might come true?"

"Exactly. You are on the edge of that ability, David. Your talent is raw, but growing in strength. Your dragon, Gadzooks, has been testing the boundaries in a bid to understand where inspiration comes from. Like G'reth, he was looking to the stars. Into the unseen shadows of the universe. It's my belief that people like you are dipping, unawares, into dark matter, into the thought world of the Fain. You may even be evolving toward them."

David paused to take a reality check. "Are you telling me I'm some kind of alien, now?"

"Missing link would be a better description. You, and others like you, are the product of human evolution and the memory of the Fain. If you need proof, just look into the sky. There is a fire star shining. Astronomers the world over have failed to report it. But you can see it. So can your dragons. Whatever happens in February, David, you have a vital role to play."

"And in the meantime?"

"You wait — and write. The fire star reaches its zenith on the fourteenth of that month."

"Valentine's Day? That should please Zanna. Are you sure there's nothing else I can do? Help to find this dragon piece, maybe? Is it possible it's hidden in the dark matter realm? When Gadzooks is back online I could write about it, see what he comes up with?"

Bergstrom shook his head. "You're commissioned to write an Arctic saga. All I want of you in the next three months is to live the life of a bear — on the page."

That brought a sharp lump to David's throat. During the writing of his Arctic scenes he had felt as if he was padding along with a bullet in his shoulder and the wind in his fur. He turned and glanced into the bleak gray sky. The snow was falling at a lesser rate now as if completion was close on all sides. "When will I hear from you?"

"When the time is right. Be patient, David. When we move, we move *very* quickly. Go home now. Elizabeth needs you. Please don't speak of these things to her. When this is over, you may tell her all you know."

David gave a minimal nod. "How do you know Liz needs me?"

Bergstrom leveled his hand. A small white dragon materialized in it. "This is Groyne," he said.

David stared at him closely. In some ways Groyne

was more of a bird than a dragon. Like a soapstone sculpture of a bird. A caricature, almost. "Is he one of Liz's?"

"No, but he watches over her at times."

David nodded again, wondering how often Groyne had been in the house at Wayward Crescent. "Why did you have him release Gretel?"

Bergstrom reached out and stroked Groyne's spine. "The potions dragon is very powerful. In cooping her up, Elizabeth ran the risk of losing her allegiance. But the decision was not entirely my doing."

"You sent him."

"I gave the order, yes, but the thought was heavily impressed on me. That came from another source."

"The Fain?"

"That, I don't know. But what took place after Gretel was released was not engineered by me. When G'reth inhaled that burning flower, his reaction to it was so intense that he connected to a deeper realm of the universe. Something wanted him out there, David."

"The force that's keeping the dragon piece hidden?"

"Possibly. Now, you must go." He moved his free hand over Groyne's head, morphing him into the talisman he carried, the one made from a narwhal's tusk.

"Versatile little critter."

"Go," said Bergstrom. A command this time, not a suggestion.

David backed away, feeling a chilling desire to drop items of his clothing in his wake. At the door he asked, "If I'm part-Fain, what are you?"

"All things to all men. I am who you see."

"Anders Bergstrom?"

"Sometimes," said the scientist.

Awakening

It took half an hour to trudge home in the snow. David, his head full of alien invasions, found Liz in the kitchen, sobbing into a tissue. Henry Bacon was at her shoulder.

"What's the matter?" David asked, darting glances at them both.

"Mrs. P.'s had a bit of bad news," said Henry.

David crouched down beside her. "Is it Lucy?"

"No, it's Bonnington."

David glanced around the kitchen. He saw Bonnington's cat carrier, open near his food bowl. The cat himself was nowhere to be seen.

"Been to the vet with the cat," said Henry.

"*You* have?"

"Couldn't let Mrs. P. drive in this weather."

"What's wrong?" asked David, lightly shaking her knee.

A fountain of sobs left Liz's throat. "He has a swelling under his tongue. That's why he's been dribbling and pushing his food around. He hasn't been able to eat properly."

David swallowed hard. "Can they do anything?"

Liz buried her wet face into his shoulder.

"Oh, no," David whispered, putting his arms around her. "I'm so, so sorry."

Henry gave a quiet cough. "Well, I'll be off. You'll call, if you need me, Mrs. P.?"

"Yes," she said, touching the corner of his jacket. "Thank you."

Henry nodded in salute and let himself out. As the door closed, David clasped Liz's hands. They felt small and frail. She was shaking lightly. He pressed them till she made eye contact. So little green behind the cloaking tears. "How long? How long has he got?"

Liz shook her head, her hair corkscrewing around her cheeks. "The vet's not sure. He wants to look at him again, after Christmas."

Some Christmas, David thought. No Lucy. Bonny dying. And the prospect of a battle to save the world looming. He took a deep breath, careful not to shudder. "Look, this may not be the best time to mention this, but what about Golly?"

Liz shook her head again. "No one lives forever, David. Not even Bonny. I think this is beyond Golly's range of abilities."

"But he's a healing dragon. There must be *something* he can do? Where are they anyway?" he said, looking up. He hadn't seen a single dragon since he'd walked in. Odd. Gretel never missed a scene like this. And where was the ever-attentive Gwillan? Stranger still, the listening dragon was not on the fridge.

Just then, he heard a noise upstairs. It was a dragon *hrrr,* but a concentrated one, as if they had all breathed fire at once. "They're in the den," he muttered. "Something's going on."

He was there in seconds. He burst in to find all the special dragons, including G'reth, arranged in a circle on Liz's workbench. Their eyes were closed and they were holding paws, murmuring softly in dragonsong. In the center of the circle was the stone dragon, Grockle, still curled up in the remains of his basket.

"Liz!" David shouted, but she was only just behind him.

"Oh my goodness," she gasped. "What are they doing?"

"I don't know, but it doesn't look good."

He gave a quick start as their eyes slid open. Each was staring at a point just above Grockle's body, creating a cone of violet light. At the apex of the cone, what looked like a holographic image of a dragon flickered into view. It had the same basic shape as a Pennykettle sculpture, but it was shimmering as though it was made from crystal, and its eyes were a swirl of violet and blue. Something fluid was sparkling in its paws.

Liz shook her head in awe. "Is that a fire tear?" she whispered.

"No," said David, quick to work it out. "That's Bonnington's saliva. I really don't like this. . . ."

But even if he'd known how to safely break the circle, he would not have had time to stop the drop falling. It dripped into the center of Grockle's stone eye, turning the iris a deep dark amber. The circle of dragons opened their mouths and blew a cloud of red smoke over his body. To David's amazement, it began to collect around Grockle's snout, where it billowed . . . then disappeared into his nostrils. "Oh my God, he's breathing," he said.

Slowly, color seeped back into the body. The scales began to soften, unfuse, and lift. The claws retracted. The isoscele turned. From the throat came the all too familiar throw of air. A frozen eye slid fully open. And where there had once been stone, there was life.

The Pennykettle dragons turned to the window, where snow was spilling in on a chute of air.

"No!" David shouted, diving forward, reaching out to pull the window shut. But Grockle had already taken off for it, kicking his empty basket aside. He was barely halfway through when David grabbed the latch and narrowed the gap. For a moment, it seemed as though he might have succeeded. Grockle was pinned just under his wings. But as David tried to grab him, the tail flicked out, lashing David's wrist. The tenant cried out in pain and relaxed just enough for Grockle to wriggle the critical extra inch he needed for freedom. He gave one fierce shriek as his trailing foot snagged between the closing window and the frame, ripping out a back claw in the process. It wasn't enough to prevent his escape.

David turned to Liz and gasped, "What do we do? How do we call him back?"

"We can't," she said, her eyes full of fear.

"But he's a dragon," David said, clamping his wrist to stem the flow of blood.

A dragon. At large. Among humankind again.

G'RETH EXPLAINS

OK," said David, closing the kitchen door with a bang. "Start talking. One of you. Now." He pointed a finger at the waiting dragons, lined up like a row of suspects on the table.

Hrrr, went Gretel, wiggling her snout. And for once that was all it translated to: *hrrr.*

"Don't get huffy," David said. "I've brought you four *conspirators* down here to explain to us, *privately,* precisely what you *think* you were doing with Grockle."

"David." Liz sighed, touching her fingers to her forehead. "Stop talking in italics. It won't do any good."

"Liz, there's a dragon on the loose," he said. "A creature known to instill fear and loathing into most of mankind. We have no idea where he is or what he's doing. I want to know why they've set him free."

"I'd like to know how they revived him," she said, hunkering down beside Bonnington's basket. The cat was curled up sweetly, asleep.

That fetched a stab of guilt into David's heart. It hurt to know how slow he'd been to detect the cat's increasing lethargy. That had to be the illness, wearing him down. He shook the thought away and turned back to the dragons. "All right, we'll start there. What's the icefire done to him? Did it cause the cancer?"

Pfff! went Gretel as if such a thing was completely unthinkable.

"Zookie?"

Gadzooks blew a faint wisp of smoke.

"G'reth?"

He was marveling at the structure of a single salt grain and simply pretended not to hear.

Gollygosh, the healing dragon, turned to speak to Liz.

"Oh, yes . . . I see," she said.

"See what?" said David, taut and impatient. Even now a rapid flurry of dragontongue tended to leave him in need of a guidebook.

Liz reached out and touched Bonnington's back. The cat stirred and gave a faintly puzzled blink, then burbled once and slipped back into his slumber. "Golly says the cancer cells are multiplying rapidly. They're young and . . ." she paused to steady her emotions, ". . . bursting with life. That combined with the power of the icefire to animate clay, plus a potion Gretel made from a lock of my hair — the red smoke we saw him inhale — and Golly acting as a kind of . . . transformer —"

"Transformer?" David said.

"That's the nearest I can translate it to . . . was enough to bring Grockle out of his stasis."

"Transformer?" David said again.

All four dragons looked at their toes.

"OK, which one of you worked this out?"

"It was the new one, wasn't it?" Liz said quietly.

G'reth flicked his tail.

"Who *was* that?" she asked.

"More to the point, where *is* that?" asked David. The mysterious hologram had faded away as soon as Grockle had started breathing.

Gretel gave the wishing dragon a prod. He stepped forward, reluctantly, and gave a little *hurr*.

"Inside you?" Liz said.

David's heart thumped.

G'reth looked at him nervously, then in a desperate flurry of dragontongue he told Liz all about his meeting with the Fain.

"Oh, no," David groaned and looked at the ceiling. Bergstrom wasn't going to like this very much.

"An alien species?" Liz's mouth dropped open.

"They love dragons," hurred Gretel. "I've commingled," she said.

They all have, thought David. He could tell by the level of excitement in their faces.

"Did you know about this?" Liz turned to him then, wonder spilling from her bright green eyes.

"A little. Bergstrom told me G'reth had made contact

with a transdimensional, prehuman species. I didn't know he'd brought one home with him." He fixed his gaze pointedly at the wishing dragon. "What else is this *tenant* going to do?"

G'reth shook his head. Nothing, he told them. The Fain was tired. The vibrations of this planet were heavy for it. It would need to rest now until the fire star came.

"Then what?"

"Then it goes home," G'reth hurred.

Liz covered her mouth. "This is amazing."

"It changes nothing," David said bluntly. "We still have a wild dragon on the loose, and another to think about in three months' time." He looked again at G'reth. "I thought you were supposed to be out there, somewhere, looking for the last known piece of Gawain?"

"Say again?" said Liz, pulling a tissue from her sleeve.

"Bergstrom claims it should be possible to stop Gwilanna if every part of Gawain is returned to the island. But there's one piece missing, which he says is protected by some kind of force that G'reth can't break through."

Hrrr, went the wishing dragon, opening his paws.

"He thinks Grockle will," Liz said, translating.

David returned his gaze to G'reth. "That's why you did this? You revived Grockle so *he* could track it down?"

Hrrr! went Gretel in the wisher's defense.

"She says it was the Fain's idea," said Liz.

"It's a big planet, guys. What hope does Grockle have?"

"A better chance than you or I," said Liz. "A dragon's sense of smell is highly developed. They can trace the whereabouts of one of their kind by following the signatures of their exhaled fire. Gawain's scent would be over every part of his body. It's as recognizable to another dragon as your twenty-four-hour deodorant is to me."

"And what if the search draws Grockle into danger?"

The four dragons exchanged a worried look.

"Quite," said David, running a hand through his hair. "We might as well sit at home and wait for reports of a strange flying creature to hit the news. A massive witch hunt for the pterodactyllike bird with violet eyes seen terrorizing the United States of America."

Liz shuddered and clutched her arms. "It won't come to that. He'll adapt. He'll hide."

"For now, maybe. He's small and agile. But what about when he starts to grow? How big is he likely to get?"

"I don't know," Liz said, tears filming her eyes.

"How will he survive? What's he going to eat?"

"I don't know," she said again, becoming distressed. "Vegetation, initially. Then . . ."

"Meat?" David's voice hit solemn. "What will he take? Rodents? Sheep? Cattle?"

"Da-vid!"

The tenant stood down, but only for a second. "He's your son, Liz."

"That's debatable," she said. "He might claim Zanna."

"Whatever. He came from an egg that *you* kindled, that could and should have produced a boy. There's something human in his genes and we must try to find him. Zookie."

The writing dragon jerked to attention.

"I need some inspiration and I need it fast." He rifled through his jacket pocket and brought out the missing pencil and pad.

"Oh my goodness," Liz gasped. "How —?"

"Long story," he said, handing them over to his jubilant dragon. "By the way, Bergstrom also told me Lucy is safe and in some kind of hibernation state, protected by a female polar bear."

"Thank you," Liz said, though the news had turned her almost as white as a bear herself.

"Zanna is alive as well."

"Oh, David. Oh, thank goodness." She stepped forward, wanting to give him a hug, but a sudden huff from one of the quartet brought David's attention back to the dragons.

Gadzooks, though relieved to have his writing things

back, was dismayed to see the tip of the pencil broken. This was no problem for Gollygosh. The healing dragon quickly dipped into his tool kit, found a sharpener, and repaired the damage. The new point seemed better than ever. Gadzooks, who looked as if he'd been storing up a novel in his days of downtime, scribbled something fiercely across the pad. Gretel and G'reth leaned in to take a look, exchanging a puzzled *hrrr* at what they saw. David closed his eyes to picture the message. It surprised him too. A name:

Arthur

He whispered it aloud.

As usual, he had no idea what it meant (at first). Insight would come a little later, from Liz. Right then, however, she was incapable of speech.

She had just fainted in a heap on the floor.

LIFE BEFORE LUCY

"Steady, steady . . ."

"Where am I?" groaned Liz, trying (and failing) to prop herself up.

David pushed another pillow under her head and eased her down again, onto her bed. "In the Ritz Hotel, having a makeover to die for."

"It *feels* like I'm dead. Why is my head so cold?"

"Golly's orders. Bag of frozen peas, on the forehead. Something to take the swelling down. You fell over in the kitchen and bumped yourself. You're now slightly lopsided, thanks to a small egg on your left temple."

"Kitchen?" she queried, looking right and left for landmarks. "I'm in my bedroom."

"I carried you up."

"You —?" Her eyes grew wide with disbelief.

"Stronger than I look," he said, squeezing a bicep. He smiled and sat down on the edge of the bed.

"I'm getting up."

"No, you're not. Lie back." Catching her shoulders, he pushed her back again.

"David, I'm embarrassed."

"You're also hurt. You had a nasty fall. One more move and I'll call Henry in. Then it'll be paramedics, a helicopter, and the National Guard."

"Don't be mean. I — ow!" she went, abandoning the protest. Frowning was far too painful. She found the bump and felt it. "Am I hideous?"

"Compared to a rhino? No."

Sighing heavily, she accepted defeat. "You could at least defrost me."

David lifted the peas, wrapped them in a towel, and put them on the floor beside a pile of magazines. He clicked his fingers at Gwillan. The dragon tapped the base of a bedside lamp. A soft rose hue lit up the room.

"Thank you," Liz whispered.

The faithful little puffler warmed up a hankie and flew in to dry her face and neck.

"How long have I been out?"

David glanced at her *Noddy* alarm clock. "Forty minutes or so."

"Forty —? Ow!"

"Lie still," he chided.

"Yes, *doctor.*" A moment passed. She reengaged his eyes. "Don't look at me like that."

He half cocked an eyebrow.

"Stop it," she said.

"Stop what?"

"Sparring. You've got that 'I need to know something' look in your eye."

He relaxed his stare, focusing for a second on her bunny rabbit slippers. For a middle-aged woman, she could be pretty sweet. "Is it coming back to you, the reason why you dropped?"

She pondered a moment, then turned her face away.

"Who's Arthur?" he asked, trying not to sound pushy.

"Don't go there, David. It won't do any good."

He moved his gaze from her face to her fingertips, watching them nipping the blanket into peaks. "I wouldn't be asking, if Zookie hadn't written it."

"He's probably trying to help you with a story, that's all."

"Liz, come on. You fainted in the kitchen. Something shocked you when you heard that name. Please, tell me. I only want to help. Is Arthur Lucy's father?"

Her eyes closed, tears welling under their lids. "How did Gadzooks *do* that?" she said, punching the blanket lightly now. "How could he possibly connect to Arthur?"

"Commingling with the Fain raised his level of vibration, bringing that name into his conscious auma. Arthur must be involved in my wish. I'm going to need your help to work out how. Who is he, Liz?"

She sobbed and a tear ran down her cheek. David raised a hand toward Gwillan. No help yet. There were moments when it was better to let people cry, he thought.

That decision bore fruit when Liz said quietly: "Do you promise me you'll never tell another living soul?"

"Does Lucy know?"

"No. And she mustn't."

"OK. I promise," David said. He gestured to Gwillan, who quickly flew a tissue to his mistress's hand.

"Cup of tea," she said, blowing. "Not doing this without."

David had already figured that. He gestured again to Gwillan, who flew behind the lamp, pushed a mug of tea forward, and warmed it instantly with his breath. "There you go. Might be slightly stewed."

"It's wet and warm. It'll do," she said. She pushed herself into a sitting position, adjusted her skirt, and stretched her legs out flat. She blew a kiss to Gwillan and circled a finger. He folded down his wings and settled back into his solid pose. "It's not that I don't trust him, but the dragons aren't ready for the whole story yet. I'm not sure you are, but . . ." She took a sip of tea. Then another. Then began.

"Twelve years ago, I lived alone — in Cambridge. I had an apartment overlooking the Charles river. A beautiful place. A kind of artist's garret."

"Were you in college?"

"No. Oh, no. I just liked that leafy part of the world. And I needed somewhere to escape from Gwilanna."

David's body height immediately rose. "You lived with her?"

"On and off, for many years. I traveled with her, learning, never really settling down. Eventually, like most people, I wanted independence and a place of my own. So I kind of ran away from her, thinking, stupidly, she wouldn't want to find me. I was wrong, but I'll come to that in a moment.

"For a while, all was well. I had money and a business that paid the rent."

"The dragons?"

"Hmm," she said, absently sipping. "I'd made other things, the usual pots and ornaments, but that *was* about the time I began to sell the dragons.

"One day, I was loading up my van with them, ready to take them to a local craft fair, when I noticed I had a flat tire. I didn't know what to do. It was a Sunday. Garages were closed. And I didn't belong to any auto clubs. So I stood for a while, looking rather glumly at my broken car, then did the only thing a damsel in distress can."

"Went for help?"

"Stamped my foot."

David spluttered with laughter.

"Magically, a voice behind me said, 'Hmm, right leg movement, but it would help if one of these was connected to the tire.' I turned around, and there was this man — holding a foot pump."

"Just like that? Out of nowhere?"

Liz smiled, reminiscing. "He confessed later he'd had his eye on me for days, but was waiting till I came out to the van because he felt too shy to approach me otherwise."

"Nice technique. What was he like?"

"Tall. Dark-haired. Lovely blue eyes. A few years older than me. Handsome in a bookish kind of way — like you."

"Eh?"

"He wore a knitted green vest. I didn't like that. And there was a pipe sticking out of his pants pocket. I wasn't sure I liked that either. He wore the silliest little glasses I ever saw. But otherwise, he was very acceptable."

"And this was Arthur?"

"This was Arthur," she confirmed. "He told me straight away my tire could not be saved, due mainly to the fact that I'd parked the van on a broken bottle. So like a true gentleman he rolled up his sleeves and put on the spare. And that was that. Within fifteen minutes he'd changed my tire and changed my life."

"You fell for him?"

"You sound shocked."

"Not shocked, just . . . surprised, given what I know about you."

"And what *do* you know about me?"

"Very little, I suppose," he said, turning red. "So . . . ?"

"So, we went out — for the next seven months. He was lovely. Shy. Funny. Charmingly eccentric. He took me to all sorts of interesting places. Art exhibitions. Poetry evenings. Jazz clubs. College functions. Picnics by the river. Walks. He loved to walk. Especially in the evening when the stars were out. He liked to dazzle me with stories about far-off galaxies and time travel and the speed of light."

David's ears pricked up. "He knew about stars?"

"Everything," Liz said, glowing from ear to ear. "Stars were his passion. He was a professor — of astrophysics. Why? Is this meaningful?"

"Perhaps," David shortened his gaze. "Did he ever talk about something called 'dark matter'?"

Liz shook her head slowly. "Not that I recall. He talked about dragons, though."

"Uh?" David grunted, almost slipping off the blanket. "How did he know about dragons?"

Liz smiled and ran a finger around the rim of her

mug. "He was Welsh, from a village in Monmouthshire. The red dragon is the symbol of Wales, remember? He was quick to wave his flag when he saw my pottery. I liked that about him. He was the first man I'd met who could hold an intelligent conversation about dragons. We used to swap myths. He even explained, scientifically, how they might have breathed fire."

"You swapped myths?" David said, going back a step. "How much did he learn? Did he know about . . . y'know?"

"No," Liz said, looking inward again. "The special dragons came later, after Arthur had gone." She picked up the tissue box and plonked it down closer, then drew one and crumpled it against her nose.

"You broke up, then?"

"Obviously."

"Sorry. I didn't mean to sound . . . do you want to stop talking?"

She finished her tea and put the mug aside. "No. You've come this far; you might as well hear the rest. But if I cry too hard you have to leave, is that agreed?"

"The house?"

"The *room.*" She gave his thigh a soft kick. "Are you sure it wasn't *you* who had that bump on the head?"

"OK, agreed. Was it bad?"

"Horrible."

David nodded, remembering his fallout with Zanna. "But it sounds so idyllic, like — excuse the mushiness — like you were made for each other. What went wrong?"

"The only thing that could have gone wrong," she said bitterly. "Gwilanna found out."

The Birth of Lucy

Right," David said, as if he ought to have guessed. "Did she follow you to Cambridge?"

"Not exactly," Liz said, staring at the window like some Wendy looking for her Peter Pan. "She picked up on my auma and came to me because she was needed — so she said."

David shifted uneasily on the bed. "This is to do with Lucy, right?"

Liz nodded lightly. "The arrival of Lucy changed everything. But if I'd known what I was, what lay in store for me, she might never have come into being."

"You can't be serious?"

"I didn't say I didn't want a child, David . . . just maybe not the way it happened." She took a deep breath and gathered herself. "Arthur and I were becoming very close. He was a good man. A decent man, with old-fashioned values. He'd never pushed our relationship beyond true friendship or asked for more than the warmth of my hand. But my feelings for him were beginning to run deeper. And that was when the problems started kicking in. I changed the dynamic. I wrecked it. Me."

"I find that hard to believe," said David. "You're one of the sweetest people I know. You couldn't hurt anyone if you tried."

"I hurt him," Liz said. "I broke his heart in so many places; I made a kaleidoscope of his life."

David screwed up his face in confusion. "How?"

"I wanted a child. I started making eggs, and dragons breaking out of them. You know what that means, don't you?"

David nodded, remembering how Grockle had been produced. Grockle: who should have been a boy with a dragon's spirit. Grockle: kindled from a large, clay egg. "You quickened a bronze?"

"Not right away. It was a few weeks before that happened. But Gwilanna could sense the change in me. Those eggs are as good as a homing beacon to her. She just turned up one day, like she did here, saying I would soon give birth to a child and I needed her protection. I thought she was crazy. She'd taught me nothing about the kindling process. All we'd ever talked about regarding children was how Gwendolen's offspring were weak and unworthy and I was Guinevere's rightful heir."

"Hold up," said David. "I'm a little bit lost. I thought Gwendolen *was* Guinevere's daughter?"

"She was a hybrid," Liz said. "Part Guinevere, part sibyl, part dragon, part earth. She came from an egg, like Grockle, like me. She was supposed to live the life of Guinevere's daughter, but somehow ended up with Gwilanna for company. All I can tell you is, it wasn't a happy union. Gwendolen left her, just like I did. When she grew to be a woman, she broke free of the sibyl's clutches and went to live among northern tribes."

"The Inuit?"

"They may not have been the Inuit then, but it's a

good enough name for them. A people who respected bears anyway. In those days, bears and humans were much alike in spirit. Gwilanna was always cursing the fact that Gwendolen's allegiance was closer to them than it was to her. But that wasn't the reason Gwilanna disowned her. Gwendolen had a child by an Inuit man. That, for Gwilanna, was tantamount to sacrilege."

"Wow," said David, sitting up straight. "I never knew that. Was it a boy or a girl?"

"A boy," Liz said. "He had a strange childhood. She sent him into the company of bears, who protected him and hid his auma from the sibyl. He was seventeen before Gwilanna found out. By then, Gwendolen had birthed five more and the boy had also parented a child. Gwilanna was outraged, but there was little she could do. The births were natural and difficult to trace. There was no way she could have stopped it."

"So are Gwendolen's offspring still around today?"

"Oh, yes. Every now and then when I was with Gwilanna we would meet someone — usually a girl — whom she would follow around and monitor for a while, just to assess their abilities. They were usually psychics or healers or stigmatics. None of that impressed Gwilanna much. She always sneered that Gwendolen's line was weak, but I got the impression she was roaming the world on the lookout for someone. Someone she might adopt as her apprentice —"

"Or remove if she felt too threatened," David muttered. He thought of Zanna then and shook a cold weight off his shoulders. The gothic girl with untapped knowledge. She must be from the line of Gwendolen herself. Why else would the bears have come to claim her? And now she was among the Inuit, too. Two sibyls. One ice cap. Not a pretty thought. He steadied his breathing and moved things on. "So what happened with Arthur?"

Liz stared at the tissue in her hands, making a series of neat, precise folds. "When Gwilanna found out I'd been producing the eggs, she forbade me to see Arthur ever again. I wish I had agreed and left with her then; it would have spared him so much pain. But I didn't have Guinevere's spirit for nothing. I was stubborn and refused. I demanded to know what right she had to interfere with my future or my happiness. Then she explained the kindling process — and how *I* had come to be a part of this world."

"You didn't *know*? But you must have been terrified. I'm surprised you believed her."

"You forget, I'd been steeped in dragon legend since the time I took my first breath. But you're right, I was awed, especially when she showed me the quickened egg. It would be a girl, she said. A girl like me, a dragon princess. If I refused to engage with her, the child would die. I looked into the egg and completely broke down. There was a beautiful, tiny fetus. I couldn't possibly let it die, but I knew I could never explain it to Arthur. Gwilanna insisted there was no way Arthur could be told the truth or live with us, even if he'd wanted to. So I made the only decision I could. I told Gwilanna I would go away with her and end my relationship with him. But that night, a full moon rose and the kindling process began. I couldn't be moved. I was so, so anxious. Arthur had been away at a conference and I knew he would come over as soon as he returned. He did, of course."

"And met 'Aunty Gwyneth'?"

"She told him I was ill and couldn't be disturbed. That only made the situation worse. He brought flowers and fruit and turned up twice a day to see if there had been any change in my 'condition.' Gwilanna's patience began to wear thin. She quickly realized that Arthur's tenacity might be a major threat to our secret. So she stepped up the pressure and told him there was someone else in my life."

David got to his feet. "Aw, that's just cruel."

"He debated it, of course, and that irked her even more. She insisted he wasn't good enough for me. Arthur thought differently. He came back with an engagement ring, demanding he be allowed to see me. She laughed in his face, but let him up. I can still remember him pounding the stairs, calling out my name, 'Elizabeth! Elizabeth!', then the door bursting open and the look on his face when he saw me holding

Lucy in my arms. He dropped the ring and backed out of the room. And that was the last I saw of him."

"I'm so sorry," David whispered, sighing into his hands. He now wished even more that he'd wiped out Gwilanna when he'd had the chance. He glanced at Liz in the dressing table mirror. She was turning a ring on her little finger. Fresh tears were clearing a path down her cheeks. Then she curled into a heap and started to sob. And David, true to the word of their agreement, lowered his head and walked out of the room.

The Long Days

November. The sky became a shroud of velvet gray. Snow fell steadily. The Earth shivered.

Television news and weather reports described it as the coldest autumn on record, while newspapers ran gloom-laden features on global warming and the greenhouse effect. Experts blamed the "premature winter" on an oscillating pattern of winds in the Arctic, driving frigid air from around the North Pole, south into the US and Europe.

People muttered about an ice age coming.

From his small house warmed by special dragons, on a comfortable sofa with a cat by his side, David Rain followed every bulletin he could, anxiously remembering Dr. Bergstrom's warning about the effects of dragon fire in the northern stratosphere. But not once did the news carry any strange rumors of leathery-winged creatures or new stars in the sky. No signs of Grockle. No hints of his death. One less worry in David's nerve-racked life.

But there were other troubles. The day after he and Liz had talked about Arthur, he received two telephone calls. The first left him shaken and hollow with guilt.

When he picked up, the caller had simply said, "David?"

"Zanna!" he exclaimed, dancing the cell phone around half a circle. He really had thought the voice was hers.

"That is so sick," the woman said. And he knew then the caller was her sister, Becky. "I thought you'd like to know we held a memorial service this morning. Some of Zanna's friends turned up from college. Didn't see you among them."

"I didn't know," spluttered David. Would he have gone if he had?

"*They* did," she said. Bitter. Remorseless. "Why couldn't you show your lousy face? You were all she ever talked about before that trip."

"I'm sorry," David said. What else *could* he say? Even though the lie was raking out his guts.

"She's gone, and you didn't even send a card."

David felt his breath coming through in stammers. "Becky, what do you want from me?"

"She loved you more than life itself and you —" Her voice broke into sobs.

"Becky —"

There was a clunk, and then she'd hung up. Number unavailable. No contact required.

Half an hour later, the *X Files* ringtone was trilling out of his phone again. Another female. Another problem.

"David? Hi. It's Dilys Whutton."

Dilys. His editor. David sank onto his bed. "Hi," he said.

"You sound hoarse. Do you have a cold?"

"No. It's just the weather."

"Dreadful, isn't it? I've been working from home three days a week. How about you?"

"Sorry?"

"Are you working? From home? *Three days a week?* OK, that's my poor attempt at subtlety. How's the book going?"

"Book?"

She gave an incredulous laugh. "Polar bears. Arctic. You can't have forgotten with all this white stuff around?"

He stared at the laptop, closed on his desk. One giant slab of silicon guilt. On the windowsill, Gadzooks barely gave a twitch. He was at rest with his eyes gently closed, notepad and pencil held to his breast. Beside him was G'reth, squatting on his tail with his paws pressed together as if he was practicing a yoga position. Somewhere inside him, an alien being was recharging its batteries, much like the dragons all around the house. Shutting down for the winter, Liz had called it. A kind of waking hibernation. "Book? Yeah. It's going . . . fine."

"How exciting! Can you tell me anything about it? Give me a few more clues about the plot?"

"I'm still doing my research."

"You writers!" she laughed. "Always cagey. What's your schedule, then? It must be hard to write and fit college in as well?"

"I quit college," he said.

"Really?"

No. It was a lie, off the top of his head. But now that he thought of it, quitting felt like the right thing to do. Stay at home with Bonnington (he stroked the cat's ears). Write. Prepare. Look after Liz.

"That's a bold move, David."

"I know," he said. His next statement was bolder still. "I'll have the book finished by the end of January."

"Wow," she gasped. "You can write that fast?"

David looked at Gadzooks again. "When I'm in the mood," he said.

"No," Liz said, when he told her of his plans. "You need an education. You mustn't quit."

He took the peel off an orange and split the fruit apart. "There's nothing there for me, Liz. I don't enjoy it, and I'm pretty sure Zanna won't go back. I have a contract to write my book. College is just going to get in the way. I have enough money from *Snigger* for my rent. Anyway, in three months' time, all my education lies in the north."

"David —"

"My mind's made up. I'm leaving."

Liz pushed her dinner plate aside. Bonnington, keen to have the haddock she'd rejected, sat up on his hind legs mewing like a kitten. There were tracks around his mouth where the dribbles had run. She dabbed the fur dry before feeding him some fish. "You frighten me sometimes," she said to the tenant. "Why did I ever draw you into this?"

"You didn't. It was meant to be," he said. "All of this is pointing to one thing: Gawain. If Grockle isn't successful — and as far as I can tell we have no way of knowing if he'll ever find that piece — there is going to be some kind of conflict on that island and I am going to be a part of it."

On the fridge top, the listening dragon shuddered.

"Everything I've gone through, the icefire, the writing, Bergstrom, Gwilanna, is leading me toward that February day. The only thing I don't understand is Arthur, what part he has to play in all this."

"I've told you everything I know," Liz said.

"What happened to him? Have any idea?"

"None," she said, allowing Bonnington up.

"You didn't try to contact him after —?"

"No. Well. OK, once." She sighed and looped her hair. "I came to Wayward Crescent after Lucy was born. I was so busy with her for the first six months, as any new mother would be. But in the quiet times, when I was alone and she was sleeping, I'd think about Arthur and wonder if he was thinking of me. Gwilanna had expressly forbidden any contact, but one day I caved in and tried to call him. There was no reply from his house, so I rang his department at the university. They told me he'd left a few months before. Quit his career. Disappeared without trace. I never tried again."

"That's weird," David muttered.

"No, not really. He was a sensitive man and he was clearly distraught and I would rather not talk about this anymore, David."

"If you told me his last name, I might be able to —"

"No," she said firmly, making Bonnington twitch. "You drop this. Now. You're not going after him, is that understood?" She pointed down the hall. "There's your room. I want to see you using it. You come out for meals and use of the bathroom! You say you have a book to write. There you are. Write it."

By Christmas, he'd completed forty thousand words. Following roughly the outline he'd given Dilys Whutton during their meeting a while before in New York, he'd begun to shape a story of the Arctic and its history, centering on a period in the late 1960s when polar bears had been hunted to near extinction. It was not the story he'd expected to write, and he'd absolutely no idea where it had come from. But throughout it, Gadzooks showed no signs of apathy and one afternoon even scribbled down a title:

White Fire

David liked it. He ran it by Liz. It was spiritual, she said. What did Henry think?

Since the onset of his writing, David had been a frequent visitor next door. Henry's study held a useful collection of books, many of them to do with polar exploration. Though skeptical at first of David's literary aspirations, Henry had nonetheless provided him with anything he needed for his research, including acquiring a few specialist books from the archives of the library in Scrubbley, where he worked. In return, David kept his neighbor informed of progress, using the librarian's commonsense reactions as a gauge to test twists and turns in the plot. The arrangement was working extremely well, until one day David walked into the study asking for a book about Inuit legends, and found himself met by a stony silence.

"What's the matter?" he asked. "Henry, what's wrong?"

Henry stiffened his shoulders. For once, all the bluster had gone right out of him. "Why didn't you tell me about Suzanna?"

David sank down into a chair. The world caught up with him and screeched to a halt. "I'm sorry. I'd forgotten how well you knew her." It was the truth, but it didn't ease the creeping sense of shame. All this time and no one had bothered to tell Henry Bacon of Zanna's "disappearance." Now, behind that granite exterior, hid a shattered and slightly disturbed older man. "How did you find out?"

"Saw her library card was canceled. Did some checking. What *happened*, boy?"

"I don't know," David said, as sincerely as he could. "I was already home when I was told she was missing. I'm sorry, Henry. Really I am. You're right, I should have told you, but I'm still in shock myself."

Henry grunted and flipped out a handkerchief. He ran it quickly under his nose. "No news of her?"

"Nothing."

"Gone, then?"

"Yes. I . . . there was a service. I'm sorry, this is very difficult."

Mr. Bacon nodded and stiffened his lip. "Liked you, didn't she?"

"Yes. She did."

"Got a dedication in mind for your book?"

That pierced David right to the core. He shuffled his feet, hardly knowing where to look.

"Bright girl. Would have been proud of your efforts. Course, I haven't read it yet. Might be useless."

David laughed, but on the inside everything was crying. Only Henry, with his characteristic old-school bluntness, could have defused a situation like that. He stood up, clutching the Inuit book. "Thanks for the loan."

Henry pointed at the shelves. "Want to see yours there one day, boy."

David nodded. "I'm working on it. I won't let you — or Zanna — down."

* * *

If such warmth from Henry was considered rare, the cordiality reached an astonishing peak a few weeks later when he invited the Pennykettle family plus tenant to join him for a home-cooked, pre-Christmas dinner. The date was December the twenty-third. Liz was so flabbergasted she almost brought Gretel out of winter stasis to provide her with a dose of smelling salts. She changed into a stylish black dress, put on some earrings, and found some Belgian chocolates for a present.

"Is this OK?" she asked David before they set out. "Too formal? Should I do something with my hair?"

David, who thought he looked shabby by comparison, in corduroy jeans and a white linen shirt, made her do a twirl on the spot. "You look great," he said. And he meant it. He'd never really seen her dressed up before. Never even thought of her as a real woman. But here she was, his landlady, with wild red hair and flashing green eyes and not a bad figure (though he tried not to look). She resembled Lucy so very much. Flawless skin. Perfect mouth. Beautiful in a childlike way. Was this what Guinevere had been like, he wondered? Wow.

What a gene pool. No wonder the dragon, Gawain, had been charmed.

Lucy, of course, could not be present. That had caused Liz a flutter or two and made her think twice about going at all. But with David's support she bravely rose above it and explained her daughter's absence by saying she was expected home the very next day (when Henry would be visiting relatives in Framingham), and would be gone again back to her Aunty Gwyneth's by the time he returned. Wasn't that a shame? Henry, who had never much cared for the company of children, took it as a kind of stoical mercy and invited them both to take places at his table.

It was a good dinner. An extraordinary dinner. Henry had cooked a spectacular turkey, which he carved with such culinary expertise that the meat almost fell into supermarket-ready slices. He had also concocted a homemade punch that he insisted could not make a goldfish dizzy but had Liz giggling after one large glassful.

As the afternoon wore on, Henry took orders for

coffee and felt his way to the kitchen. While he was gone, David turned in his chair and cast his eye about the room.

"What you after?" asked Liz, covering her mouth to stifle a bubble of returning punch.

"Remote," said David. "It's Saturday. Want to check the soccer results."

"You can't do that. You're a guest in someone's house."

"I used to live here," David reminded her. "Henry won't mind. Besides. . . ."

"Wozz the madder?" Liz said, befuddled by the pause.

He had stopped at the edge of the shaggy white rug as if he was suddenly afraid to cross it. "Something's happening," he said, putting out his hand. The air above the rug was rippling like a heat haze. Everything beyond it, the TV, the sideboard, was swimming way out of focus, as though his eyes were wrapped in a layer of polythene. Then, something extraordinary happened. At rug level, a wicker basket pulsed into view. It was the one Liz had found when Lucy had been taken. The one that Snigger had been jailed in and released from. He was in it again now, gnawing at a corner. Chewing through it. Breaking out. *This can't be right,* David thought, his brain all at sea. But when he tried to say so his voice was muted, as though he was caught in a waking nightmare. The air shimmered again, and suddenly he understood what was happening. He was seeing a replay of Lucy's abduction — or rather, a second or two after that incident. The air movement was a rip in space, a rip that was fast resetting itself. But not fast enough to beat a nimble squirrel. Snigger leaped forward, and with a pop as quiet as a soap bubble bursting, he completely disappeared. The wicker cage dissolved from view.

The room returned to normal.

David swept around. "Did you see that?"

Liz was falling forward, holding her head. "Feel tired," she mumbled. "Brainz gone to sleep."

"There was a disturbance," said David. "Some sort

of time slip. I saw Snigger, going through a kind of wormhole. I thought you told me you'd released him in the garden?" He shook her to her senses.

She blinked and said, "Snigger?"

"Do you remember letting him go?"

Her green eyes swam, but it wasn't the drink. "No," she said.

"But you must. Where's the basket?"

"Bazzket?"

"The cage you found?"

She shook her head. "I don't know what you're talking about."

"Black or white?" said Henry, coming through with a tray.

David answered for them. "Liz'll have black. Good and strong. I need to run back home for a moment."

"Now? What's so urgent, boy?"

"Thought I heard the phone ringing. Might have been Lucy." And he was gone before the first drop of coffee was poured.

In the hallway at number 42, Gollygosh was fixing a set of Christmas lights. "Come with me," David told him, snapping his fingers. "I might need you to wake G'reth."

Hrrr? went Golly, who didn't think it was quite in order to bring a wishing dragon out of his winter stasis.

"It's important," said David, going into his room. He crossed to the windowsill, where he found Gadzooks pacing crossly back and forth. "What's the matter? Zookie, what is it? Did you sense what happened next door just now?" He glanced at G'reth. The wisher hadn't moved a single scale.

Gadzooks gave a snort and turned his pad. Scrawled across it was the word:

Far

"Far what?" asked David.

Zookie whipped his tail. *Hrrr,* he complained.

"You were interrupted? This is only the start of a word?"

Gadzooks tapped his pencil hard against his teeth.

"What stopped you?"

The dragon slid his eyes toward G'reth.

"The same force that's stopping him completing his mission?"

Hrrr, went Gadzooks, settling down in a heap.

David looked into the dark night sky. "Something's playing games with us, isn't it?" he said. "Something with the power to change the course of events?"

Something with its finger on the pulse of the universe.

The question was, what?

Christmas came. Although they'd agreed not to buy each other presents, David gave Liz a pair of amber earrings — green to match her eyes. She in turn gave him a sculpture: a sleek white polar bear.

"New line," she said, sheepishly. "Exclusive to you. Thought you'd like it. Something to keep your writing focused."

"It's great," he said.

"You have to name it, you know."

"Is it —?"

"I didn't use the icefire. No."

"It won't —?"

"David, just give it a name."

"Thoran," he said. "The hero of my book." There was wisdom in its eyes. History in its paws. Determination in the set of its jaw. "If I could choose to reinvent myself, I'd be a bear like this." He stood up and gave her an enormous hug. Her body shuddered and he knew she was crying. "Hey, hey, what's the matter? Shush."

"I miss Lucy," she sobbed. "I've never had a Christmas without her before."

"I know," he said quietly. "I miss her as well." He ran a hand between her shoulder blades and knuckled her back. "Zanna, too." He thought about the black feather under his pillow. *Wherever you are, merry Christmas,* he wished her.

"Oh, David, what's going to happen?"

"I don't know."

She dropped her head deeper into his shoulder, her soft red hair creeping under his collar. "It's all so strange. I never thought I'd fear Gawain, but I do."

David closed his eyes, trying not to picture the dragon in his mind. Everything had been so quiet lately, but in two months' time . . . "Bergstrom has plans. We'll find Lucy, I promise."

She eased back, bouncing her fists off his chest. "You're an idiot. You can't take on a dragon."

"People said the same about Guinevere, once."

She laughed through her tears and beat him again. Behind them, Bonnington's tail brushed the Christmas tree, making half the ornaments shudder. "Arthur used to call me his Guinevere," she said.

The clock chimed softly. David raised a hand and moved the hair off her face. "Who could possibly blame him?" he said, and let her cry into his shoulder again.

In the dictionary, there were over two hundred words or phrases beginning F-A-R. None of them delivered any spark of understanding. But the mystery of that Christmas dinner remained. Though he checked the room carefully while Henry was away, David could find no evidence of a wormhole, nor a single squirrel hair in the white tufts of the rug. But for two things, he might have put it down to Henry's fruit punch: Liz had no memory of letting Snigger go, and the wicker basket was nowhere to be found.

Mystified, he returned to his writing. The story unfolded, but it was different now. With every passing week he felt an expectation growing, as though he was being carefully monitored. Not by anything he could name or see, but by the auma of the universe, pressing in around him. Dark matter. It moved with his fingers as they hurried across the keyboard. And he sensed it shadowing his every thought. Zanna, drawing within range of the Tooth. Ingavar, already prowling the ice. Grockle, out there, seeking his fire. Lucy, dreaming of a girl by a stream. Bergstrom and his talisman, readying for battle. Gwilanna in a damp cave, waiting, plotting. In the sky above them all, a fire star coming.

The book, *White Fire,* drew to a conclusion. With it, the weather began to improve. Cold bright sunshine. Tangible rain. Colors came alive through the windows again.

Dragons awoke: Gretel first, hurrying Gruffen and others along. G'reth, still nursing the rejuvenating Fain, remained on the windowsill, taking his time. From its high point on the fridge, the listening dragon broke all the winter news. The house breathed. The calendar turned.

The month of February arrived.

David paced his room, ever more anxious that his time was approaching, wondering why Bergstrom hadn't been in touch. On his desk lay almost three hundred sheets of paper. His part of the bargain. The story, delivered. Twice he'd called the Polar Research Base, only to hear the boring answering machine. He thought back to his parting with Bergstrom at the college. *When we move, we move quickly,* the scientist had said. David checked the calendar. February the ninth. Talk about cutting it close.

It was February the eleventh, midmorning, when it all changed.

David was in the front room cradling Bonnington. The cat was dying, in progressively slower stages. Sleep had replaced all forms of activity. Any pursuit now was in the cat's dreams. "Why can't you help him?" David asked Golly. The healer was sitting on the arm of the sofa. Lately, he had kept a much closer vigil. Gretel, too, was never far away, sweeping the air with soothing lavender. G'reth was on the coffee table, looking on.

Hrrr, Golly whispered, so as not to wake the cat. Bonnington was paws up, snoring peacefully, making small wet bubbles on his pink-tipped nose.

"How can you say it's all right?" David said, wiping a dribble from Bonnington's mouth. "He's dying, Golly. He's going away." Behind the gum, he could see the swelling, raising the tongue.

But the healing dragon had nothing to add. He simply folded his wings, blew a faint wisp of smoke, and fixed his big blue eyes on the cat.

David sighed and lifted Bonnington's paw, slipping back through his memories of their time together. He was wondering if Bonnington was doing the same, revisiting ridge tiles, fences, walls, his treasure trove at the bottom of the garden, his basket in the kitchen,

David's blanket, when all of a sudden the atmosphere shifted and the dragons stirred.

"What was that?" David said, laying Bonnington on the sofa. He was about to stand up when he felt a slight tingling sensation in his hand and a rather strange clearing calm in his head.

I am Fain, said a voice from the center of the calm. *Shall we commingle?*

If you like, said David, thinking rather than saying the words. It was a tentative offer, for he no longer felt quite part of the room. And everything in it was tinted blue. Besides, if the thing was inside him already, he didn't seem to have a lot of choice . . .

You have a high vibration, said the Fain. *You attract.*

Attract what? said David.

Everything, it said. *The universe moves within you and without you.*

David shook his head.

Do not wobble, said the Fain. The room swam violet.

Sorry, but I don't understand you, said David.

You have connections, it said, *to Godith.*

You mean through Gadzooks? And Golly and G'reth?

More, said the Fain. *You are one with Arthur.*

David sat forward, concentrating hard. What do you know about Arthur? he asked.

He is becoming like us. Like Fain.

Changing things by the power of thought?

Arthur is reaching out, it said.

How can I find him?

You already have.

The mailbox rattled, making David jump. Instantly, the Fain disconnected from his auma and returned to its favored host, G'reth.

Seconds later, Gadzooks landed breathless on the sofa. He dropped a small white envelope at David's knee.

It was addressed to David, in shaky green writing.

42 Wayward Crescent, Scrubbley.

By airmail. Postmarked Scotland, UK.

David tore it open as Liz walked in.

"This came," he said. A folded sheet of paper.

Gretel snatched the envelope and pawed at the ink.

"Hey, what the —?" David tried to snatch it back, but she hurred aggressively and flapped away.

Gadzooks, meanwhile, was growing more and more agitated.

"He wants to see it," said Liz, nodding at the note.

David, still wondering what the Fain had meant about Arthur, slowly opened it. Two words, in the same green ink:

Farlowe Island

Hrrr! went the writing dragon, beating his wings.

Liz knelt and cupped her hands around his body. "What's the matter with him? What does it mean, that note?"

David chewed his lip, his eyes darting back and forth. "At Christmas, he tried to write a message beginning F-A-R. Something stopped him before he could finish. I'd bet my last chestnut this was what he had in mind."

"But who's sent this?" she said, taking it from him, fighting to keep it out of Gretel's clutches.

"Don't know," David muttered, going over to the shelf where Liz kept a number of reference books, among them an atlas. He flipped it open at the British Isles. "There," he breathed excitedly. "There, it exists." He showed Liz the map. "Farlowe. It's one of the Scottish islands."

"I've heard of it," she said. "It's a holy place, owned by monks. It's famous because it's shaped like a cross."

"Monks," David muttered, tapping the map against his chin. "Monks . . . Wait, that must be it!" He snapped his fingers and looked Liz in the eye. "Where do people who drop out of society go?"

Before she could answer, Gretel was tugging at the letter again.

This time, David caught her and turned her to face him. "This ink. What is it?"

Gretel's eyes grew wild.

"What *is* it?" he repeated, this time in dragontongue.

Blood, she hurred.

"Dragon's?"

She nodded.

A rippling *hrrr* ran through the house.

"I have to go," said David, snatching up his jacket. "I can book a flight over the Net."

"Flight? Flight where?" said Liz.

"Go? Go where?" said Liz.

"To Britain. To Farlowe. To him. *Arthur* is there, Liz. I think he's found what Bergstrom needs."

"David, slow down!" She hauled him back. "This doesn't make sense. Even if it *was* Arthur, why would he write to you? He doesn't even know you exist."

"I think he does. I think he's been sending me clues all along."

Liz glanced at Gadzooks.

"Yes, via him. Zookie didn't write Arthur's name for nothing. He's a physicist, Liz. A man who loves stars and the stuff of space. I think he knows about something called dark matter and how to control it — us included. He's on that island, and that's where I'm heading."

"But why would he send you this letter?" she said, anxiety running right through her voice.

David paused to think. "Why does anyone light a beacon?"

"You think he's in trouble?"

"I just know I have to find him."

And without another word, he dashed out of the room.

Part Three

FARLOWE ABBEY, TEN DAYS EARLIER

"Enter."

The door swung slowly back and the tall, stooping figure of Brother Vincent stepped into Abbot Hugo's office. The abbot was sitting with his back to the door, on a dark oak pew with a fleur-de-lis pattern cut into the backrest. There was no movement in the fabric of his robe, but his head was not bowed and he was clearly not at prayer. All the same, Brother Vincent did not approach. Humility and rank forbade such arrogance. Instead, he clasped his hands together and waited, muttering on a downward slant: "You wished to speak with me, Abbot?"

"Yes. Close the door."

With a nod of his tonsured head, Brother Vincent pushed the door until it clicked against the keeper. The sound echoed madly in the hollows of his chest, beating at the fear he felt rising there. Doors in the abbey were rarely closed, to demonstrate trust and openness. And though speech was not forbidden within the Order, it was usually restricted to arranged times and emergencies. To be summoned, thus, meant all was not well.

"Come and sit beside me, brother."

Vincent shuffled across the floor, his sandals barely raising a sound from the boards. Although the island was deep in the last throes of winter, the modern heating system at work in the abbey meant there was no need for shoes indoors. He joined the abbot on the three-seater pew, resting his hands in the hollow of his lap and fixing his gaze through the wide arched window across the green acres of pasture land that ran away eventually down to the sea.

Hugo took off his wiry brown spectacles. From somewhere deep within his bushy white beard, his lips produced a stream of warm, wet air. The small round lenses of the spectacles clouded. Using a fold of his habit as a duster, he wiped them clear before looping them back around his ears. On a table at his side lay a small wooden box. From it, he took out a folded piece of paper. It crackled drily as he opened it out.

"This was on the floor of the chapel," he said, disapproval evident in the jut of his chin. "There is no identifying mark, but it was found in the spot where you are known to kneel." He ran a myopic eye across it. "Is it yours, brother?"

Calculations. Vectors. Stellar trajectories. The final approach path of the star. Brother Vincent tried not to seem ruffled, but the gulp in his throat as he swallowed his guilt must have sounded like a cannon shot. Abbot Hugo was a watchful, perceptive man. He knew the answer to his question already. What he was seeking here was admission.

"Before I joined the brethren," Vincent said, "I had a substantial interest in astronomy. God's hand was never more at work than in the stars. Sometimes, their movements lure me still."

Abbot Hugo sucked in through his nose. It was deeply indented and hooked like a beak. His presence about the abbey could always be detected from the sound of his pinched, headmasterly breathing. He pressed his thumbs together till the skin turned white. "I know the contents of our library very well. I have never seen any book in there relating to astronomical procedures, or any kind of ephemeris giving planetary positions. You have no telescope in your cell. And yet you are able to write and draw figures which suggest you have computed something of great importance in the heavens. What do you have to say about that?"

Rain slanted into the windows, strumming jazzily against the glass. Brother Vincent closed his eyes, time and space peeling back through his mind. It had been raining that autumn evening, on the bridge above the river where he'd seen a comet arcing brightly across the sky. In that place where her hand had first reached for his . . . and where he had tried to say his last goodbye. The pattern of that night was embroidered on his memory. White fires, burning in the sea of his grief. What need did he have of books or ephemerides? What *could* he say that the abbot would understand? How was it possible to speak of his loss to an old man dressed in a stone colored cloth, who had never loved anyone other than his God?

Abbot Hugo coughed into his fist. "You understand why I must ask you this?"

Brother Vincent lowered his head.

"If you have no access to scientific data, then it must be assumed you are using the stars to give weight to prediction. The penalty for any act of divination would be instant exclusion from the Order."

"No!" Vincent leaped up straight, rocking the pew's uneven feet. He slid to his knees and gripped the abbot's robe. "Don't send me from the island. Please. I beg you." He placed his forehead against the abbot's knees.

Eyes plumping behind his spectacles, Abbot Hugo

placed a hand on the younger man's shoulder, pushing him away to a comfortable distance. "Are there more of these papers?"

"Yes, Abbot. Yes."

"You must show them to me. They may have to be destroyed."

Brother Vincent pressed his hands to his face.

"You spend a great deal of time at the folly. Is that where most of this . . . writing is kept?"

The folly. A gray stone tower to the north of the island. A place of meditation. A place of secrets. Brother Vincent drew back into himself. "I go to the folly in search of peace. All the writings are in my cell. In the drawer of my escritoire."

The abbot touched his beard as he pondered this reply. His gaze flickered briefly to a curtained-off enclosure, returning quickly as Vincent looked up. "Gather them and bring them here, tonight. Speak to no one of this. Go now. I will pray for you."

"Thank you, Abbot." Vincent rose up humbly and headed for the door.

"Oh, Brother Vincent?"

"Yes?"

Abbot Hugo was now tipped slightly forward, his hands squeezed together under his chin, the chain of a crucifix trailing from them. "The ink on the paper: It's a most unusual color. In a certain light, it seems to glow green."

Brother Vincent allowed himself to swallow again, confident this time that he was too far away for his fear to be detected. "I . . . dilute the ink with alcohol," he said.

"Alcohol?"

"From the perfumes," he added, thankful that God had guided his eyes toward a row of bottled scents on the abbot's shelf. The island was sustained by its sales of dried herbs, candy, and colognes. Brother Vincent, with a history of science in his background, was one of the accomplished members of the Order. "I was writing down a recipe for Brother Malcolm and the ink and the alcohol ran together. I liked the color. I found it soothing."

"Intriguing," said the abbot. "Peace be with you, brother."

"And you, my Lord Abbot," Vincent said quietly. With a courteous nod, he backed out of the room.

The rain lashed the windows again, masking the sound of a curtain swishing back.

"Well?" said Hugo, to the monk who came to join him. His name was Brother Bernard Augustus. He was short and his legs were bruised at the ankles. His face was round with kindness and concern.

"His soul is aching. His voice betrays it."

"He's hiding something," the abbot said quietly.

Brother Bernard spread his fingers, touching their pudgy ends to the window. "I fear for him. The history of this island is dark."

"Then find out what he is keeping from us."

"You wish me to follow him? To spy on my brother?"

A bell clanged, low and rich with persuasion. The abbot parted his hands. "Eleven years ago, before he came to the brethren, Brother Vincent tried to end his life by throwing himself off a bridge into a river. No one has ever found out why. That torment is rising in his eyes again. Something evil is preying on his heart. All I want to do is protect him, Brother Bernard. All I want to do is understand."

In the Fields, Next Day

Brother Vincent!"

The voice came calling out from some way behind him. Turning, he saw the stumpy figure of Brother Bernard Augustus hurrying along the flattened grass track. They were halfway between the monastery chapel and the folly at the northern tip of the island. A knot of uncertainty rolled into the center of Vincent's chest. He had never been followed out here before.

Red-faced from the hurry, Bernard came puffing up, resembling a small, very overweight puppy. Wisps of ginger hair from his freckled head were falling forward, sticking to his brow. A brittle wintry rain was in the air and the grass underfoot was slippery and muddied, but he had neither changed his sandals nor raised his cowl.

Brother Vincent bit his tongue in silent reproach. Direct exposure to the harshest elements was one form of penitence he had not yet considered. He shook his head, chiding himself for such scorn. Even now, after all these years on the island, the monastic principles did not always sit comfortably with him.

"Brother Bernard. What brings you chasing me here?"

Bernard patted his brow with a handkerchief. He puffed his chest and blew a round breath of air. It solidified into a larger ball of mist. "What a glory it is to be out in the wilds, even in the bleakness of a February morning."

Vincent bowed. That he could not argue with. Isolation was a route to inner peace, but his mind, just then, was anything but still. What did this winded brother want?

Bernard opened his chunky hands. His smile was almost as wide as his reach. "I'm sure you remember that ornithology is an amateur pastime of mine. I was merely wondering where that was nesting?" He pointed beyond. Brother Vincent turned to see a large black bird skitter down from the sky and land just a yard or two away. It strutted a few steps and pecked the earth, then threw back its head and screeched at the men.

"Fascinating, don't you think?" Bernard said, wiping the handkerchief hard across his mouth.

"It's a crow," said Vincent. His heart was thumping but his voice was even. Beneath the folds of his habit, his bare knees seemed to have welded together. He blinked as a snowflake landed on his eyelid. "Why would it be of particular interest?"

"Ah!" Bernard rubbed his hands together as though he was attempting to spark a fire. "At the risk of sounding overly precocious, I must correct you, Brother Vincent. I believe that is a raven, not a crow. It has a fan-shaped tail and a beak more rounded than its smaller cousin. Its presence here is most beguiling."

Vincent dragged his gaze away from the bird. "Why is that?"

Bernard's eyebrows hopped and he smiled again. "Because we've never had a single raven here before."

He brushed past to stand a little closer to the bird. It dipped its beak and stared back fearlessly. With an elegant ruffle of its flint-black feathers it put its wings into the wind and was carried away north. Bernard twisted, cupping his eyes. "Magnificent," he breathed. "I first saw it on the roof of the chapel. That was just over a week ago. This morning, I observed it again through my binoculars. It was circling the folly, of all places. I know you like to spend time out there. I was wondering if you had seen it, brother, and could possibly tell me if there is a pair?"

Brother Vincent drove his hands into his wide, loose sleeves and continued his measured walk along the path. "You must forgive me. While my heart contains joy for all God's creatures, during prayer my eyes are trained only within. I know nothing of this bird. Peace be with you. Good day."

"Brother, wait." In a matter of clumping strides, Bernard was back at the other man's side. "If you have no objection, I would like to join you at the folly today and hopefully answer my question myself."

In the distance a soft wave landed, spilling its hollow yawn into the caverns cored out of the island by the motions of the sea. Brother Vincent paused and rolled his shoulders. "The folly is not a place of comfort, brother. I . . ."

"I have provisions," Bernard interjected, cheerily. He patted a knapsack strapped across his shoulder. "Cheese, bread, and a flagon of water."

Vincent looked to one side.

"Forgive me, I have been too presumptuous," Bernard said, clasping his hands together and bowing. Snowflakes fell across the yoke of his shoulders, patterning his brown, slightly threadbare cowl. "I have no wish to disturb your meditations. I will walk the coast path and observe the bird from there."

"No," said Vincent, recovering quickly. "The island retreats are there for all. It would be a pleasure to share bread with you at the folly. Excuse me if I seemed anything less than grateful for your offer. Come, let me guide you. I know a route less likely to wet the toes."

Brother Bernard nodded graciously and fell into step.

For a few strides they walked on in silence, then it was the taller monk who spoke again. "May I ask a question about this bird? You seem excited yet puzzled by the presence of it?"

"Indeed," said Bernard, his heavy feet slapping against the grass, spraying his companion's ankles with water. "Members of the *Corvidae* tend to cluster. Why one should choose to cross eight miles of water and settle here is a mystery, brother."

"Perhaps something attracted it," Vincent said quietly.

"Other than your excellent recipe for chocolate, I cannot think what. Though I did read an article the other day which the ignorant or misguided might argue was the cause. It was to do with, of all things, spiritual awareness."

Brother Vincent felt a shudder topple off his shoulders and leave an ice-cold trail down his arms. "To know God is something we strive for every day. Why be so dismissive, brother?"

"The subject matter was monkeys!" said Bernard.

The leader came to a sudden halt. "Monkeys?"

"On a group of South Sea islands."

Vincent shook his head in puzzlement, throwing off his cowl. The cold wind immediately punished his ears. He flipped up the cover and continued walking.

"It was a scientific study," Bernard said, "which set out to determine if the monkeys were able to solve a simple problem. Sweet potatoes were left on a sandy beach for them. The monkeys found them and sensed they were good to eat, but were put off because they were covered in sand. Then one day, a wise old monkey, on the remotest island of the chain, washed her potato in the sea and ate it. Monkeys nearby quickly learned to follow suit, until most of them were cleansing their food in that way. Then something extraordinary appeared to happen. When the number of monkeys exhibiting such behavior reached one hundred, monkeys on islands miles away suddenly began washing their potatoes as well, even though they'd had no contact with the original troop! The author of the piece proposed a preposterous explanation —"

Vincent cut in and said without a pause, "That the skill had been attained by enough members of the group to form a critical mass, so that awareness of the skill was then transferred to every monkey through their group consciousness."

"Precisely!" Brother Bernard exclaimed. "You astound me, brother. How did you guess?"

They were at the base of the folly. Brother Vincent unlatched the door and bade his fellow monk follow him in. There was nothing on this level but a winding staircase and dampness leaking from the circular walls.

As his foot found the first worn hollow in the stone, Brother Vincent said, "There is a theory called the Law of Attraction, which proposes that whatever we think about, we bring to us; whatever we desire, we create."

Brother Bernard Augustus lifted his habit and trod his way carefully up the stairs. "A law, Brother Vincent? Surely the only law of creativity is that which the Lord himself commands? Would it not be the greatest of profanities for you or I to think we could — shh! What was that?"

As he'd climbed through the hatch to the next floor of the folly, something had scuttled across the wooden boards.

Brother Bernard closed his hands in prayer. "Are there rats here? Forgive me, I do not like rodents."

"Only one," said Vincent. He dropped down on one knee and opened his hand. A small lithe figure jumped onto his palm, ran the length of his arm and vanished behind his neck. "This is my companion," he said. "Quite tame." When he turned, there was a gray squirrel sitting on his shoulder.

Brother Bernard stared in astonishment. As in the case of the single raven, he had never seen a squirrel on the island before.

And certainly not one that smiled.

Prayers in the Folly

On the first floor of the folly was a lectern as old as the abbey itself. It faced a broken window which looked out onto the open sea. Gulls, and sometimes fishing boats, crossed by, but for the most part there was only water and sky. It was here that Brother Bernard leaned a forearm. The desk was often used for standing prayer and he found himself muttering a biblical passage, hoping it might explain this apparition now chirring softly into Brother Vincent's ear.

"I do not understand this," he said, somewhat flushed. Out came his sweat-soaked handkerchief again. "How can squirrels and ravens arrive on the island when they have never been present before?" He watched Brother Vincent feed a peanut to the squirrel. It shelled it in seconds and chirped for another. "Perhaps the tourists?" he added, gesturing hopefully. There were many every year. But not through the winter. He pulled his hands tight together again, troubled.

"You should rest," Vincent said. "The walk here saps the strength from the knees." He drew up the only chair in the room and sat Brother Bernard with his back to the window and the rustling sea. Bernard slipped his knapsack of provisions to the floor, noticing something by the foot of the lectern. A scrunched-up piece of paper. He reached for it, only to find his arm gripped at the wrist.

"Allow me," Brother Vincent said. A weak light bounced off his glassy blue eyes. He picked up the paper and squeezed it in his fist.

Brother Bernard sank back, bristling nervously. Glancing around, he could see other balls of paper. Evidence that Vincent had been lying, at the abbey. Oh, why had Abbot Hugo given him this task? There was nothing spiritual about distrust.

"You seem anxious. Is something on your mind, Brother Bernard?"

The chair creaked as Bernard shifted his weight. He prayed quickly for guidance, and made a bold decision. "Brother, the abbot is concerned for your welfare. He fears you are fighting demons in your mind and has asked me to watch over you. I am not altogether at ease with his request. I don't know what to do."

Brother Vincent walked to the window and guided the squirrel onto the ledge. "You must do what the Lord dictates," he said, "and follow the path of righteousness. I see questions in your eyes, worry in your movements. What is it you wish to know?"

Brother Bernard ran a hand across his gleaming crown. "These . . . papers. What are they? There: It's out!"

"Mistakes," said Vincent. "Unforeseen errors. Passages I'm not quite comfortable with."

"Passages?"

"For the past few months, I've been writing a story. Here, at the lectern." He patted it as though it were a faithful friend.

"A work of fiction?"

"I thought so, once." There was a tremor in Vincent's

voice. He ran his little finger down the squirrel's back. It darted up his arm again, back onto his shoulder. "Let me guess," he said, stepping forward. "Abbot Hugo has told you I tried to take my life. He would like to know why, in case I try again. If I tell you the circumstances, will you swear to me you will not speak of my story till after I am gone?"

"You're leaving the Order?"

"Shortly, yes."

Bernard let his arms fall loosely at his side. "So many surprises."

"There are more," said Vincent. He dropped the ball of paper into Bernard's lap. "Look at it. Please."

Bernard smoothed it out. It was three-quarters filled with the same green ink that he had seen on Vincent's sketches of the heavens. "What will I learn from this?" he asked. He glanced at the page and saw the word "dragon." Immediately, his warm heart cooled.

"Many years ago I knew a woman," Vincent said. "I was in love with her. She with me, or so I thought. One day I discovered she had mothered a child that could not have been mine. I was devastated and threw myself into a river. I was rescued and taken to a hospital. When I recovered, I chose to find spiritual sanctuary, here. In the past few months, I have."

"But this . . . ?" Bernard passed a hand across the page.

"That is my catharsis," Vincent said. "My explanation for the birth. It exonerates her virtue and keeps our love alive."

Bernard blinked in confusion. He looked again at the word "dragon." "Liz," he muttered, finding a name.

"Elizabeth. That was she."

"And this explains her . . . infidelity?"

"There *was* no infidelity," Vincent insisted. "No other man involved."

"Then who was the father?"

Vincent looked away.

Bernard slowly folded the paper. "Brother, you have been my companion for ten years now. In all that time you have never once stepped off this island. How can you know what you cannot know, or convince yourself of a truth just imagined?"

Vincent pushed his tongue between his tightening lips. He stepped backward and turned to the wall. There was a grating sound of stone against stone. When he turned back to the light again, there was something in his hands. It was long and curved with a sharply pointed tip.

"What is that?" Bernard said, fear rising in his throat. The myths about this island seemed suddenly very real.

Vincent held the artifact as though it were a pen. "This is a dragon's claw," he breathed.

To the Cavern

Brother Bernard shook his head wildly and threw his weight against the base of the chair. A leg squealed, gouging a scratch on the floor. "No, you mock me. There is no such creature. How can you speak of such things in this place?"

Vincent looked at the fallen knapsack. "Give me your water."

"What?"

"Your flagon."

Bernard shook his head. "I —"

Vincent dropped down and tore at the buckles. "Watch," he said, uncorking the flagon and tipping it until the water lapped the neck. He dabbed the point of the dragon claw into it, then spread the crumpled paper on the floor and proceeded to write the letter *G* on its reverse. "A gentle squeeze brings forth a kind of ichor. The colder the water, the better the flow."

Ichor? The blood of the gods? Lord, preserve us! Bernard turned away with a hand to his head. Now he understood why the abbot was concerned. Brother Vincent had clearly turned quietly mad.

"I found it after years of meditation," said Vincent. "Day after day I pleaded for an answer. One night it appeared. There, in the center of this floor, lit by the light of a distant star."

"Brother, you must pray with me," Bernard beseeched him. He fell to his knees and began to beg for mercy and understanding.

"But this *is* my prayer," Vincent insisted. He knelt opposite Bernard and shook him into silence. "With this, I have touched the heart of the universe. I have uncovered that which cannot be seen. I have brought forth life where there was only clay. I have looked through the eyes of God."

"NO!" Bernard shouted. "This is blasphemy! Delusion. Your mind has taken leave of its senses. What proof do you have that what you say is real?"

Chirr! went the squirrel.

Brother Vincent smiled, for there was the answer. "His name is Snigger. You will find him in the early body of my texts. I brought him here, through space and time. The raven . . ." He looked absently towards the window. "The raven is a messenger of love from the north."

"I must leave here," Bernard said, turning left and right in search of the hatch. "Please return with me, brother. Let the abbot . . . let the Church redeem your soul!"

Brother Vincent laughed. "On the fourteenth day of this month, the world will change. A new dimension will open to us all. A chance for all souls to find redemption."

Bernard shook his head.

"I can prove it," said Vincent, with steel in his voice. "Ten minutes, brother. Ten minutes that will change your grasp on reality."

Beneath the weight of his habit and the scapula

which covered it, Bernard felt the quickening thump of his heart.

Vincent crossed the floor and lifted the hatch. "Follow me," he said, descending swiftly.

In a matter of strides, he was through the door and heading toward the cliffs.

"Where are we going?" Bernard shouted, struggling with the pace and the breath-snatching whistle of the coastal wind.

Vincent walked on and did not turn. Suddenly, he was gone from view, stumbling down a man-made path which slanted through a wet dune and onto a narrow beach covered with rubble from the cliffs above. The sea, as if taunted and enraged by his presence, crashed against the rocks and threw spray into his face. Still he walked on, crossing the stones with a jaunty balance, resembling a puppet suspended on strings.

He was sitting on a ledge at the mouth of a cavern when Bernard finally caught up.

"Well?" cried Bernard, struggling against the snarl of the sea.

"Closer," Vincent shouted, beckoning to him.

Bernard lifted his habit and looked for a step. But long before his leg was off the ground, his heart was firmly in his mouth. From within the cavern he could hear a sound. A low, guttural, rumbling cry. An animal of some kind. A large, wild creature. He crossed himself and urinated down his leg. The voice was like nothing he had heard on God's earth.

Grrrrr-ockle, it went.

WITH GROCKLE, THE DRAGON

Brother Bernard Augustus had been a historian all his life, from school, through the best theological college, and now here, as librarian of Farlowe Abbey. He had documented many interesting studies and knew that this island had once been the center of a myth surrounding the wrath of a dragon. Long ago, too long for records to be kept, and therefore confined to the hearsay of centuries, it was said that a dragon had nested on the site of the ruined bell tower, where the original priory had stood. Fearful of her presence, two monks had climbed up into the belfry and oiled the staples of the unused bells, freeing each clapper without a sound. Waiting for a stormy night, a night so bitterly condensed with rain that a whole wing of dragons would be worthless of flame, the abbot had ordered the bells to be tolled. The clatter had driven the mother from her nest. The monks, hiding in the shadows of the balustrades, had leaped up and pierced her egg with spears. The mother, witnessing this dreadful act, had unlatched her jaw and issued a scream that had shaken the tower and split it asunder. The crash of stone brought every bell down. The abbot had been covered by the largest of them, trapped underneath like a wasp in a jar. Only then did the mother dragon descend, mantling her giant wings against the rain, before releasing a boiling flame that melted the brass and the abbot with it, until they flowed like the yolk of her unborn young.

Until that day on the rocks by the cavern, Brother Bernard had told himself that stories like these were invented by charlatans and religious scaremongers. Now, with the ocean cooling his feet, spreading its solemnity up through his bones, he believed every word. His perception of truth, as Brother Vincent had suggested, had changed forever.

He had seen a demon.

The creature, squatting, was probably no bigger than a very large dog. But each time it gave out its savage *grrr-ockle,* the bellows of its lungs would lift its shoulders and its wings would arch into folded peaks. It was a monster, as tall as a teenage child when it stretched its ugly, scaly knees. He shuddered at the sight of its bladelike talons, as long again as the toes they grew out of. And its face! Its hideous pointed face. Those repeating teeth. Those rolling yellow eyes, laced by capillaries of bright green blood, centers darker than the wells of space.

"Magnificent, isn't he?" Vincent said. He dipped behind a rock and threw a limp hare at the dragon's feet. Holding the kill with a single talon, it used the other foot to tear the skin apart.

Brother Bernard vomited onto the rocks. In swept the sea to wash away the stains. Bernard wiped his mouth clear of the bile, but the agonies in his mind were not so easy to cleanse. "Where did it come from? Why is it here? What wickedness brought it into this world?"

Brother Vincent adopted the pose of a saint. "Why

do you fear him, brother? He is a gift of creation. A protector of the Earth. A child, no more than a few months old. He has flown here in search of his ancestor's claw and is recovering from a journey, long and harsh. Look at his flank, injured, but healing. During his flight, he struck into a line of electrical cables and was almost killed. For days, until hunger drove him forth, he had to take refuge on an old church spire, assuming the stillness and guise of a gargoyle. His powers of survival and adaptation are remarkable. I learned yesterday that he has the capacity to draw the blood from the surface of his scales until they turn the color of —"

"Stop!" Hands lodged against his brow, Brother Bernard rocked to the swell of the ocean. "It ails me enough to see you abiding by this beast. How can you speak as if you know it? As though it were some kind of pet? The fires of hell are in its belly. This . . . *child* will grow and kill us all!"

Vincent shook his head. "The creature has no fire. Its birth was misgoverned and it fell into a stasis, resembling stone. It was revived by extraordinary means and came here to find salvation and purpose. For me, he is a miracle of universal consciousness. I wrote of him. And he appeared."

Bernard shot a glance at the dragon again. *Grrr-ockle,* it rumbled, tilting its head. Its amber eyes swiveled and focused upon him. The choice between loathing and understanding seemed too wide to breach for a moment. Nevertheless, for the sake of his brother's soul, Bernard Augustus knew he must try. "Tell me, in plain words, how this came to be. Did you conjure this creature or is it real?"

Vincent picked up a pebble and threw it to the sea. "For ten long years I have suffered," he said, "trying to understand why Elizabeth betrayed me. I begged the Lord to show me a motive and He, in His mercy, sent me that claw.

"I had no idea what it was at first, but Elizabeth had always believed in dragons and that was all the reason I needed to assume it was no ordinary talon. When I touched it, I felt inspired. My only thought was to write with it, and once I'd discovered its strange proclivity for producing an endless supply of ink, I began to work on a story.

"I let the claw guide my hand, always believing that what was written would be the will and compassion of God. Soon I was documenting Elizabeth's life, with her then grown daughter, in a place called Scrubbley. The story led me far and wide, from suburban America to the wasteland of the Arctic, but always staying connected to an ancient world of dragons. I assumed that the only purpose of this venture was to build something noble from the ashes of my sorrow, a means to alleviate the welter of my grief. But as the writing took me over, there came a revelation. In time, I wrote of a procedure through which a child, touched by the spirit of a dragon, could be delivered from an egg kindled by a human mother, without the need for a human father."

Brother Bernard closed his eyes.

"Suddenly, light returned to my soul. I started finding more than amusement in the story: I began to find hope. Its world developed and drew me in. As the pages flew by, I knew I had created something far greater than a shelter for my hurt, a legend so convincing that in my mind I had reached out and touched a new reality. Even before this dragon appeared, I knew that Elizabeth's love for me was pure." He turned his head and looked at the baby dragon, grazing its teeth against the side of the cavern. "Now I know for certain."

Brother Bernard steepled his fingers, shaking them as if to make a cocktail of his words. "You are saying you were recording *true events,* even though you thought at the time it was fiction?"

Vincent threw another hare to the dragon. "His role in the story was to seek out the claw. You see him before you. There is your proof."

"But how can that be? The laws of physics —?"

"All wrong," said Vincent. "Misunderstood. Consciousness binds the universe together in a vast, invisible realm which physicists label dark matter. With the aid of this claw, I have been able to access that realm and change the universe from within."

A cloud rumbled across the sun, sending out the first hard shrapnel of rainfall. Brother Bernard found it a welcome relief, for his skin was beginning to simmer with sweat. Dark matter. The words were the essence of turpitude and evil. Nightmares were tranquil compared to this. "How?" he said, as though he'd swallowed a boulder. "How can you change the order of things?"

Vincent raised his cowl against the rain. "One day, I tried an experiment. I went back to a section of my manuscript and altered it. I wrote that a squirrel, captured by the villainess who deceived me and turned me away from Elizabeth, had escaped through a narrow wormhole in space."

"The squirrel in the folly?"

"Yes. Until then, I had no idea that the claw had the power to alter matter or the flow of time."

"But this is merely coincidence," Bernard rasped. He threw out his hands. "The squirrel might have come from anywhere."

"You are a tide's lap away from a dragon, brother. How can you possibly deny what you see? There is no such thing as coincidence."

"But if this were so . . ." Bernard paused, becoming

flustered. He shook a raindrop off his nose as he searched for his words. "If this were so, such a power would be . . ." He shook his head, unable to face the outcome of his thoughts. He looked up in great fear. "How does the story end?"

"With him," said Vincent, nodding at the dragon who was now retiring back into his shelter. "In the darkness, there is a fire star shining. In a few days' time, it will reach its zenith. When it does, he will fly the claw north, to a dragon, waiting, like him, to be reborn."

"And you?" said Bernard. "What will you do?"

Brother Vincent spread his hands and caught the rain in his palms. "I will go home to Elizabeth," he said.

Asleep in the Folly, 2 A.M.

In the beginning was the auma, and the auma was all there was.

All things were visible then.

There was no future. There was no past. There was only the now.

And the auma *was* the now.

For an unknown time, in an unknown space, the auma existed as a pure white fire.

Then, for no reason, for there was no reason, it began to expand.

And time began.

The auma reached out, filling no space, for there was no space for the auma to fill. But in time, it reached out to such an extent that holes appeared in its innermost structure.

Into the holes came a new energy, darkness.

And a binding force which the auma knew as G'ravity.

With G'ravity, the auma reshaped itself, folding in, billowing out, making nothing at first but ripples and contours and patterns of light.

Thus it explored the nature of Geometry, finding stability in aspect and symmetry and ratio and mass.

And in time, the auma gained in mass and, gathering itself, assumed a figure.

And the figure it assumed was a perfect winged creature.

And the creature was a dragon.

And her name was Godith.

By now, darkness was all around. Godith spread her wings far into the void and knew she could no longer touch her own eternity.

So she desired to replicate herself, to reclaim the space she alone had created.

She turned inward, then, to the fire within, and in one immeasurable instant of time, she opened her mouth and spoke the first word: *hrrr*.

And the word flew out to every corner of the universe.

And this is how the world began.

The sea raged. The rain beat down. Darkness shrouded the small stone folly. On the first floor, underneath a blanket of burlap, the monk who had taken the name Brother Vincent dreamed of a gold-rimmed pocket watch.

The dream was always the same. The hands of the watch were always traveling backward, quickening into a spinning blur. In the glass, he could see time passing. Ten years of prayer. Ten years of solitude. Ten years of life without Elizabeth.

When the hands stopped, she was always there. Her flashing green eyes. Her soft red hair. Cradling a child that belonged to them both. It was a girl, and when he reached out and touched her hand her tiny pink fingers would curl around his thumb and there was joy in his heart, and truth, and light.

Light.

It swam above him. Through the voiles of his eyelids, it pushed the night aside. There was a clink of metal. Or was it glass? Vibration in the floorboards. Footfall? How? His eyes half flickered. There was Brother Bernard, kneeling by the window, still muttering softly in prayer. When the thunder broke and the rain had come, shattering the air in a wall of leaden drops, he had chosen to shelter here, in the folly. For six long hours, he had asked his Lord in heaven for guidance.

It had come in the form of Abbot Hugo.

"Wake him," the abbot's voice said.

Vincent rolled over. Six of the Order. Two with lanterns, swinging on poles. "What is this?" he said. He flashed a glance at Brother Bernard. A green light flickered off a small silver object in the fat monk's palm. It was a cell phone.

"NO!" Vincent launched himself toward the

trapdoor, but was caught by Brother Malcolm Cornelius, an ex-marine, a man of great strength.

"Do not make me tie you," the abbot said, images of lanterns in his sad brown eyes. "We have the beast captured and bound."

"You don't know what you're doing. Set him free," said Vincent, so fraught with anger that the words left his mouth on a bubble of froth.

Brother Bernard, crying tears of remorse, crossed himself.

"Abbot." Brother Peter, a monk with too little skin for his cheeks and the posture of a vulture from the shoulder blades up, stepped into view. In his hands was a wooden box. He opened the lid to reveal a stack of papers. "This was in the roof space, hidden by burlap."

Abbot Hugo nodded. He removed the top sheet and read the first words: *Housing Available.* His brow creased into a puzzled frown. "We searched your cell," he said to Brother Vincent, who was tugging without hope against the grip of Brother Malcolm. "There were only blank papers in your desk. You lied to me, brother — to protect this *miscreant* you found in the caverns."

"Please," Vincent begged. "A few more days and the creature will be gone."

The abbot's disbelief was barely hidden as he said, "Where to, brother?"

"The Arctic wilderness. If you stop this, we are all endangered."

Abbot Hugo tilted his head, his beard brushing through the neckstrings of his cowl. With a sigh, he dropped the sheet back into the box and gestured Brother Peter to take it away. He studied Brother Vincent with a mixture of compassion, suspicion, and regret. Mostly regret. He stepped up close, close enough to whisper in the younger man's ear. "What has become of you, Arthur?" he said.

Vincent whispered back. "For the love of God, give the claw to the dragon."

Abbot Hugo stood away and switched his gaze to Brother Malcolm. "Take him to the abbey and lock him in his cell."

Tooth of Ragnar, Same Day

She was a mile out to sea, or rather out to ice, trying to establish where the dragon's head lay in relation to the snow-packed contours of the island, when the Fain arrived. It could not be seen, but she felt it approach. So fast, so close, there was no time to react.

Nothing had ever scared her more.

She looked to the sky. The star was bright, but not yet shining on the summit of the island. Her calculations were not inaccurate. How, then, had the Fain come through the portal?

"Why are you here? What do you want?"

The wind moaned and swept about her feet.

"Take a form," she snapped. "Let me see you."

The ice creaked. Her skin began to prickle. Commingling. The thing was *inspecting* her.

"I am Fain, like you. One of the old ones!"

The air pulsed, pressing against her eyes.

"We can help one another! Our purpose is the same. All I want is to bring the dragons back."

Her blood surged. Her nerve ends crackled.

Cold boomed in the tunnels of her ears.

And then it was within her. One with her.

The Fain.

It filled her limbs, raised her hairs, flowed between the crevices of her toes.

Highly evolved. Superior. A killer.

Why is the dragon made stone? it said, plugging directly into her brain.

She had one chance before it finished her: change.

Its tear was stolen, she said, through thought.

It paused to consider the truth of this. And in its rest, its lapse of concentration, she became a raven and broke herself free.

Ten wingbeats. That was all she got. As she banked

toward the island her feathertips froze. Her beak tipped and she plummeted down.

Her bird brain hummed as the Fain returned.

Where is the dragon's fire? it said.

Cark, she snorted. Her last act of defiance.

Then she was extinguished. Glassy-eyed. Inert.

Gwilanna, the sibyl of ancient ages.

Now a raven, sealed in a block of ice.

Brother Vincent's Cell, Two Days Later

They had captured the dragon with a dead hare drugged with Brother Cedric's sleeping pills. It was lighter than expected and two of them, Brother Malcolm and the one-time circus performer, Brother Terence, carried the limp body up to the clifftop. Crudely, with a roll of mailing tape, they had lashed the wings tight to the creature's body, then bound it with ropes to an open trailer, hooked to the back of the only vehicle on the island, a Land Rover. It woke as they were transferring it to a cobbled enclosure in the disused stable block. Such a scream of anguish did it give that several of the brethren fled from its presence. It was left to Brothers Malcolm, Terence, and Feargal to secure the beast with chains: two around its ankles to stable posts, one from its neck to the crossbeam in the roof. Its wings they left taped. Its tail they caught and wrapped in burlap.

Its heart they left to break by itself.

When Brother Vincent heard what they had done, he wept.

Brother Bernard, in attendance (by his own request), wrung his hands together in despair. "You must eat," he said. He looked at the tray on the floor of the cell. Red cheese. Bread. A tall glass of water. Twice a day delivered. Twice a day untouched.

"What will they do with him?" Vincent asked, his voice low and falling apart.

Bernard coughed into a sweat-stained handkerchief. "The abbot is seeking advice from the mainland."

Vincent raised his head from his bed. His face was a picture of torment and betrayal. "Advice? From whom?"

"I believe there is an envoy coming," said Bernard, turning his face away. There was such hostility in the younger monk's eyes that for a moment he thought about calling for assistance. But he gathered his composure and steadied his gaze beyond the window where, of all things, he saw a raven circling in the dusk. "This is good fortune, brother. At least the creature was not instantly killed."

"Better that it had been," Vincent said bitterly. "If you wish to atone for what you have done, take a spear and drive it through the dragon's heart. The fate that awaits it is worse than death. They will take him away and take him apart. Piece by piece, in the name of science, they will destroy all hope this world ever had."

At this, Brother Bernard threw up his hands. "How can you continue to ply such . . . irreverence!" As he wheeled around, the door of the cell clicked open and a stern-faced Brother Malcolm looked in. "It's all right," Bernard said, mopping the blood pressure out of his brow. "We are having a discussion. A private discussion." Brother Malcolm cast an adverse glance at Brother Vincent, then softly closed the door.

Bernard brought his hands together in a knot. "By the cavern, you talked about things that had happened to the creature, such as it flying into cables. But when I looked through the latter pages of your story, there was no mention of any misadventure. Did you fabricate this? Or conjecture it because the creature was scarred?"

"No," said Vincent. "He told me what had happened — in his own tongue."

Brother Bernard reeled. He found the window frame and stumbled against it. "You speak to this thing?"

Vincent, sensing hope, swung himself into a sitting position. "If this could be proven, would you believe my claims that the creature is more an angel than a devil?"

Bernard felt for his chest. His heartbeat had doubled its pace in seconds.

"You have an interest in ancient languages, do you not?"

"I must leave," Bernard muttered. "For your health, please eat."

"Speak to him, brother. Simply, in any tongue the Inuit people might recognize. His vocabulary is limited. He is only a child, but he *will* understand."

Brother Bernard paused with his forehead on the

door. “What you’re asking goes beyond all my levels of faith.”

“You will find new ones,” Vincent said. “Speak to him, before this envoy comes. He brings danger in his wake. I can feel it in my bones.”

“Danger?” Bernard looked back, startled.

“A wind from another world,” Vincent said, closing his eyes and concentrating hard. “And where there is a wind, there is sometimes a storm. Help me, brother. Help us all. Go to the barn and speak to the dragon.”

Stable Block, Next Morning

Brother Bernard." Brother Terence rose from his three-legged stool just inside the door of the stable block and bid his fellow monk good morning.

Bernard dipped his head in acknowledgment. Beyond the taller man's shoulder he could see the dragon, hunkered to the ground, making what comfort it could of its shackles. Somewhere deep within Bernard's heart, a shred of compassion wriggled uneasily. "Is the creature calm?"

"It cries and whimpers like a dog," Terence snorted. "And stinks of something most ungodly whenever it opens its vicious mouth. What news from the abbot?"

"He has sent me to feed it," Bernard replied. He unwrapped a hare from a roll of paper. A droplet of fresh blood fell onto the skin between his sandal straps. He knelt to clean it, noticing the dragon's head following his movements. Not for the first time, he said a swift prayer.

"I would rather starve it," Terence sighed. "Its rancid feces are making me ill."

"The abbot needs it alive," said Bernard. "Go. I will stand by the beast for an hour. Has it shown any signs of making fire?" He looked worriedly about him. There was a great deal of wood in this prison cell.

"None," said Terence, pushing back the door. The dragon shied away from the light. "For a fiend from hell, it thankfully gives us very poor value." He gave an orderly bow and walked away, leaving Bernard alone with the dragon.

The ghastly yellow eyes rolled up to look at him. No threat present, merely helplessness. For a man who had striven to love all God's creatures, it troubled Brother Bernard to see this animal humiliated so. But if, as the general attitude suggested, it had not been created by the hand of heaven, then they could take no chances with it. And yet here was he, having slain a hare, having left his prayers to deceive a fellow monk with an order from the abbot when no such order had ever been given. If this dishonesty should ever be exposed, many difficult questions would have to be faced. But maybe none so difficult as that which had kept him awake through the night: Could this creature converse?

"Are you hungry?" Bernard said, without offering the hare.

The nostrils flared but the head went down. To all intents and purposes, no response.

Bernard steadied his nerve and tried again. "Are you hungry?" he repeated, but this time in a dialect he had learned in his days as a missionary among natives of the Canadian High Arctic.

Amazingly, the dragon lifted its head. A membrane slithered half across its eyes, narrowing the gaze to terrifying slits. Bernard's bones almost rattled the cobbles. Had the creature understood him? Were those scales, flexing and changing color on either side of its head, ears? He lifted the hare out of the paper and dangled it by its large back paws. "Eat?" he said, in the northern tongue.

The dragon tilted its head.

"What are you?" said Bernard.

Grrr-ockle, went the creature.

Answer or involuntary response? The growl had a strange onomatopoeic resonance, but other than that it made no sense. He threw the hare to it. It fell just outside the neck chain's reach. The dragon stretched, chomping its jaws in frustration.

Irritation and pity ravaged Bernard's soul. Finding a broom with a head that was almost as bald as his, he pushed the meat into the dragon's path. It gathered it and quickly sliced out the innards, gorging itself on the soft red offal.

For a man who abstained from animal flesh, this was almost too much to bear. What was he *doing* here? How could this savage beast possibly communicate? Was this a means of confirming Brother Vincent's sanity or an act of sordid curiosity on his part? Which of them was the lunatic, truthfully?

He looked at the creature again, sucking fur from between its teeth. It burped as if it was grinding stone. Bernard shuddered and turned away, sickened. He was almost at the door when the dragon made another sound, deep within its throat.

Waaarrtttrrrr.

A vortex of fear whirled the monk around. "Water? You want water?"

The dragon opened its jaws to show a parched black tongue, stained here and there with streaks of hare blood.

Bernard pushed a hand across his throbbing brow. Was this a dialogue or an acknowledgment of need? He stumbled backward, nodding his head. He filled a bucket from the tap outside and took it back, nudging it forward with the brush. The dragon bent its head and drank, lapping in the manner of a domestic cat. When it was done it tipped the bucket over and rolled it back to Bernard's feet.

Waaarrtttrrrr, it croaked.

He filled it again.

It took five to quench the dragon's thirst. After the fourth, it squatted and sprayed a jet of urine, drenching the moldy straw behind it. The stench was horrendous. There were white marks on the creature's feet where it had stepped unavoidably in its own excrement and the scales had crusted over with some kind of fungus. It was hideous. Inhumane. It was written in the holy scriptures that man should have dominion over animals . . . but how could the brethren stoop to such tyranny as this? Bernard decided there and then he must speak with the abbot. Make a plea on the creature's behalf. The animal was intelligent and clearly suffering. But one trick with a bucket would not convince the Order to show it mercy. To end the persecution they would have to see a much higher level of sentience. And so he spoke again, this time more pointedly:

"Where did you come from?"

The dragon raked the ground. It seemed to understand, but its answer was vague and made no sense.

Zannnnnaaaa, it growled.

"Zannnnaaa? What is Zannnnaaa?" Bernard said, frowning.

The dragon swung its head. The chain links rippled in the flashes of daylight streaking through the holes in the derelict roof.

Muuuuūtthherrrr.

The word rumbled around the stable. In a glassless window high in the gable away to their right, the raven landed with a flutter of its wings. A tic developed at Brother Bernard's mouth. "Mother?" he whispered.

The dragon whimpered.

"Then who is your father?"

With another fierce toss of its head, the dragon graarked as though the question was worthy of a bolt of fire. But no fire came. That area of its body still bound by mailing tape bulged with the instinct to spread its wings. But there was no release. Its muted tail pounded the floor in frustration. Its talons raked the earth. It gave no answer.

"Tell me," said Bernard, his throat growing sore

from the demands of a language so lacking in vowels. "Who is your father?"

Caarrkkk! went the raven, making Bernard jump. This bird was beginning to make him uneasy. There was a dark light in the center of its eye. Why was it so often in attendance to the dragon? Was it some kind of familiar? he wondered. A spirit that served the needs of the creature? He heard footsteps nearby. The raven heard them, too. With another moody *caark,* it circled the barn and swooped back into the open air. Startled voices remarked upon it: Brothers Terence and Peter. Bernard centered on the dragon again, "Quickly. Your father?"

The yellow eyes closed. The arches of the nostrils flared like trumpets. *Gaaaawwwaaaaaainn,* said his distant descendant, Grockle.

Bernard backed away with a hand against his throat.

Gawain.

That was all the proof he needed.

Abbot Hugo's Office

Abbot Hugo, I must speak with you, urgently."

The abbot's hand was raised before Brother Bernard was halfway through his sentence. He immediately slowed to a halt, lowered his head, and spoke an apology.

The abbot's hand drifted sideways and pointed absently to the pew seat. He himself was in the leather chair at his desk, hunched forward, reading Brother Vincent's manuscript.

Brother Bernard chose to stand. For the next few minutes he waited patiently, gathering his thoughts as the abbot meticulously turned the pages, lifting them gingerly by the corner and laying each one facedown upon the last in crisp and perfect register. Finally, after reading a page barely one-third filled with the looping green script, he sat back in his chair and removed his glasses.

"What am I to make of this?" He sighed, widening his hands above the leaves of paper as though addressing the cast of characters within.

"Abbot —"

"Is it the work of a madman or a genius?"

"I have only glimpsed through it. I cannot comment. May I speak with you about the creature?"

Abbot Hugo seemed uninterested. "It appears to be a children's fable, and yet . . ." he paused and hung the arm of his spectacles off his lower lip, ". . . there is a definite substance to it. He spoke of this story in the folly, did he not?"

"Yes," said Bernard, trying not to show any sign of impatience. "He claimed it was a fictionalized account of true events."

The abbot gave a burp of incredulity. "Explain."

Now Bernard cursed his slackness of tongue. Five hundred years ago, Brother Vincent would have been sealed alive into these walls for a single mention of the word "dragon," and though his fate in present times would be far less devastating, any affirmation of his beliefs would be met with ridicule and almost certain expulsion from the Order. But to lie would be a sin in itself. Perhaps an outline of the theory of dark matter, followed by the evidence accumulated at the stables, might be enough to persuade the abbot to review these happenings without any prejudice?

"He . . ." But from the beginning, Bernard was stumbling for a choice of words. "He was a physicist before he came here."

Abbot Hugo rocked his chair at a pace befitting his age and stature. "He was. Go on."

Bernard turned to the window. "He believes that reality is not what it seems. If I understand it correctly, he has a theory that contemporaneous events, that is, those happening at identical times but in a different place, can be accessed via a realm of the universe he labels dark matter, a realm invisible to you or I — though he leaves the impression that all of us, all humankind can attain this ability, through an expansion of consciousness."

Abbot Hugo clicked his tongue, a sound he only made when considerably displeased. "Is he taking a drug?"

Bernard turned sharply to face the old man. "A drug?"

"How is he achieving this . . . growth of awareness?"

Bernard slipped his tongue between his lips. They felt cracked and dry. "By using the claw. He seems to think it amplifies the process. He believes, in his . . . cloud of confusion, that dragons are the guardians of the dark realm. My Lord, the creature —?"

Once again, Abbot Hugo raised his hand. "I have been trying, unsuccessfully, to write with this artifact, but I can manage no more than a droplet from it. Did he demonstrate the process?"

"Yes, but —"

The abbot raised a hand for no more interruption. Built onto his desk was a stack of box drawers. Turning the knob on the middle one of three, he slid the drawer open and removed the claw from it. "Please, be good enough to show me."

Bernard loosened his shoulders. Any protest was

pointless. "Very well. Your water." He pointed at a half-filled glass.

Abbot Hugo slid it across the desk.

"Should I write on the manuscript?"

The abbot shook his head. He tidied the two stacks into one and turned it all face up. Then he took a piece of paper no larger than the size of a small chocolate wrapper from a pigeon hole next to the set of box drawers and pushed it within Brother Bernard's reach.

Bernard dipped the claw and squeezed it gently. As he did so, he felt an odd euphoria sweeping through him. A pleasing dizziness he could neither comprehend nor begin to explain. He touched the claw to the paper, squeezed again to produce a flow of ink, and wrote the words "Farlowe Island" across it.

"Intriguing," said the abbot. "Let me try."

But before he could, his attention was drawn by a commotion in the corridor. "What is this?" he demanded, whirling in his seat as the door burst open.

Brother Peter stumbled in, collapsing to one knee. "Wickedness," he panted, reaching for his heart, which seemed in imminent danger of seizing. "Brother Terence . . ."

"What of him?" the abbot said, going to Peter and catching him before he could fall any farther.

"Blinded," he gasped, gripping Abbot Hugo's habit so tightly that the cloth was ripped apart at the collarbone.

"By the creature?"

Peter nodded and fell into a faint.

"Attend to him," Abbot Hugo said, and swept out of the room.

In the corridor, monks were running back and forth, calling for aid and medical supplies. Two cells away, behind a locked door, Brother Vincent was shouting to be released. In the stable block, no doubt, the baby dragon was being stoned with the vilest of words, if not rocks themselves.

And yet Brother Bernard somehow knew that, for the moment, his place was at the abbot's desk. He squeezed the pen again and a new and bizarre impulsion came over him. From the pigeonhole above the paper supply he removed a matching envelope. He looked at Brother

Vincent's manuscript. On the very first page was the name of a character and his address:

David Rain,

42 Wayward Crescent,

Scrubbley, Massachusetts

U.S.A.

This he wrote on the envelope and sealed the note inside it.

Then he went to the aid of the dragon.

Stable Block, Midday

Four monks were clustered around Brother Terence where he sat, propped against the outside of the stable door. Brother Cedric, a retired physician, was holding a cotton pad against his eyes. Bright red blotches on his cheeks and neck suggested he'd suffered some kind of burns. Something yellow (was it vomit?) was splattered down his habit which was wet with copious amounts of water. One leg was twitching uncontrollably. A mumbled prayer was issuing from his lips. There was a halo of deep-rooted fear around him.

Bernard caught the arm of Brother Sebastian. "What happened?"

"The creature spat at him."

"Was it provoked?"

"Does it *matter*? Our brother, Terence, may be blinded. He cannot open one eye; the other is clouded by the creature's vile discharge."

"Has he said nothing of the incident at all?"

"He is mumbling prayer and will not respond to questions. I tell you, this thing should be removed from our world and sent back to the pits of hell it arose from."

Brother Bernard nodded, but said nothing in agreement. He patted Sebastian lightly on the shoulder, prayed for healing to be sent to Brother Terence, and hurried along to the stable block.

"Approach with care," the abbot said, from several yards to the right of the dragon. His voice was calm but his manner solemn. Brother Malcolm, standing slightly forward of him, had the mood and posture of a dragonslayer. The creature itself had withdrawn into a shadowed corner of its pen. Only the occasional blink of light glinted off its leathery green scales.

"I cannot understand this," Bernard said. "I was with the beast not minutes ago and it was perfectly calm. It made no attempt to attack me."

The abbot took no heed of this. Raising his hooked nose he said to Brother Malcolm, "Find a large sack."

Malcolm immediately searched the pallets where wheat and barley had once been stored.

"What are you planning to do?" asked Bernard, feeling a sense of unease creeping over him.

"Do you pity this beast so much?" asked the abbot.

Bernard laced his fingers. "I don't believe it's a demon."

The abbot turned slowly to look at him. "Brother Terence would not agree." And it seemed to Bernard there was a sight more malice in the old man's eyes than he'd seen in any parlay with the dragon.

Malcolm reappeared, shaking ears of straw from a dusty sack.

The abbot pointed to a loose stack of wood. "Choose a piece of board. Something large enough to shield us from any further spittle."

Bernard looked in horror at the sack. "You plan to hood it?"

"There is a monk outside who may never see again. Neither will the beast, for now."

"Abbot, this is monstrous."

"The *wood,*" he growled.

"Allow me," said Malcolm, throwing the sack into Bernard's midriff, who caught it as though it were his prison issue.

"You intend to kill it?"

"I am waiting for an emissary," the abbot said. "He will decide what is to be done."

"Is he part of the brethren?" Bernard asked, nursing a feeling of nervousness. He had not shaken off Brother Vincent's warning: *danger, a wind from another world.*

"That is not your concern," said the abbot.

"But if the Order has always been exclusive to the island, then why —?"

"You worry me," said the abbot, cutting him off. "Increasingly, I find your mood infected by the same misguided sentiments that have addled Brother Vincent."

"The creature should not be tortured," Bernard snapped, switching the emphasis back to the dragon.

But the abbot merely turned and addressed Brother Malcolm, who was holding up a sizeable piece of board. "Advance with caution. Brother Bernard seems not to fear the beast. Let him stand close enough to cover its head."

Brother Malcolm lifted the shield, showing forearms bruised with naval tattoos. But as he set off, Bernard stopped him and said, "I will do this alone."

"What? Are you deranged?"

"The creature has intelligence," Bernard said grittily. "Already, it cowers in the comfort of shadows. If I spring at it suddenly from behind a board it may attack again. Protect yourself if you must." He stepped into the open.

The yellow eyes watched him fearfully. He took two steps forward. The dragon reared its head. Another step and its talons ratcheted the ground. One more. Its ear scales lifted. "Do not resist," Bernard whispered in the tongue, matching his voice to the level of its growl.

"They will kill you if you try. Trust me. I will help you." And he opened the sack and in one fluid movement ran it over the dragon's head.

The baby creature bucked against its chains. *Zaaaannnnnaaaa,* it cried, sneezing, almost blowing the sack away. The material caught against its scales and held.

"Brother, step back," the abbot shouted.

But Bernard had a question of the dragon first. "Why?" he asked. "Why did you spit at Brother Terence?"

And the answer was both confusing and frightful.

Biiirrrrdddd, the dragon whimpered.

Bernard swept around and looked at the gable.

There in the window was the raven again.

"Come away," the abbot insisted.

Brother Malcolm drew Bernard clear.

"This place is forbidden," Abbot Hugo said. To Malcolm, he added: "Have it well guarded." To Bernard: "You may leave."

"Abbot, this dragon —"

"Go, Brother Bernard."

Bernard looked once more at the pitiful creature, then bowed his head and hurried outside, almost fainting as the colder air hit him. He staggered over to a disused water trough and sat upon it, panting, clutching his side. What was happening in this once holy place? Dragons, ravens, burnings, torture. And here he was at the center of it all. He pulled the envelope from the pocket of his habit and stared at it as though it were a sentence of death.

"Brother, are you hurt?" Cedric came up and laid a hand upon his shoulder.

Bernard shook his head. "How is Brother Terence?"

"Not as bad as I feared. The injury is more in his mind than his eyes. I believe he saw something which greatly disturbed him before the creature chose to attack."

"Has he spoken of it?"

"I cannot say; his jabberings are meaningless."

Bernard let out a beaten sigh. Something must be done here. Something which might persuade the abbot to review this creature in a sympathetic light. He tapped the letter against his thigh. "Has the boat arrived from the mainland yet?" Once a week, on this day, a small boat came to bring supplies.

Cedric nodded. "Yes, it moored half an hour ago. Brother Ferdinand and Brother Rufus are helping it unload, taking care to make sure that any visitors are kept well away from our secret."

Our secret. His own inclusion made Bernard want to retch. "I missed prayers this afternoon. I must go to the chapel. Would you grant me a request?"

"Of course," said Cedric.

Bernard handed him the letter. "Please add this to the postal collection. . . ."

Point Scarrow, Canadian High Arctic

The bear was in the road, waiting for him. Sitting. Staring. Squinting through the snow. Every aspect of its body shape spoke of provocation. It was here to mount a challenge. To make itself *known*.

Something in the natural order had changed.

He brought the pickup to a halt and switched off the engine, but left the headlights blazing at the bear. Five miles on the odometer. Five miles south of the polar research base. He glanced at the radio and opened a channel.

"Russ."

"Anders?"

"Got a situation."

"Don't hear your engine. You broken down? Don't say those relays have burned out again?"

"It's a bear, Russ. Down near Scarrow."

"Jeez, what's a bear doing there at this time of year?"

"Don't know. I'm about to take a look. You might want to come down with the can."

"You got time for this? What about your flight?"

In his pocket, the narwhal talisman buzzed.

It sensed danger. Very great danger.

Bergstrom looked behind the seat at the loaded rifle. "Bring the can," he said, and cut the radio link.

Then he stepped out of the pickup, unarmed.

Snow danced in the warmth of the headlights. Silhouetted by their lazy beam, he walked forward at a nonaggressive pace.

Ice clouds dusted around the bear's paws. It altered its stare, but not its position.

Ten yards from contact, Bergstrom stopped walking.

The bear twisted a forepaw, flexing the claws. "Heavy," it said. "Powerful, but cumbersome."

Not a bear, then. A being inside a bear.

"You are Fain," said Bergstrom.

"And you are . . . interesting," the ice bear said.

"How did you come through the portal early?"

The bear blinked as if the question wasn't worthy of respect. "I am tracing a young Fain which broke the continuum. You have been close to it, shaman. You radiate Fain."

A break. G'reth. What had the wishing dragon brought back with him? Bergstrom stayed his breath. "What is your purpose with the young Fain?" he said.

"To retrieve it. To punish it. Then to cleanse this world of dragon. No image of Godith will travel back to the Fain."

"Why?"

"That is not important. Where is the fire of the dragon called Gawain?"

"Hidden."

"Speak the location — or die."

"Why can't you detect it?"

The squint shortened. "I will find it, shaman. And come back and burn your body to ash."

The wind shifted, rolling the snow. Bergstrom moved a hand and the lights of the pickup shrank to black. In that moment, he threw himself forward, changing in the blur to the shape of a bear. His teeth sank into the neck of the Fain. But it was strong and crushed the air out of his lungs with one gigantic closure of its paws. As he slid to the road, the Fain hit him with a blow across the back of his head that neither man nor bear could have possibly withstood.

When Russ found him, twenty minutes later, his fur had been shredded with bloody lines and the airstream falling out of his snout was less measurable than the weight of any snowflake.

The lights of the pickup were on once more, drilling softly through the night.

The vehicle's driver was nowhere to be found.

Russ radioed a major alert. Dazed, he stood over the wounded bear, aiming a handgun at its head.

Compassion demanded that he end its suffering. But though his firearm shook and his trigger finger shortened, curiosity stayed his hand. Might they learn more with the bear alive?

He put away the handgun, and returned to his truck for a tranquilizing gun.

And it was then, while his back was turned, that something squeezed out from beneath the stricken body and rolled a short distance across the road. It was a piece of bone, cut long ago from a narwhal's tusk. The etchings on it were moving rapidly, trying to detect further traces of the Fain. But the being had gone, to continue its search. And so the talisman obeyed its primary order: In emergency, turn into the dragon, Groyne, and seek out David Rain. . . .

Abbot Hugo's Office, Farlowe Island, 1:35 A.M., February 12th

Once, in his childhood, temptation had turned Brother Bernard's head. In Mr. Suneet's, the convenience store, before the modernization had happened and electronic eyes had recorded all movement, he had stolen a tube of candy. He remembered the occasion well. How he had waited by the magazine rack, until the chubby Mrs. Vickers had come down the aisle and stopped to examine the birthday cards, blocking the view from the payment counter. In that instant, he had turned away from righteousness. Away from his parents. His Sunday School. From good. Pocketing the candy had been the easy part. Leaving with them was a different matter. His legs, powered by a burning rush of guilt, had raced him too fast toward the door. He had bumped Mr.

Cardle, the blind man with his dog. The collision had produced a variety of sounds, but the only ones Bernard remembered were the candy, rattling like pellets inside their tube. "Hey!" Mr. Suneet had called. And Bernard had run. At twelve years old, he had become a thief. He had never been caught and the evidence was spilled down a drain within minutes. But his punishment was harsh and would last his life long. His mind was stained with indelible shame — and he could never go back to that shop again.

He was thinking of these things as he slipped into Abbot Hugo's office in the early hours of that February morning. If caught here, his life would be all but over. For this was Mr. Suneet's shop again. Only now, the risks were so much greater. Beyond this island, there was no shelter. No place to run. No drain wide enough to swallow his guilt.

But the questions in his mind would not die down. Throughout the five long days of prayer and meditation, the motive for the creature's attack on Brother Terence had dogged him. Its chilling accusation that the raven was involved cast a shadow far wider than the common viewpoint, a consequence he dared not contemplate too far. And what of his own irrational decision to send a message to Wayward Crescent? What was he hoping to achieve by that? It made his head spin just to think about it, writing to a *character* in a book? Vincent. He must be allowed to talk to Brother Vincent, even though it meant breaking into his cell. Between them, they must formalize effective measures to persuade Abbot Hugo that these incidents required a level of scrutiny beyond narrow-minded bigotry. Everything must be brought into the open. Everything.

He clicked on a flashlight, panning its weak beam over the wall until it struck the metal safe where the keys to every part of the monastery were kept. Bare-footed, he crossed the room and opened the case as quietly as he could. The key to Brother Vincent's cell would be on the bunch with the bright orange tag. Locating it proved less than easy. The safe was never locked, but the contents were often moved around. In the flashlight's glare, every tag looked the same. Steadying his hand, he sifted through them, wincing if a loose key scraped the casing or tangled awkwardly against its hook. What should have taken seconds was moving into minutes when he at last identified the correct group of keys, dropped them in his pocket, and turned for the door.

That was when he knew he was not alone.

An intruder. Down at floor level. Small claws catching against the boards.

Bernard shuddered and clicked off his light. If this was a mouse or, heaven forbid, a rat, he did not want to draw its attention.

But the visitor was neither mouse nor rat. To Bernard's astonishment, a squirrel entered the veil of moonlight filtering in through the tall arched window. It sat up on its haunches and twitched its nose, trying to focus on a scent of some sort. Twice it half-turned and poked its nose again. Then, with an effortless burst of agility, it leaped up onto the abbot's desk.

Bernard watched with a kind of dazed fascination as it hopped toward the box drawers and reached up to sniff at them. It scented the frame of each drawer in turn but seemed most drawn to the central one, the one containing the dragon's claw.

By now, an idea was brewing in Bernard's mind that he was not the only thief in the room that night. But the outcome of this fantasy seemed so ludicrous that, even when the squirrel gripped the painted wooden handle and began to twiddle it as though it were an acorn, he still did nothing to intervene. There was a pause. The squirrel rested and flagged its tail. Then, with hardly a space between the actions, it clamped the drawer knob between its teeth, yanked it open, and leaped inside.

"No!" gasped Bernard and lunged across the room.

Too late. A stream of bright gray fur poured out of the drawer with a dragon's claw clamped tight between its jaws.

"Stop!" Bernard shouted.

The squirrel skidded to a halt on the corner of the

desk. *Chuk!* it throated, its dark eyes popping at the sight of human presence. With a whip of its tail, it turned in a flash and leaped off the desk.

Bernard went in pursuit. But the race was never on. His shin collided with the corner of a footrest, knocking it over with a dreadful clatter. He reached for it, slipped, and shoulder-charged the shelves of perfume bottles. There was a crash of glass. Something pooled in the doorway. The nimble-footed squirrel leaped over it and was gone.

Suddenly, a light went on. Bernard froze in terror. Abbot Hugo's face stared out of the doorway. His eyes panned the room, taking in the key safe and the drawer slid forward and tilting down. He inspected it. Empty. "Replace it," he said.

Bernard covered his face.

"Replace it!" roared the abbot.

"I don't have it," Bernard wept. This was madness. A nightmare. The claw, literally squirreled away. How could he explain it? How?

The abbot turned, hearing footsteps close by. Brother Malcolm appeared, still tying the cord of his nightrobe. "I heard voices, breaking glass . . ." His words tailed off into disbelief.

The abbot plunged his hand into Bernard's robe pocket and pulled out the keys with the bright orange tag. Were they being taken or being returned? He threw them into Malcolm's hands. "Check that Brother Vincent is still in his cell."

Question marks appeared in Brother Malcolm's eyes, but he knew not to argue with the abbot's will. As he hurried away, Hugo turned his ire on Brother Bernard again. "What were you hoping to achieve by this?"

"The truth!" Bernard cried, sinking back against the desk. "There are things occurring here that *you* refuse to see. Things that could change our world forever. The creature you have bound and treated so badly may be closer to God than you or I or any church ever built."

"This is a sickness," said the abbot, appalled. He crossed himself. "First Vincent. Now you."

"Since when was the truth an illness?" shouted Bernard.

The abbot turned his head. Brother Malcolm had returned, pale-faced. "I cannot rouse him."

The abbot's gaze narrowed. "Is he dead?"

Malcolm gulped and shook his head. "He is sitting cross-legged by his window, praying. I cannot shake him from the pose. He seems taken — by some kind of trance."

"He must be working without the claw," muttered Bernard. "Bending the universe by his will. It must have been him who sent the squirrel."

The abbot seized him by the neck of his habit. "Stop babbling. What have you done with it?"

"I have done nothing," Bernard said, his cheeks growing red with rage. "The claw has been taken by a force you could never comprehend. But my guess is that it will not be long before you know precisely what became of it."

For if the claw was not on its way to Vincent, then it was surely on its way to the dragon.

In this, Brother Bernard was correct. Even as the thought had entered his mind, the squirrel was scrambling across the courtyard into the shadow of the stable block. In a blink it had wriggled beneath the padlocked door and bounded into the dragon's pen. The creature, sensitive to any warm blood, lifted its head and twitched its nostrils. Although it could not see the small gray messenger, the cargo it carried raised every flexible scale on its body. It growled and punched its head forward. Lively and fearless, the squirrel swerved away and dived between the dragon's open legs, taking care not to brush the talons with its tail. It dropped the claw as close to the injured back foot as it could. Then it turned and whisked back into the dark.

A quietness came upon the hooded prisoner. Somewhere here was a shadow of the past. The scent of history. A trace of greatness.

Instinctively, its feet moved toward that place, claws spreading wide above the dank and rotting straw. Like a compass needle, the claw of Gawain jumped and flickered, aligning itself with the toes of the foot. The dragon, Grockle, set his foot down. And just as the tooth of the ice bear Ragnar had melded to the jaw of his descendant, Ingavar, so the claw of the last great dragon, Gawain, joined the body of his distant son.

With it came a tingling sense of belonging. Connection to the Earth. Wisdom.

Power.

Wayward Crescent, Late Night, February 12th

She liked to read in bed. Magazines, mostly. Something glossy. Homes and gardens. Although she had never been particularly house-proud, and the garden was defaulting to a "wild" state, Elizabeth Pennykettle liked to imagine that something better could always be achieved.

That night, however, the night the Fain invaded her home, she had been unable to settle. The magazines lay unread on her blanket. Her cup of hot chocolate had already cooled leaving a milky skin on its surface. For an endless time she sat among her pillows, staring at the wall, worried about Lucy, terrified for David.

Gwillan was the first to notice the change. He gave a short *hurr* of surprise and flew from her table to the small corner bedpost, arching his wings and tufting his ears.

"What is it?" Liz said, sitting forward. She, too, was aware of something now. She gazed at several abstract places, before deciding that the presence she could feel descending was centering itself around the Dragon's Den. Throwing off the blanket, she leaped out of bed, wearing nothing but a pair of blue cotton pyjamas.

Gwillan called out again as the air filled with an urgent sense of pressure. Perfume bottles rattled on the dressing table. Books fell sideways on their shelves. The lights went out, then pulsed back in. There was a breakage somewhere in the Dragon's Den.

"Hide!" Liz shouted to the terrified puffler, and ran, barefoot, along the landing.

The wave hit her the moment she opened the door. She screamed and was thrown back against a rack of shelves, bringing it and many dragon sculptures crashing down around her. A picture of Lucy flew off the mantelpiece and crossed the room tumbling like the blade of a propeller. Several items on the workbench were swept to the floor. The anglepoise lamp took a sharp uppercut, banging back against the wall and snapping its springs. The lightbulb popped and fell from its housing. Chips of broken clay were everywhere.

Suddenly, there was a mighty roar and Gruffen grew to three times his size. This had always been a planned defense against any kind of break-in or attack. Built into the guard dragon's auma was a key which allowed him to manifest a magnified image of himself as the fire-breathing monster the human race fondly assigned to his species. But the enemy here was far from human.

The Fain twisted into him, and finding nothing but a minimal outflow of auma, stole his fire as quickly as a wet thumb puts out a candle. The guard dragon lapsed into his solid state and fell to the floorboards, snapping his tail. The door clattered and the air in the den became still, though elsewhere in the house the whirlwind continued.

"What's happening?" Liz cried to any dragon who could answer. She crawled across the floor to her beloved Gruffen and was met there by a shaken G'reth.

Hrrr, he explained in a trembling voice. The Fain he had brought back into the house was being chased by a larger, evil one.

Liz wiped a bloodstained hand across her mouth. "Close down. All of you. Now." And staggering to her feet, she hurried downstairs.

The outcome of the chase was never in doubt. All the master Fain was seeking was a suitable host to drive the upstart into for a time. To lock it away until the work at the north of this planet was done. Then to return and punish it properly.

It found what it sought in the Pennykettles' kitchen. A fur-covered quadruped of low intelligence, whose auma was now in gradual decline.

All Bonnington had ever wanted was a quiet life. A warm basket. A tickle of the ears. The occasional bowl of Chunky Chunks. When the young and terrified Fain flew into him and was locked into his cells by its more advanced pursuer, all prospect of serenity ended. Yowling wildly, he bolted around the kitchen before trying to throw himself out through his catflap. He missed and hit his head against the plastic frame, knocking himself out cold in the process.

Trinnnnnggg!

The doorbell rang.

Rap! Rap! Rap!

Someone walloped the panels.

"Mrs. P.!" cried a voice. "Are you all right?"

"Henry, go back home!" Liz shouted. She was in the hall now, trying to sense the location of the Fain.

"Heard noises! Sounded like you might be in trouble —"

His voice stopped abruptly.

"Henry?" Liz called. "Henry, are you all right?" She slid back the bolt and opened the door a crack. "Henry? Agh!"

He was inside in a moment, examining his hands, rolling his shoulders. A blue light swirled around the pupils of his eyes. "Aged," he said, "minimal power."

"No power whatsoever. Let him go," Liz said.

His arm came up and took her by the throat, forcing her backward down the hall. "You have many connections," said the Fain.

"I'm not your enemy," she croaked, as he stretched her neck fully till her head went back and made contact with the wall.

"You have history with the dragon in the north. You are hybrid to its auma. And you have *offspring*."

"Please," Liz said, though the word was barely audible.

"I sense the dragon's fire in this place."

Liz waggled a hand towards the kitchen. "Take it. In the cold box. Go."

"Minimal. Where is the rest?"

"Don't know," she said, trying to shake her head free. Something cold and inhuman spiked her brain. She cried out in terror, her fingernails gouging paper from the walls.

"You speak the truth," said the Fain, then chillingly added, "yet you still have something to protect."

"No!" she squealed, as his left hand came up to cradle her skull and make a full circuit throughout her head.

The human eyes blinked. "Your . . . creations have touched my world. They are working for a master. Where is he?"

"He went away. Please, leave us be."

"Where is he?" growled the Fain, using the masculine edge in the human host's voice.

"I can take you to him," a quieter voice said.

"She's lying!" Liz cried, recognizing the voice of the betrayer.

"Sleep," said the Fain, and threw her, collapsing in a heap, to one side.

The figure of Henry turned around to see a small clay dragon, sitting on the stairs.

"I know where he is," she said, and proudly displayed her bouquet of flowers.

Dunlogan, Scotland, February 13th

They traveled as Henry Bacon and clay figurine. Human male, insignificant sculpture. For the Fain, a being capable of moving through the vastness of space and time purely by the power of conscious thought, it was drudgery of the highest order. Bones, muscle, blood, skin. How did these humans cope with such oppressive vibrations? Why did they still submit to G'ravity?

The Fain looked through its human eyes, studying the clay on the table in front of it. The clay seemed to be enjoying the passage, as though it had traveled on one of these cumbersome vehicles before. It was here with some kind of stratagem, of course. But he would snuff it out when his work was complete. For now, it merely intrigued him to observe how this creature, cleverly constructed in the image of Godith and animated by a spark of genuine dragon fire, would interact with the master it called "the David." What did this human mean to the clay?

The vehicle, the thing they called "train," halted. The dragon shook its flowers, indicating they should leave. Henry rose from his seat. He glanced briefly at the human that had challenged him for payment and was now slumped against the window opposite, then left the carriage with Gretel in his hands.

They reached the dockside on foot. It was raining heavily by then. The materials covering the human's skin had become far weightier still, and it was this that attracted the attention of a man, sheltering beneath a brightly colored awning over a wooden hut decked with fishing nets.

"My goodness. You are soaked!" The man stood up. He was tall and bald-headed and dressed in gray. Under his arm was a leather briefcase. On his feet were a pair of sandals.

"What are you?" said Henry.

The man appeared confused. "My name is Brother Darius. I am a man of God. Please, take shelter."

"You are traveling to the island."

Brother Darius looked to one side. "The island is not open to tourists at the moment. You would need special dispensation, I'm afraid."

"I travel where I please," Henry said. And throwing Gretel aside (she flew to the awning), he stepped closer, then suddenly collapsed to the ground.

During that second of brief confusion, Brother Darius was still himself. But as the Fain left Henry and invaded the monk, it quickly learned the nature of this brother's mission and used the muscles around his mouth to pull the lips into a satisfied smile.

A jeep drew up. Two figures in wet weather clothing got out. One, a bearded man with no other hair said, "Is it you who'll be wanting a boat, brother?"

The other, spotting Henry's prostrate body, hurried over to crouch beside him. "Och, now. What's this?"

"I do not know him," Darius said.

"Mebbe a drunk," muttered the man. "Did you see him go over? This chap's barely alive, Dougie. He needs a hospital."

"You take him," said the bearded man, thumbing at the jeep. "I'll take this brother across to Farlowe."

Farlowe Island, February 13th

At two o'clock, the fishing boat docked on the jetty. Brother Darius, dressed in a plain gray habit, stepped off and strode purposefully along the landing stage. Hiding in his cowl was a potions dragon. High above the waterline, thunder rumbled, gathering the boat back into the gloom.

Brother Feargal, sent to wait for an unnamed visitor, turned his umbrella and hurried across the planking to greet the stranger. Despite the persistent rain, the gray monk's cowl lay flat against his shoulders. Crowns of water were breaking on his head. There was barely any color around his puckered mouth. He looked up, his dark eyes drilling through the drenching rain.

"Brother, let me shelter you," Feargal said, tilting the umbrella like a spindly toadstool.

The gray monk raised a hand, a movement that seemed to pause weather and time. "Thank you . . . brother, but I find the rain refreshing."

Brother Feargal looked aghast. "You will suffer a chill. The winter is barely done and —"

"I do not feel the cold," the gray monk interrupted, speaking with such an air of supremacy that Feargal, awestruck, stumbled back a pace.

"As you wish. Where are your belongings?"

"I have no need of belongings," said the monk. The briefcase he had dropped overboard on the crossing.

"I see," said Feargal, though he was clearly confused. "Come, let me guide you, the abbot is expecting you." He turned for the narrow path between the rowan trees, only to see that the stranger was already making for it.

"Thank you. I can find my way."

"You have visited the island before, Brother . . . ?"

"Darius," he said. "You may call me Brother Darius."

Feargal nodded. An unfamiliar name. And the dark gray cloth, unusual also. "Forgive my curiosity, Brother Darius, but may I ask what Order you are from?"

"I do not belong to any Order," said the monk, as though to suggest it was some kind of insult.

Feargal, sensing a warning note, bowed and decided he would not dig deeper. This visitor, this emissary (as the rumors among the brethren had it) was clearly some kind of high-ranking official. But what kind of monk had no fellow brothers? It set a troubled nerve ticking in Feargal's head.

"Have you traveled far?"

"I am here," said Brother Darius. "That is all that matters."

"Yes, of course," mumbled Feargal. "I . . ." He rubbed his head. Was that rain beneath his fingers or pearls of sweat? What was it about this man that disturbed him so?

They passed through the gardens, dead now of flowers, and on toward the gift shop, closed for the winter. Here, Brother Darius paused a moment and directed his gaze toward the roof.

There was nothing on the tiles but moss and rain. Feargal, with a nervous squint, inquired, "What is it? What do you see?"

"A shadow," the gray monk said, and turned his powerful gaze to the priory, at its stone walls planted in the lush wet rise of green embankments. "There is a dragon among us."

The tic in Feargal's head became a major shudder. Clumsily, he brought his hands together. A carousel of raindrops flew off his umbrella. "The island is stained by its presence," he jabbered. "Have you come to deliver us, brother?"

The sky opened and lightning flashed beneath the clouds. Briefly, within it, the shape of a wide-winged raven could be seen, circling above the stable block. Brother Darius made a strange kind of rumble in his throat. “There are many forces at work here,” he said. “And soon, brother, you will see one more.”

And he smiled a smile that had little to do with joy and much to do with malice.

Then he walked on toward the monastery.

Alone.

Abbot Hugo's Office, Fifteen Minutes Later

"This is it," said Abbot Hugo. "The results of his labor. Allegedly written in the blood of the beast, through the use of its claw — which has disappeared, still unaccounted for."

He stood away from his desk, allowing Brother Darius to view the manuscript. The gray monk cast his eye at the papers, then slowly withdrew a hand from his sleeves. He picked up the top page and sniffed it carefully. "Have you read this?" He quietly put the sheet aside.

Abbot Hugo nodded. "Our unworthy brother, Bernard Augustus, believes the story is a means for Brother Vincent to purge his emotions of a past relationship."

The gray monk nodded, and shifted his gaze across the room. "Where is the claw?"

Bernard, sitting on a stool by the window, sat up slightly, popping his jaw.

"Answer him," Abbot Hugo commanded.

"I believe the dragon has it."

"By what means?"

"I saw a squirrel take it," Bernard said, flushing brightly and breaking sweat. The gray monk's stare was so invasive. His eyebrows, black and sharply arched, were like tunnels hiding heaven knew what.

"Nonsense!" Abbot Hugo snorted, blowing fiercely into a tissue. "You expect us to believe that a *rodent,* a creature of low intelligence, broke into my drawer and removed the claw?"

"He is telling the truth," Darius said darkly.

The abbot's eyes swelled with disbelief. "But that's preposterous. How can you —?" His speech was interrupted by a knock at the door. "Yes! What is it?"

Brother Malcolm stepped in. "Abbot, forgive the interruption, but I thought you ought to know that Brother Terence is running about the corridors, prattling wildly about his attack. He is saying he saw —"

"An angel!" cried a voice, and in burst Brother Terence, eyes as large as hard-boiled eggs. He ran to Brother Bernard and clamped his hands, shaking them as though they were a cup of dice. "An angel, brother. A dark-haired angel." He jumped towards the abbot. "She appeared before my eyes!"

"Restrain him!" cried the abbot, as Terence fell against him, clinging to his robe like a wild dog.

"I will deal with this," Brother Darius said, stopping Brother Malcolm before he could advance. He tapped Brother Terence lightly on the shoulder. As he turned, Brother Darius gripped his wrist and pulled it down as if striking a lever.

Terence, swaying slightly, stared back mesmerized.

"You saw an angel," said Darius. "Describe it to me."

"Hair," pined Terence, his pupils expanding. "Hair as dark as the perfect night. Wings, brother. Beautiful wings. I tried . . . I . . ." With a pained expression, he stretched out a hand.

"You tried to touch her?"

Terence nodded, helping a tear stream down his cheek. "I meant no harm. No harm at all. But the creature . . ." He stood back. "No! No! No!" And suddenly he was buckling up, covering his face.

Brother Malcolm caught him around the midriff as he fell, and took him down to the safety of the floor.

"There!" snapped Bernard, rounding on the abbot. "He was trying to touch an angel and the creature protected it. Doesn't that prove that —?"

"It was not an angel," Brother Darius cut in. "Merely a spirit, in the guise of a bird."

"Bird?" said Bernard. He searched the bald-headed face for more.

"On my walk here, I saw a raven. A bird often associated with portents and spirits."

"Is it friend or foe?" Bernard gulped.

"That depends on which side you stand," said Darius.

"Oh, this is beyond me!" the abbot blustered. "Birds. Squirrels. Mystical scribblings. I applied to the Elders for advice upon this creature, and the sooner it is done, the sooner my brethren can return to their sanity. Please, shall we go to the stables and finish this?"

"No," said Brother Darius, gathering up his sleeves. "First I will commingle with Brother Vincent."

"Commingle?" said the abbot. "What kind of phrase is that?"

"He means to mix, to share thoughts," Bernard muttered, trying to reason out why his head was suddenly so full of doubts about this monk.

The abbot ran a troubled hand across his brow. "Oh, very well, if you must. This way —"

A knock. Yet another monk appeared at the door. Brother Rufus, striking a timid pose.

"Not now," said the abbot, sweeping past with Darius and Bernard close behind.

Brother Rufus bowed to him, quietly grateful. He had been guarding the restless dragon when, of all things, the lightbulb in the barn had blown with a pop that had showered the floor with heated glass, scaring him nine-tenths out of his wits. It did not take a genius in electrical wiring to know right away that the cause was not simple wear and tear. He had tracked the problem to this piece of cable, taken from the base of the central support. He twisted it once or twice in his hand. Teeth. One could see the indentations. Sharp teeth, gnawing through the plastic sheathing. Annoying, but what was done was done. He had better light a lantern and return to his duties.

Teeth. Yes.

Probably a rat.

Abbot Hugo's Office, Ninety Seconds Later

It was a nuisance, but it had its worth sometimes. He had bought it to record important messages when he was away at prayer. It would cut in after just four rings. The manual had instructions on how to change that, but manuals irritated Abbot Hugo, almost as much as telephones themselves.

That day when it cut in, a woman left a message. In a clear but troubled voice she said: "My name is Elizabeth Pennykettle. I wish to leave an urgent message for a student called David Rain, who I believe may be with you any moment now. Please tell him to call me or come straight home. It's very important. I believe he's in serious danger." {PAUSE} "And if . . . if a monk called Brother Arthur is among you, please tell him I never really went away. . . ."

Stable Block Barn, Same Time

A tearing. He thought he heard a tearing sound. A crack not unlike the sharp snap of cardboard when the staples are torn from the walls of a box. Coming, he thought, from the dragon pen.

Snap!

Yes. There it was again. He tilted the lantern, swinging amber light deeper into the barn. The hooded creature was half in shadow. But half was all that Brother Rufus needed to see.

A wing! Heaven help us! A wing extending! The mailing tape ripped through, torn along the ventral line of the chest! As the full extent of his horror gelled, the dragon struck out fitfully, crashing the wing into a stack of hay bales. The wire binding them was sliced in an instant, severed so fiercely the ends coiled into zinging pigtails. The dry air filled with flying grass seed, topped by the dragon's unearthly squeal. Brother Rufus threw his lantern aside, bolted for the courtyard, and screamed for help.

The dragon, Grockle, still growing in strength, yanked on his neck chain, straining it taut. On the third time he did this, he caused a small movement in the purlin above. The ancient timber, stout but riddled with wood-boring insects, cracked at its center and pulled into a *v*. With another wild tug the purlin snapped and the chain flew clear, lashing its captive with a clatter of steel. Rafters creaked. A rotted timber fell, shattering on the anvil of the cobbled floor. Near to it burned the abandoned lantern, its yellow light flaring as the oil it drew upon spilled from its well. Though unsafe, there was no real danger of combustion. The lamp lay on stone, with little loose straw around. It would take a deliberate act of arson to cause a blaze of unstoppable proportions.

But that was precisely what was in Brother Vincent's mind.

The squirrel had done him such good service. Now it would undertake one last mission. Drag the lantern into the straw and set the stable block alight. Then would come the final proof that the dragon, Grockle, was a savior to them all.

Lying out, in his state of heightened consciousness, he pictured the squirrel clamping its teeth around the lantern top. But it was hot, and the little creature squeaked and jumped back. The lid of the lantern, loosened by the bite, fell away slightly from its glass walls. A naked tongue of flame poked out.

Vincent's eyeballs flickered under their lids. Another way. He must find another way. This thought line was too ambitious for the squirrel. Perhaps if it laid a bridge of straw between the hay bales and the —

"Wake!"

The word fell into his mind like a pebble breaking the waters of perception. The squirrel, the dragon, all disappeared, replaced by a rushing sense of fear.

"Wake!" the voice commanded again.

A concentrated force of heat above his eyes. When

he opened them, he felt a hand on his forehead and stared up into the face of death. Its colorless mouth gave a smug little twitch. "It's over, brother," the thin lips said.

Erasure. Darkness. The blades of wickedness cutting and stirring his memories into sludge. Brother Vincent, Arthur, physicist, monk, cried out and clutched at the corners of his mind, as voices elsewhere were shouting for sanctuary. *The dragon is empowered and breaking loose! God in his mercy, save us all!*

But the loudest shout of all was that of Brother Peter. Scrawny of body, burly of lung: "FIRE! FIRE IN THE STABLE! FIRE!"

Brother Darius, hearing it, snatched away his hand. He scowled at Brother Vincent, as though the man had outwitted him.

"Fire?" called the abbot, hurrying out of the cell.

Brother Bernard rushed to Brother Vincent's side. He pored over the body, feeling for a pulse. "Is he revived?"

"He is empty. No longer any threat."

"Threat? To whom?"

STABLE BLOCK BARN, SAME TIME

FIRE! FIRE!

"Lead me to this hybrid dragon."

"What *are* you?" said Bernard, standing in his path. "What have you done to this man?!"

In a move so swift Bernard didn't see it happen, Darius clamped a hand across the fat monk's forehead. "Well, well. Even you have been an instrument in this comedy."

Grimacing, Bernard sank to his knees.

"Now," said Darius, leaving him gasping. "Now the finale begins."

By the time Brother Bernard had regained his senses, the barn in which the baby dragon had been chained was already a mass of crackling flame. He arrived to see cinders spitting high into the air, and smoke, coaxed by the falling drizzle, winding eastward toward the sea. The large outer wall was standing proud, charring rapidly at its base. But the lower one closest to the monastery itself had begun to fall inward, drawing down the roof. It was here that the abbot had positioned the brethren, with long poles, planking, anything they could find with which to push the wall in farther, to foil any chance of the fire migrating. With a grinding crack! a row of panels went over. Rafters buckled. The roof caved in. The stench of melting roofing felt tarred the air. A great crown of debris, sparks, and ash erupted from the ground and blew back in a cluster. Several brothers cried out or dropped to their knees as the embers caught on their clothing and skin. But in contrast to the wretched, piercing screeches issuing from the burning pyramid of wood, their shouts were merely whispers on a distant wind. Bernard's stomach squeezed itself out like a sponge.

The creature, the dragon, was trapped in the blaze.

"How was this started?" he cried, falling down. He looked through the smoke at the blackened faces. Brother Malcolm was tottering, exhausted, through the debris. He was covering his ears to block out the screeches.

"Who started this?" Bernard shouted again. He struggled up and pulled Brother Malcolm around. "Who set it on fire?" He shook the man hard.

"It was escaping," Malcolm mumbled. "I . . . there was a lantern . . ."

Graaarrrrrkkkk!

"Brother, what have I done?"

"Pray for it!" said Bernard, making Malcolm kneel. "Pray for it!" he screamed, running to the others, purging them with swipes of an illusory stick. "It feels pain! It cries out! It has a soul. PRAY!"

And one by one, each brother, including a dazed and despectacled Abbot Hugo, settled to his knees and began to beseech his Heavenly Father to send this creature to a better place.

Only one, Brother Darius, did not join in. He was looking back an impossible distance, beyond the gardens and the rowan trees, toward the jetty where another small boat had just docked a passenger. A young man, a civilian, was sprinting along the stage, clearly heading for the source of the blaze. Brother Darius turned his face to the sky, the color blue running through his sharp gray eyes. There, a far greater distance away, the fire star was starting to reach its zenith. Less than a day before the portal opened fully. He returned his gaze to the dragon and the monks.

With a sudden inward rush of air, the fire consuming the barn went out.

Startled gasps cut short the prayers. The brethren looked to one another for guidance.

A wisp or two of smoke twizzled out of the pyre. Blistered, shriveled relics of timber cracked and shifted, finding new levels. The shoulder of the dragon poked through the mess. Bloodless. Gray. Like solid stone.

Then, as the rain increased a little and the dying wood hissed and the earth around it fizzed, a shade of green rose through the dragon's shoulder, forming into a pattern of scales. A breath of movement rippled the wood.

Then the mighty wings came out.

Fragments, some as large as untouched rafters, flew out sideways in both directions. What did not strike the flesh of human skin, splintered windows, charcoaled walls, or simply came to rest in the open fields.

The dragon rose. Its body, flushed with its newborn energy, grew in girth again by the length of a scale. The manacles around its feet and neck burst like useless paper hoops.

Brother Bernard, one of the few uninjured, watched it shake away the last flakes of wreckage and turn its eyes on the screaming humans. "Please," he begged, "we only want to help you."

The dragon snorted a sulfurous blast, powerful enough to knock Bernard over.

"Don't hurt me," he begged, scrabbling in the dirt. "God have mercy. Please, don't hurt me."

The eyes slid, the wings gyred. The creature, head back, roared at the rain. And where there had once been water, there was steam.

"Grockle!" cried a voice. "Grockle, it's me!"

But by then the young dragon had taken to the sky. And the only further signs of fire after that were those short blasts flowing out of its throat as it banked instinctively toward the north.

DAVID AND DARIUS

"Arthur? Which of you is Arthur?"

The young man, David Rain, skidded to a halt, squinting through the smoke at the bodies and the wreckage.

"Help me!" croaked a voice nearby. Brother Cedric, blood pouring from a wound to his ear, gripped David's knee with the strength of a monkey.

David knelt and tore the sleeve of Cedric's habit, using the cloth as a makeshift pad. "What happened here?" he asked, laying Cedric down with his palm holding the bandage in place.

But Cedric, delirious with pain and dread, could only gaze at the sky and burble, "God bless you. . . ."

David left him and ran toward Brother Ferdinand,

who was limping to the aid of Abbot Hugo and others. "Please, help me. I must find Brother Arthur."

Ferdinand, his long chin blackened by smoke, shook his head and almost fell. "No one here goes by that name."

David blew a raindrop off his nose. "One of you must know —?" Suddenly, he felt a hand on his shoulder. He turned to see a smaller, tubbier monk.

"Are you . . . ? Are you *David*?"

"Yes."

Brother Bernard closed his eyes and almost wept. He interlaced his fingers and bit a knuckle. "Then everything Arthur told me is true."

David put a hand out to stop the man shaking. "Where *is* he?"

"Come, I will take you to him."

"You will not," said a voice.

Standing in the smoke was a bald-headed man, his hands resting in the sleeves of his habit.

"Who are you?" said David, aware that Brother

Bernard was melting away as though to clear the ground for some kind of duel.

"You command the clay figures," Darius said. "You are a friend of dragons."

David looked the man up and down. "You're Fain," he whispered. But nothing like the one G'reth had brought back. An overwhelming aura of deep malevolence surrounded this man, this shell of a man, perhaps. Then came another shock. From out of his cowl, a small figure fluttered into the air. David gave a start of recognition: Gretel. "What's she —?" He stopped himself. "You've been to the house."

Gretel, annoyed that he'd spoken out, flicked her tail and waved a paw across her mouth.

Darius took a step forward.

David instinctively took a step back, a long cold horror seeping through him. "If you've hurt Liz or the dragons, I'll kill you."

"You are not capable," Darius snarled. "Nothing on this torpid planet could move at the same vibration as the Fain."

"Why are you here?" David asked it, suddenly aware that he had not been deserted after all. Bernard had circled around behind the gray monk and was picking up a heavy piece of wood from the pyre.

"To cleanse this world of dragons."

"Why, when they're dying out on your homeworld?"

The human lips puckered into a smile. "You have been making connections, human."

David stroked the wet hair off his forehead. "I've got powerful connections, trust me."

Darius advanced again. "The shaman bear and the sibyl I have dealt with. All that remains are you, the clay creatures, and the hybrid dragon."

David glanced into the sky. There was no sign of Grockle. "Why didn't you kill him while you had the chance?"

"The hybrid will go to the island," said Darius. "When the portal opens, he will call all dragonkind to his side. There is a pure fire hidden somewhere in the north. Its reading is diffuse, but the hybrid will find it."

David leveled his gaze. "I wouldn't bank on it."

For a small man, Bernard had remarkable strength. Though the skin of his palms was blistering with the heat, he brought a burned rafter down with such crushing force on the gray monk's head that the man appeared to be driven slightly into the ground. As he buckled, Bernard roared and swung at him again. Darius went over and fell, mouth open, hard to the cobbles.

Gretel immediately flew to David and pushed her flowers right under his nose.

Hrrr! she went. *Don't argue, just sniff!*

David took in the scent and staggered back, blinking.

"Evil," Bernard panted, shedding tears of despair, crying out as if confession was all that was left to him. He threw the murderous rafter aside. "I felt it in his touch. He damaged Arthur. Come, I will take you to his cell."

But then it was David who was crying out suddenly. He dropped to his knees, pitching forward.

"What ails you?" said Bernard, reaching out, and was immediately thrown aside by a force which left him sprawling on his back.

David scraped at the weeds between the cobbles.

The world pulsed and came back tainted blue. The Fain was inside him, seeking knowledge.

The clay figures. Why were you chosen as their master?

A trail of vomit left David's mouth.

What do you know about the dragon-made stone?

His eardrums buzzed. His brain would not respond.

You are unclear, the Fain said irritably.

Blankness. Tumbleweed blowing through his head.

A bear, it said. *I read an image of a bear with a sacred tooth. This is your primary connection? A fable?*

David's mind was empty of answers.

Where is the tear of the dragon Gawain?

Lurching forward, he vomited again.

You are trivial, said the Fain. *Unimportant.*

And it left him and returned to its previous host.

As if he had not had to witness enough, Brother Bernard was now about to face the horror of what he'd thought was a dead man, rising.

"I am leaving," said Darius, slurring the words. Within the deeply cracked skull, the brain was hemorrhaging and barely functional. But there was still enough auma present in the body for the Fain to regenerate its energies for travel.

The man who had once been Brother Darius shimmered, turned gray, then dropped again, this time never to recover.

Bernard let out an anguished cry.

"Don't worry, it's gone," David said. Dizzily he got to his feet, wet stains marking both knees of his jeans. "The man you think you killed was already effectively dead, possessed and stripped by an alien life-form called the Fain."

Bernard put his fingertips against his temples, as though his head might fall apart at any moment. He was about to say, "Aliens?" when he jumped back again, startled at the sight of a dragon appearing in David's hands.

"This is Gretel," David said. "She was made by a woman called Elizabeth Pennykettle, who Arthur was in love with once."

"He still is," said Bernard, looking pained.

David nodded and stroked Gretel's wing. "She just saved my life. She gave me a potion that stopped my mind being read by the Fain."

"But —?"

"She can move. You won't see her in her animated form. Only when she's solid like this. We talk, too." And he asked Gretel what had happened at the house.

She told him quickly, explaining how she had led the Fain away before it could hurt Liz any more.

David gently kissed her head. "Go. Find more flowers," he whispered, and threw her upward into the rain. He turned to an openmouthed Brother Bernard. "I need to follow the Fain to the Arctic."

"The Arctic? From here? David, it's impossible."

"Take me to Arthur. He'll know what to do."

Bernard gave an anxious gulp. "Brother Vincent — Arthur — was laid low by Darius."

"Low?"

"Insensible. As if in a coma."

David closed his eyes and gave a sigh of defeat.

It was short-lived, broken by a *hrrr* from Gretel. She buzzed past his ear, drawing his attention to a shimmering in the air.

David put out his hand again. And this time it was the dragon, Groyne, who materialized into it.

Part Four

Tooth of Ragnar, February 14th

Lucy had always been a late sleeper, but even she knew that her current "nap" was far more extended than a Sunday morning rest. She opened her eyes in complete darkness, immediately aware of something warm and extremely large lying beside her. Her underfed stomach at once tried to retch as the stench of the animal's sweat and feces entered her cold but sensitive nostrils. The movement made it shuffle a paw. Lucy yelped and paddled her feet. In turn the bear growled and lifted its head.

"Are you him?" Lucy chattered. "The bear who came before?" She crossed her fingers and shut her eyes tight. It made no difference at all to her vision, but she felt a little safer for it.

The bear slid away from her and rocked to its feet.

Another winter through. More ice in her joints. Alive, but groggy. She yawned at death.

"Help," said Lucy, whimpering a little. She coiled up, fearing she might be trampled.

But the mother bear, used to dealing with young, lowered her snout and nudged her aside, then turned her face to the bitter draft of air flowing down the tunnel.

Snow, laid thick on the mountainside. Ice, beginning to think about melting. Air, looking for a warming sun. She could scent the end of winter approaching.

But above all this, she could scent male bears.

They were commonplace, of course, but never in this quantity. Every male from the western runs must have descended on the island. Either that, or her old snout was playing tricks on her. Or death had yawned at *her* instead.

No, the child was real. She remembered her, sleeping on the floor of the cave. A trace of Sunasala on her furless skin. Were the bears here for the *child,* perhaps? Was she a wonder? A spirit among men? She shook herself down and snorted at the tunnel. Whatever the answer, she had made a pledge, and she would do exactly what she always did. Go outside. Make herself known to the ice. Check conditions. Protect her young. Even this girl. To the point of death.

“Lord, there are two humans approaching.”

Ingavar tipped his snout to the wind. “From which direction?”

“South and west of the island, where the ice is clear of ridges.”

Ingavar let his steady gaze roll, then squinted back at the Tooth of Ragnar. It was magnificent, he thought: black against the moody reflections of the ice, its hollows tinted yellow by the light of the star, layers of purple-gray sky above it. Ragnar’s island. Sunasala’s denning place.

His heritage.

“Is one of them the girl we spared?”

“We cannot tell.”

Ingavar focused on the end of his snout. “Find them. Surround them. Stop their progress.”

The bear dipped his head in salute.

"Wait — is the pack in place?"

"They are situated evenly around the island. If the creature appears, we are ready to attack. There is still no scent of the Lord Thoran. Do you wish me to send a party in search of him?"

Ingavar ground his lower jaw, feeling for the tooth of his ancestor, Ragnar. This was a mystery he could not fathom. Where was the creaky, starseeking Teller? He looked back high above his shoulder, where the star he'd been following for so long now was shaping a strange void out of the darkness. "Thoran will find his own way," he said, hoping that his words showed no imbalance between optimism and fear. "Be prepared."

The bear bowed and was ready to sweep away when he turned again and said, "Oh, there is a female denning on the island. She was just seen at the lip of a cave."

A muscle twitched above Ingavar's eye. "Were there young?"

"We have no scent of any."

Ingavar puffed his chest. "She will be greatly troubled

by our presence. If she brings out cubs, they are not to be harmed. Chase her and her young away, if you can."

"Calm the dogs!" snapped Zanna. "Calm the dogs. You won't get hurt if you just stand still."

Tootega said, "Nanuk is all around us. I pray they eat you first."

"Y'know, for a hunter, you're such a bore."

Despite his terror, the Inuk said, "What does this mean, 'bore'?"

"I rest my case," Zanna said. "Shoot nothing. Let me do the talking."

She took off her mittens and flipped back her hood. With one shake of her head, her black hair, still festooned with charms, fell out across the shoulders of her furs.

Ordering the dogs to stop their yapping, she set off toward the nearest bear.

"Ai-yah," wailed Tootega.

"Shut up," she said, "or you and that sled go down an icy hole."

Thirty paces from the bear, she stopped and pointed to the space between them.

The bear looked down, and saw the mark of Oomara burned into the ice.

Instantly, he lay down in front of her. Around the circle every bear did the same.

"I am Zanna," she said. "Daughter of Gwendolen. Sibyl of the North. Defender of the ice. Like you, I am here to protect the island. OK, that's the speech. Now, one of you stand up and take me to Ingavar. . . ."

"Excuse me. Please, don't growl, but —"

The bear swung around and snorted in surprise.

"Hhh!" went Lucy, jumping to attention with her arms squeezed tightly by her sides. "I'm just hungry and I needed to stretch my legs. And, y'know, use the *bathroom*?"

The mother bear squinted.

"Ohh," Lucy wailed, "you're not him, are you? You don't understand anything I *say*?"

The female snorted again and peered back at the open cavemouth. What was this manchild thinking of? There were more males roaming than claws on her feet. If this girl was scented, they might attack.

"Can I look?" said Lucy, cupping her eyes, even though the light outside was little brighter than it was in the cave. She could make out the color yellow, she thought, and remembered the star she'd seen before she slept. She edged forward.

Ruuffe, went the bear, forcing her back.

"Hhh! All right, I'll stay in the cave. Where's Gwilanna? You haven't eaten her, have you? You didn't have a raven for breakfast once?"

Ruuffe.

Lucy dropped her shoulders. No Gwilanna. That was a worry.

Around and about them, the body of the island rumbled gently. Lucy touched the wall and said hello to Gawain, then drew the isoscele out of her pocket, where she'd placed it for safekeeping while she'd climbed the tunnel. "This is part of him," she said, and held the piece up for the bear to see. One loose ray of starlight made it glint.

And somewhere in the distance a creature called.

Lucy Pennykettle's jaw dropped open. "That . . . that was a *dragon,*" she said.

The shoulder wound no longer ached, but sitting occasionally made Ingavar stiff. He was standing up, stretching, turning a circle, when he heard the same call that Lucy had picked up from the cave. Far away, he saw a terrible shape in the sky.

A great bird — that was how Thoran had said it would look — was approaching across the expanse of sea ice. He could see its long wings beating in the half-light, whipping it on toward the island. To his left, he heard a bear give an open-throated growl, carrying the warning out to the pack. But why was the bird in open sky and not rising from stone as Thoran had suggested? What was happening here?

With a whoosh that drove an ice cloud into his face, the dragon swept over Ingavar's head, circled the island, and landed on the very tip of the Tooth.

Grraaaarrkkk! it cried, mantling its wings and jerking its head, up and down, up and down. The ice around Ingavar seemed to respond with a mighty lament, as if it was making a humble petition to be known to the creature or remembered by it. He looked back quickly at the star. Its beam, though short of its highest point, was weaving something out of the darkness.

A tunnel of light was beginning to form.

"Grockle. It's Grockle," Zanna gasped.

Tootega sank to his knees. Bears all around. Now demons in the sky. Only death could be at the end of this.

The bears quickly reviewed their orders. Five turned left toward the island, one remained as escort for the travelers.

"Where are they going?" Zanna demanded.

"Take stand," said the bear in his stilted tongue. "If creature come to the ice, we kill it."

"By whose orders?"

"Lord Ingavar."

"*What?*" Zanna turned on her heels, looking north for any sight of him. "Ingavar wants to kill the dragon?"

The ice bear flexed its claws.

"Something's wrong here," Zanna breathed. "Something's way out of place. Where's Gwilanna? Have you seen another sibyl, like me?"

The bear shook his head.

"Any men? Inuk with hair like a bear?"

The bear blinked and blew a cloud of vapor. "Walk. I take you to Ingavar."

Zanna stared into his almond eyes. "No, Nanuk. You obey me now." She kicked Tootega. "Pass me the binoculars." Tootega put them into her hands. Turning the sights, she focused on Grockle, watching his talons raking the snow. She dropped the elevation and focused again. "Oh my God," she gasped.

"What you see?" said Tootega.

A cavemouth, a bear, and a redhaired child.

"Lucy," said Zanna. "Lucy's here."

Ingavar sensed a movement behind him. "Thoran?" he grunted, for the shift in pressure felt like the way a Teller or a spirit bear might approach.

But that which closed on him was not a bear.

The Fain invaded his wounded leg and flowed on up through his shoulder and neck. Roaring, he leaped back the moment he felt it, taking all four paws clean off the ice.

You cannot resist, the Fain said, in thought.

Ingavar backed up, pounding the ice, thrashing his head from side to side until the muscles of his neck were loose and raw.

We are allies, said the Fain. *You plan to kill the dragon.*

Ingavar roared again and pawed his ear.

You are strong, but you cannot break free of me, bear.

"What are you?" growled Ingavar, looking for water, hoping to see some sign of this being.

I am Fain, it said. *And I am tired of this heavy, ponderous world.*

And it concentrated half its energy flow into Ingavar's lower gum. With a grinding twist, it forced out the tooth which Ragnar had lost so long ago. It bounced once between Ingavar's paws, staining the sea ice red where it fell.

This island was raised by force, said the Fain. *You, by force, will lower it again.*

And it lifted Ingavar to stand on his hind legs, then brought his full weight down to crush the tooth.

The ice zinged and a running fissure appeared, snaking fast toward the island. At the interface of ice and rock there was a boom. The island shook, torpedoed low down. Snow fell in slabs from its western face. A plangent shock wave traveled out in all directions, causing splits and disruptions in the landfast ice. When Ingavar looked up to see what he had done, the base of the island was spreading apart and the first splinters were showing higher up the cliff face.

The dragon, Gawain, is broken, said the voice. *Now we remove the hybrid as well.*

Lucy screamed and screamed. "What's happening? What's happening?" Another shower of rocks hit the floor of the cave and this time the ground beneath them fractured. For the second time, she was thrown off her feet. There was wetness on her elbow and she knew she was bleeding. Clutching it, she tried to squirm toward the cavemouth, barely visible because of the dust. The island rumbled and she heard a great crack, and the whole world seemed to lurch to one side. Lucy, along with the rest of the debris, found herself piled up against a wall that itself was in danger of tearing apart. "Gawain! Help me!" she cried in dragontongue, but it was the female polar bear who came to her aid.

Frightened by the sudden noise of the explosion, she had lost her footing just outside the cave and tumbled several yards with a torrent of snow. When her slide had stopped, she looked up to see the island breaking apart, losing rocks like a bird shedding feathers.

The girl. She scrabbled back to the cave. Loping inside, she scented Lucy and dragged her out by the folds of her clothing. In the open, she almost lost her to another slide of snow when the clothing ripped and they were separated briefly. But Lucy, clever and aware of the danger, rolled herself into the mother's flank, then pulled herself onto the ice bear's back.

"Gawain is waking up," she panted.

But the truth of it was, Gawain, like the island his body was a part of, was slowly crumbling into the sea.

"Change of plan," said Zanna, pulling the binoculars away from her eyes and thrusting them into Tootega's hands. "See that big bear dead ahead?" She pointed in the direction of Ingavar. "Quickly!"

He looked. "Male bear. I see."

Zanna took the binoculars back. "That's the one we saved in Chamberlain. He's attacking my dragon and destroying the island. Something's gone horribly wrong here, Inuk, and you and I might be the only ones to right it."

"Where is David? You said David come."

Zanna tightened her lip. "David's probably dead," she said quietly. She pulled the rifle out of the sled. "This time, don't miss, OK?"

With an anguished cry, Grockle spread his wings. The perch beneath him rumbled and sheared away, then fell clear of his grasping feet. As he hovered, he saw the entire island collapse. First, the basal layers disappearing, spilling waves of water across the ice. Then, as the middle strata came down, the whole substance of the apex crumbled inward, disintegrating into a well of rubble. And there among the falling chunks of stone were legs and wings and lastly an eye. A petrified eye was the last Grockle saw of his father, Gawain, before the surging water took him.

Immediately, he let forth a belt of fire that lit a candle all over the north. A personal aurora to his father's memory, and a sign to his aggressor that revenge would be sought.

His yellow eye looked at the fissure in the ice and followed it back to where the bear that had created it arrogantly sat. With a whup of his wings, Grockle dipped and joined the end of that watery runway. Ice chunks crashed and pulverized below him as waves, displaced by the island submerging, spread their energy across the ice shelf. He opened his mouth and flamed it all, creating a spectacular channel of fire that the water hadn't doused by the time he had set the bear alight. He watched it turn from white to black, saw the fur and blubber melt back to the muscle, the muscle burning along with the bone. Its ashes fell into the Arctic Ocean, and where they floated, he flamed them, too.

He came down on an ice floe and cried at the sky, not knowing that the enemy he thought he'd destroyed was now about to turn its attention to him. . . .

Tootega had faced many dangers in the north, but none so strange as this. His sled, his dogs, had all been drowned by the tidal wave flowing out from the island. A wave that would have taken him as well, but for the good fortune of stepping the right way across a cracking floe and not into the fire this monster had created. And now here it was, barely paces distant. The two of them, alone on a raft of ice, floating aimlessly out to sea.

Its nostrils twitched as it turned to him, and he could see in its monstrous yellow eye that it was suffering. He knew how that felt. His life, his beliefs, were as much at sea as this piece of faltering ice. He was tired, and about to be turned to ash if this creature's killing wasn't done with yet. That was no way for an Inuk to die. He had the rifle in his hands. He laid it at his feet. What use were bullets now? He turned to the water to be with his dogs.

That was when the Fain came into him. In an instant it learned of his intent, stayed his action, and turned him around.

Pick up the weapon, it said.

And the hunter that had once been the Inuk, Tootega, prepared to put a bullet through a dragon's skull.

It was the easiest of targets, for the unsuspecting dragon had twisted its head, seduced by the glow falling out of the sky.

It amused the Fain that it should happen this way, with metal poisoning the dragon's dull brain. Its death would be the worst of slow vibrations, a fitting punishment for its failure to lead him to the fire of Gawain.

Graark? it queried, awed by the sparkling tunnel of light. It gyred its leathery wings toward it, sensing that a better world was close.

Shoot, said the Fain. *Let it be ended.*

Tootega's finger squeezed the trigger.

Lucy had been lucky. Polar bears, as she soon discovered, were wonderful swimmers. The mother bear had hardly put a paw out of place as she'd hurried away from the dying island and plunged into the ice cold waters of the Arctic. She had swum because her life depended on it. And the life of this precious child.

Just how precious, she was soon to discover. As they

bobbed along with the outflowing tide, the girl suddenly sat up and tugged at her neck, clearly trying to make her change her course. She heard voices, human and polar bear, and altered the shape of her swimming stroke to bring herself in line with them.

The girl was suddenly hauled off her back. And there on the ice stood another, older girl, surrounded by a group of male bears.

"Zanna!" Lucy cried.

Zanna pulled her in close. "This is crazy. What are *you* doing here? And look at your hair. It's blazing red."

"Gwilanna brought me."

"Gwilanna? Where is she?"

"I don't know. And I'm really, really cold."

"Warm her," said Zanna to one of the males, as Lucy fell exhausted to the ice. The bear lay down and gathered her in, aided by the female who by now had dragged herself out of the water.

Suddenly, a bear barked, "Creature! It come."

And all of them turned to see Grockle's attack.

"He kill Ingavar," said one, running farther up the ice.

Zanna shook her head. "That can't be Ingavar."

The bears, five in all, exchanged angry glances.

"Ingavar would not destroy the island," Zanna told them. "Bad spirits are working here."

"You sibyl. Make magic," the largest bear said. "Or we attack creature."

Zanna crouched beside Lucy and gripped her hand. "Gwilanna must have brought you here to raise Gawain, Luce. How is the star involved in it?"

"I don't know," said Lucy, "but —"

"Inuk," said a bear. "Inuk with creature."

Zanna raised her binoculars. Tootega, with a gun. Grockle distressed. The situation didn't look good. "What, Luce? Hurry."

"I saw a drawing in the cave of a tunnel in the sky and people going up it and a dragon at the top. And I found this." She handed Zanna the isoscele.

"Gawain," Zanna gasped. And in a microsecond

she'd connected with Grockle and knew exactly what he must do. "Fly," she called out to him. "Fly to the light." And gripping Lucy tight, she called on the spirit of Gwendolen to aid him.

A gunshot ripped through the air.

But the dragon, Grockle, had already moved. The moment he entered the circle of light, he was gone, transported to the world of the Fain.

"We did it," said Zanna. "We saved him, Luce."

"But where's he gone?" she said. "And — hhh! Look!" She pointed urgently across the ice. Another figure had appeared beside Tootega.

It was David Rain.

"You know, I preferred you as an evil monk. Would have made killing you a whole lot easier."

The Fain swung around, hardly able to believe what was happening. The hybrid gone, and now this irritating human present. "You. How?"

"Told you, I've got connections," said David. In his right hand he held the Inuit talisman. "A few hours gathering flowers around the abbey and Gretel was able to restore some of Arthur's vital memory. He taught me how to use the shaman bear's talisman to physically travel through space and time, instead of just dreaming it, like I'd done before." He opened his hand and let Groyne fly free. "Go to Lucy. Take her home."

"Your creations will all die with you," said the Fain and thought about using the rifle again, but grunted scornfully and threw it aside. The gun slithered across the ice and dropped into the sea. David's attention was briefly caught by movement in the water farther behind. Zanna was arriving on the back of a bear. He had to make this fast.

"You've failed," he said. "My 'connections' will put Gawain back together and send him through the portal, along with the one you call the hybrid. Irks you, doesn't it? To see a healthy dragon in the dark matter plane? A dragon untainted by the virus you've been spreading to wipe them out."

The fingers of Tootega rolled into a fist. He knelt

down and picked up a loose scrap of ice. "How did you find this connection?"

"Commingling's a two-way process," said David. "It's amazing what you learn from the young of your species, who want nothing more than to praise Godith."

"Die," said Tootega, and threw the ice. In midair it changed to a pointed spear, piercing the center of David's chest.

David cried out and dropped to his knees, his left hand clasping that portion of the ice still sitting proud above his chest.

"It will be slow," said Tootega, throwing another. Its point sank into David's heart. "The ice will stop your human blood and freeze you to death from the inside out."

"No," said David, reeling slightly.

"I am never wrong," the Fain said back.

"The ice will transform me," David breathed. "You're the one who's going to die."

"Nothing on this world can touch me, human."

"I'm not thinking of this world," said David. His head fell low. In his mind's eye, he turned for what he knew could be the last time to his beloved writing dragon. "Are you sure?" he asked.

On his pad Gadzooks wrote down the word:

Icefire

So be it.

"You've been seeking the fire of Gawain," said David.

"Where is it? Speak and I will kill you quicker."

"You're standing on it. The ice is his fire tear. And *that's* what's seeping into my blood."

Puzzled, Tootega looked about him. The ice rocked, the ocean rippled. A strange dark wind began to blow. For the first time in its life, the Fain felt *cold.*

"I was sworn to secrecy," David said, giving out a little breath of discomfort. "If I speak of the fire, in the presence of the tooth, the spirit of Ragnar will be at my shoulder." He stared into the absent, hooded eyes. "Say hello to Ingavar. I think you've already met."

As Tootega turned, a spirit paw punched through the center of his chest, and tore out the Fain, striking it dead. The body that had once been the hunter, Tootega, fell to the ice in a lifeless heap. The spirit of Ingavar raised its paw again and drew three short lines in the dead man's head. A hole opened in the ice beneath the corpse, and Tootega joined his dogs in spirit.

"David! David!" Then it was Zanna, scrambling headlong across the ice. She dropped to her knees to cradle his head.

"Hi," he said, having difficulty swallowing. "Guess this means we're back on again?"

"Why?" she said quietly, swaying over him. "Why did you have to do it?"

He lifted a hand and played with her hair, amused by the number of Inuit charms. "Got your feather. It's under my pillow."

"Don't do this," she sobbed. "I don't want to lose you."

He swallowed again and looked up into her face. "Your eyes. They're so beautiful. Please don't cry."

"David, don't. Stay with me," she begged.

The ice rocked. Three bears, maybe four, had climbed onto the floe.

David ran his fingertips over his lips and pressed them onto her cold, white cheek. "Know what day it is?"

She sniffed and shook her head.

"Valentine's. Don't s'pose you sent me a card?"

She shook her head again. "Missed the mail."

"No problem. Put out your hand."

She leveled it for him. And gathering his own hands together in a circle, he placed an invisible gift in her palm.

"What is it?" she said, trying hard not to cry.

"A Valentine dragon — anonymous, of course."

She laughed and pulled her hair away from her mouth. "What's its name?"

He blinked once and touched her face again. "It'll come to you," he said.

Then his eyes closed slowly and his head fell into the crook of her arm.

"No," she wailed, and pulled him to her. "Stay with me. Please stay with me."

One of the bears gave a gentle snort.

There were four on the floe, lying down together. Farther out, on other floes, she could see more. At David's feet sat the spirit of Ingavar.

"Not yet, I want to hold him," she said.

And they waited, heads bowed, until she was ready to lay David down and move aside. Only then did she tell them, "Do what you must."

The spirit of Ingavar set himself down at David's shoulder. One by one, the four bears stood. North, south, east, and west. On a signal they rose together and pounded the ice in unison.

The piece holding David and Ingavar broke and committed them both to the lapping water.

"My love," said Zanna, and looked into the sky.

In the heavens, the fire star went out.

EPILOGUE

Wayward Crescent — Three Days Later

Charming. That was the word that leaped to mind as soon as Bernard stepped out of the taxi. Despite the rain, the Crescent had a wonderful, welcoming feel. He knew his decision to come here was right.

He paid the driver and picked up his only pieces of luggage: a small bag containing his personal effects and a covered birdcage that Brother Peter's budgerigar had once occupied, home now to a restless gray squirrel.

Number 42. After all he had witnessed on the island, this in some ways was the strangest sight of all. *Here there be dragons,* he thought. He smiled inwardly and walked down the path.

The door opened before he could touch the bell.

And there she was. Mrs. Pennykettle. Arthur's love. Green eyes and flowing red hair. Elizabeth.

"Hello, I am Brother Bernard Augustus," he said, and shook her hand formally, knowing no better approach.

She smiled warmly and invited him in.

"And this must be Lucy?" he said. The girl was incredible, almost a carbon copy of her mother.

Lucy's sparkling eyes went straight to the cage. "You've brought him," she said, hunkering down and lifting the cover.

Chuk! went the squirrel, making everyone laugh.

"Please, come through," Liz said politely, directing Bernard toward the kitchen.

"Mom," Lucy said, blocking his way, "shouldn't you tell him about . . . ?"

"Oh, yes," Liz said, clapping her hands at her breast. "I must warn you about our cat."

"Do you like them?" asked Lucy.

"Very much," said Bernard. "What breed is it?"

Lucy wiggled her nose. "Well . . ."

"Oh, he's just a plain brown tabby . . ." said Liz, ". . . sometimes."

"Sometimes?"

"Cup of tea?" she said brightly, and bundled him down the hall.

On the kitchen table were three or four clay figures. Bernard put the birdcage beside a cat bowl, which seemed to be filled with slices of raw meat. He shook his head and pointed to the dragons. "Your sculptures, I 'met' one on the island."

"Gretel, yes. She's with her mistress, Zanna . . . David's partner." She and Lucy both looked away a moment.

Bernard bent forward with his hands on his knees. "And these beings, they move?"

"Not that you would notice," Liz said.

Lucy stepped forward to introduce them. "This is Gadzooks. And this is G'reth. And this is Golly, the healing dragon. He's mending Gruffen."

"They have medical skills?" Bernard stepped back in amazement.

"Spiritual would be a better word," Liz said. "Please, sit down." She put a plate of cookies in front of the monk, which Bernard took to with great delight.

"I have seen so many strange things," he said. "The events on the island have opened our eyes to aspects of our faith we never thought existed."

Liz filled his china cup with tea. "Yes, I wanted to ask about that. Will the 'events' be spoken of beyond the island?"

Bernard shook his head, spilling crumbs down his habit. "As historian to the brethren, it's my duty to record what happened, but I assure you the documents will be filed away safely and — oh, what was that?" He paused, hearing a kind of juvenile roar.

"Oh, that was just Bonnington . . ." said Liz.

". . . the cat," said Lucy.

"It has a most unusual purr," said Bernard.

"It varies," said Liz. "Anyway, you have some news for us, I hope?"

"Yes." Bernard brought his hands together, beating them softly on the table. "Your neighbor, Henry Bacon, is still recovering. He was taken to the local hospital in Dunlogan, officially suffering from mild amnesia. I think you can expect him home in a few days."

Pff, went Lucy, blowing back her fringe.

Liz gave her a "that'll do" look. "And Arthur?" she said, with a tentative gulp. "On the telephone you said he was . . . unwell?"

Bernard lowered his head. "May I speak freely?"

Liz looked at Lucy and nodded.

"Arthur — the man I know as Brother Vincent — is changed. This being, this Fain, damaged his mind. Your dragon, Gretel, achieved some remarkable results, but Arthur's journey to recovery will be long and may not have a conclusive ending. And there is something further you should know."

"Go on," Liz said, drawing a tissue from a box.

"He is almost blind."

"Blind?" said Lucy, dropping her jaw. "So he won't recognize Mom anymore? Or see me ever?"

Liz sank into a chair.

"I'm sorry to be the bearer of this news," said

Bernard, resting a comforting hand on hers. "We will care for him, of course, but —"

"No," said Lucy. "He's got to come here."

"Lu-cy?" Her mother choked back a sob.

"I want to meet him, Mom."

"That's not our decision."

"We can help him," Lucy said to Bernard. "If I ask him to, will he leave the island?"

Bernard sat back and dropped his hands on his stomach. "I . . ." He paused a moment, praying for guidance. "It *was* his intention to return to your mother."

"There," Lucy said triumphantly.

Her mother mouthed, "stop it." "Lucy, this is complicated," she said.

In the birdcage, Snigger did a little twirl.

"We should take him to the library gardens," said Lucy. "Arthur should be there when we let Snigger go."

There was a pause. Bernard stirred his tea. "What of David?" he inquired, switching the subject. "His departure from the island was nothing short of miraculous. Between them, he and Arthur have turned the laws of physics on their head. Did he reach the far north? What happened exactly?"

And now it was Lucy fighting back the tears.

"Is he safe?" asked Bernard, worried for her.

"David did what he had to do," Liz said. "He's still in the north. He may be there for some time."

At that moment, there was a *brr-up* from the hall and Bonnington padded in.

"Ah," said Bernard, grateful of some light relief. He turned to greet the cat, but jumped back and almost fell off his chair. "That's . . ." He waggled a finger at it.

Lucy looked down. "A tiger," she said. "Oh, cool, he's grown those saber teeth, Mom."

Bernard gaped in astonishment at Liz.

"I did warn you Bonnington was *different*," she said.

SCRUBBLEY LIBRARY GARDENS, FEBRUARY 29TH

Come on," said Liz. "We've been through all this once before. And it's even colder now than it was last time. Just open the cage and let him go."

"That is one well-traveled squirrel," said Zanna. "Why didn't you just let him loose in your garden?"

"I did," said Lucy. "But he wanted to come here — when *you* were ready. Mom, did you bring the food?"

"Yes-ss." She sighed. "Here's his commission for helping David with the nutbeast story." She threw Lucy a plastic bag filled with peanuts.

Zanna blew into a tissue and laughed.

"You OK?" Liz asked her, stroking her shoulder.

Zanna closed her eyes and nodded.

"It's fitting," said a voice, "that the story should return to the place it began."

Liz patted Zanna's arm and walked the short distance along the path to where Arthur was sitting on a low stone wall, listening to the rustle of the leafless trees. He reached for Liz's hand. She took his, knelt with it, and kissed his fingers.

"David is with us in spirit," he said.

"He's with us in a bit more than that," said Zanna.

Liz threw her a questioning look.

"I'm having his baby," she said.

"Oh my goodness," said Liz, drawing in such a gulp of air that birds deserted the surrounding trees.

"His baby?" gasped Lucy, standing up at once. "You're going to have —?" She stared in awe at Zanna's tummy.

"Oh, Zanna," Liz cried, and threw her arms around her. "When did you know?"

"This morning," she sniffed, and gave a quick shrug. "Come on, guys. It's just a baby."

"It's David's child," Arthur said, smiling.

"And Gwendolen's," Liz whispered, touching Zanna's cheek.

Zanna sniffed again and looked down at her feet. "We gonna let this squirrel go or what?"

Liz took her hands and rocked them proudly. "You're going to need help. I want you to come and live with us, OK?"

Zanna's pale face twitched into a frown. "Kinda crowded," she said, struggling to talk. "Us four, the dragons, and a crazy leopard — or whatever he's transmoggified into this morning."

"We'll talk about this later," Liz said happily. She squeezed Zanna's hands and turned back to Lucy.

"Oh, there's one other thing," Zanna said.

Liz and Lucy gave her their attention again.

"Gadzooks gave me a note this morning." She pulled a tissue from her sleeve and clamped it in her fists. "It said *G'lant.* It's the name of my Valentine dragon. He said the name would come to me. He wrote to me, Liz."

Liz took her in her arms and hugged her tight. "It's

not over," she whispered. "Not by a long way." And she glanced at Arthur and signaled to Lucy.

And Lucy let the squirrel go.

. . . until the stars have blinked their last,
wherever on this Earth you walk,
he will arouse, excite, inspire,
my Valentine, my one dark fire . . .

Chris d'Lacey is the author of several highly acclaimed books for children and young adults, including the first two books in the *New York Times*–bestselling Dragon series, *The Fire Within* and *Icefire*.

He works as a research scientist for Leicester University and lives in Leicester, England, with his wife.